T0356832

FLAMES *of* ANARCHY

OTHER BOOKS BY JERRY BORROWMAN

Historical Fiction

An Ocean of Courage and Fear

Nonfiction

*Why We Fought: Inspiring Stories of Resisting
Hitler and Defending Freedom*

*Catastrophes and Heroes: True Stories of
Man-Made Disasters*

*Invisible Heroes of World War II: Extraordinary
Wartime Stories of Ordinary People*

*Compassionate Soldier: Remarkable True Stories of Mercy,
Heroism, and Honor from the Battlefield*

BY BERNARD FISHER AND JERRY BORROWMAN

*Beyond the Call of Duty: The Story of
an American Hero in Vietnam*

FLAMES of ANARCHY

JERRY BORROWMAN

SHADOW
MOUNTAIN
PUBLISHING

For Marcella Borrowman, my best friend and wife,
for her encouragement in writing this story

© 2025 Jerrold J. Borrowman

All rights reserved. No part of this book may be reproduced in any form or by any means without permission in writing from the publisher, Shadow Mountain Publishing®, at permissions@shadowmountain.com. The views expressed herein are the responsibility of the author and do not necessarily represent the position of Shadow Mountain Publishing.

Portions of this book are historical fiction. Characters and events in this book are represented fictitiously.

Visit us at shadowmountain.com

Library of Congress Cataloging-in-Publication Data

Names: Borrowman, Jerry, author.
Title: Flames of anarchy / Jerry Borrowman.
Description: Salt Lake City : Shadow Mountain Publishing, 2025. | Summary: "In 1908, anarchist Angel Casimer and the shadowy forces supporting him try to wreak havoc on the United States. One of his targets, Senator Jason Ellis, and his childhood friend, a former Pinkerton detective named Andy Pettit, must join forces to try to stop him"—Provided by publisher.
Identifiers: LCCN 2024055111 (print) | LCCN 2024055112 (ebook) | ISBN 9781639933860 (hardback) | ISBN 9781649333575 (ebook)
Subjects: LCGFT: Detective and mystery fiction. | Novels.
Classification: LCC PS3602.O779 F53 2025 (print) | LCC PS3602.O779 (ebook) | DDC 813/.6—dc23/eng/20250117
LC record available at https://lccn.loc.gov/2024055111
LC ebook record available at https://lccn.loc.gov/2024055112

Printed in the United States of America

1 2 3 4 5 LBC 29 28 27 26 25

CONTENTS

CONTENTS

AUTHOR'S NOTE

In our day, acts of terrorism threaten peace around the world. Attacks such as those in New York, Pennsylvania, and Washington DC on 9/11/2001, the bombing of a passenger train in Spain, subway attacks in London, and innumerable acts of violence in the Middle East are often carried out by religious extremists who feel their place in the world is threatened. Smaller but no less unsettling acts of violence against schools and other public places leave us anxious, not knowing if it's safe to go about our daily lives or to travel abroad. Our feelings of uncertainty and dread sometimes seem unprecedented, like this is something new in the world.

But as it turns out, it is *not* new. More than a century ago, in the last decades of the nineteenth century and the first decades of the twentieth, a worldwide movement known as anarchism used bombings and assassinations of prominent public leaders around the world to destabilize governments and the existing social order. The anarchist Leon Czolgosz shot US President William McKinley on September 6, 1901, in Buffalo, New York. The president died of gangrene from the bullet wound on September 14, and his vice president, Theodore Roosevelt, ascended to the presidency. Shortly after becoming president, Roosevelt declared that terrorism was a "crime against the human race."

Anarchists and other revolutionaries also used bombs and bullets to target heads of state, beginning with Tsar Alexander II of Russia and killing the French president, the prime minister of

Spain, the empress of Austria, and the king of Italy from 1881 through 1900. Seven attempts were made on the life of England's Queen Victoria and one on her eldest son, Albert, who later became King Edward VII. The most serious act of terror among all of these, of course, was the murder of Austrian Archduke Franz Ferdinand at the hands of anarchist Gavrilo Princip in the small Austro-Hungarian town of Sarajevo (now part of Bosnia and Herzegovina) on June 28, 1914, precipitating the first world war.[1] These attacks were most often motivated by labor interests who felt that the world unfairly favored the aristocratic and wealthy at the expense of the commoners who created their wealth. Their goal was to redistribute political and economic power by destroying the governments that the anarchists believed protected the unworthy ruling classes.

Featured in this book are a number of fascinating historical figures whose lives were affected by the anarchists, including President Theodore Roosevelt and his wife, Edith; Prince George (later King George V) and Princess Mary of Wales; and Kaiser Wilhelm II of Germany, who was also the subject of multiple assassination attempts. These historical figures interact with fictional characters to tell the story.

The primary fictional characters are Senator Jason Ellis of New York and his wife, Patricia; Pinkerton detective Andy Pettit; Angel Casimer, an idealistic and violent young anarchist; and Big Jim Fitzsimmons, a union organizer who directs Angel Casimer. Taking a broad sweep of history, the book ranges from New York City, Washington DC, Chicago, and on to London, Berlin, and St. Petersburg. All dialogue is a product of my imagination, although I've studied the historical characters to imitate their

---

1. See "President William McKinley: Assassinated by an Anarchist," historynet .com; accessed 25 April 2024.

personal styles of speaking as authentically as possible. I hope you enjoy the story.

1908 was also the year that the Federal Bureau of Investigation was authorized,[2] giving the federal government domestic police powers to oppose the anarchists. The debates of those days about the cost to privacy and individual liberty that might result from this new national exercise of power sound remarkably similar to the debates that rage today over the proper role of national security agencies in the first decades of the twenty-first century. Perhaps it's fair to say that technology and times change, but people remain the same.

---

2. See "A Brief History of the FBI," https://www.fbi.gov/history/brief-history; accessed 24 April 2024.

CHARACTER LIST

HISTORICAL CHARACTERS

Tsar Alexander II
H. H. Asquith
Margot Asquith
Karl Benz
Charles Bonaparte
John Wilkes Booth
William Borah
Tommy Burns
Joseph Cannon
Andrew Carnegie
Clementine Churchill
Winston Churchill
R. J. Cunninghame
Leon Czolgosz
Gottlieb Daimler
Benjamin Disraeli
Albert Edward (King Edward VII)
Charles W. Fairbanks
Franz Ferdinand
Joseph Benson Foraker
Prince George of Wales
Princess Mary of Wales
Jay Gould
Charles Evans Hughes
Philander C. Knox

Robert M. La Follette
Vladimir Lenin
Sinclair Lewis
Abraham Lincoln
William McKinley
J. P. Morgan
Tsar Nicholas II
Tsarina Alexandra
Adolph Ochs
Allan Pinkerton
Gavrilo Princip
John D. Rockefeller
Edith Roosevelt
President Theodore Roosevelt
Leslie Mortier Shaw
James S. Sherman
Jean-Baptiste Sipido
Bill Squires
William Howard Taft
Leon Trotsky
Cornelius Vanderbilt
Queen Victoria
Kaiser Wilhelm II
Empress Augusta Victoria

FICTIONAL CHARACTERS

John Adams
Mr. Anderson
James Arens
Angel Casimer
Senator Jason Ellis
Patricia Ellis
Jim "Big Jim" Fitzsimmons
Maxim Koslov
Matthew Porter
John Penrod
Andy Pettit

Tom Scanlon
John Schumster
Ed Smith
Jeanette Smith
Jefferson Smithson
Doctor Stoddard
Joan Talmadge
Lane Talmadge
James Timothy
Kurt von Oetle

CHAPTER 1

DEATH TO THE TYRANT!

Washington, DC
January 1, 1908

Angel Casimer shivered as he crouched next to a tipped-over baggage wagon on the passenger platform. The platform's roof was mostly blocking the freezing rain, but some was getting through. Normally his small body gave his movements the grace of a feral cat, but not now. After four hours of pretending he was fixing the wagon's axles, his joints were stiff and painful. In this early hour the platform was mostly empty.

"I am here stranded as the imperialist president, Mr. Theodore Roosevelt, travels in grand style in his own railcar from New York. And he is not even so courteous to be on time," Casimer whispered, his voice trembling more from indignation than the cold, as if the train's lateness was intended to inconvenience him. *Soon enough he will feel my rebuke when beneath his feet his Pullman car explodes!* Casimer thought to himself. He smiled at the thought of the havoc he was about to wreak by killing the most popular president in US history. *And then will the world know the name "Angel Casimer," and our glorious vision will advance as never before!*

Casimer calculated that this day's act would have a far greater impact on world opinion than had President William McKinley's assassination at the hands of an anarchist in 1901. It was that murder which had brought Roosevelt to power. *Roosevelt is a popular leader, but today his death will shake the earth and thunder down through history!*

Casimer and the men who sponsored him had carefully selected the spot at the magnificent new Union Station, not half a mile from the Capitol. Killing him in the heart of Washington, DC, would destroy the confidence of the political establishment as they came and went. *If even Roosevelt can be killed at Union Station, they will reason—who among lesser mortals can feel safe?* Casimer relished the thought that his act of violence would be painted on a brand-new capitalist canvas that the world could not help but notice.

Hearing voices on the adjacent platform, he took a quick peek over the wagon's deck. The two guards walked by, oblivious to just another worker in a flat cap and boiler suit. Casimer blew into his hands to warm them. *When will he get here?*

Almost at the point of despair, the ground began to tremble beneath his feet, which meant another train was approaching the station. Anxiously, he peered to the northeast to see which track the approaching locomotive would be switched to. This had been happening all morning, trains arriving and being switched to various platforms. None so far had been switched to track 1, reserved for very important persons (especially the presidential train). When the colossal iron locomotive entered the switch at the far end of the station, bellowing great clouds of steam into the frigid morning air, Casimer squinted anxiously. When the giant beast lurched to the left, he exulted, *Yes, it turns onto track 1! This is it! This is the opportunity! Be steady, Angel! Be steady!*

Casimer was stationed on the platform between tracks 1 and 2 so that he could be both close and far enough away from the blast when it happened. He wanted to see the moment when Roosevelt's private railcar rolled over the dynamite he'd placed at four a.m. when all was quiet. The blasting machine was cleverly hidden in a barrel beside the turned-over wagon. When the train reached the dynamite, all Casimer had to do was remove a section of barrel, push down the plunger, and wait as the explosion rained shrapnel against the wagon's deck. Then he'd run like every other worker in the yard, invisible to anyone looking for a mad anarchist.

Slowly, slowly, the train made its way to the front of the platform as the engineer carefully slowed the speed of the train to bring it to an easy stop when all cars were at the siding. "Not yet. Not yet!" Casimer's hands were shaking so badly that he forced himself to concentrate. *When it arrives, I pull the front off the barrel. I push the plunger as hard as I can. I wait as hell explodes around me. I run, avoiding any guards or police.* As the enormity of the act he was about to commit washed over him, he thought of the people who would suffer and experienced a momentary wave of regret. *But you must act, Angel. This is the right thing! How else to bring about a new world for the working classes?*

As the train finally slowed to a crawl and then to a stop, the locomotive released one final blast of steam with a shriek so loud that it startled Casimer. He fumbled pulling the front of the barrel off, exposing the blasting machine. But he quickly recovered, checking the position of the Pullman car at the rear of the train. *Not exactly there, but close enough. That's why I placed several sticks along the track!* He ducked behind the wagon's bed. He had lost his fear of being heard above the noise of the smoldering loco-motive. He shoved the plunger into the blasting machine and shouted, "Death to the tyrant!" And with a massive roar, the plat-form behind him erupted into chaos.

CHAPTER 2

AN INTERRUPTED JOURNEY

15 miles from Washington, DC
January 1, 1908

"'Slide trombones that yowled like a cat in torture.'" Senator Jason Ellis laughed as he read from the *Chicago Daily Tribune*.

"What did you say?" Theodore Roosevelt said, looking up from his copy of the *New York Times* on the first day of his last full year in office.

"I'm sorry," Ellis said. "I shouldn't disturb you."

"No, I'm interested. What's your article talking about?"

"New Year's Eve on Times Square. Apparently, it was astonishing. Adolph Ochs didn't set off fireworks this year. He had an illuminated electric ball lowered at midnight from the top of his new building to mark the New Year."

"Yes, I think I'd heard he'd planned that. But slide trombones?"

"Ah, yes. 'Slide trombones that yowled like a cat in torture.' The *Tribune*'s correspondent said people were using those along with," he glanced down at the newspaper, "'cowbells, streetcar gongs, and sections of pipe rasped with files till they gave forth bellows that carried for blocks.'" Ellis laughed again. "The reporter goes on to say that the cacophony was deafening." He was pleased when Roosevelt smiled.

Senator Ellis glanced around at the rich furnishings of the president's private Pullman, the elegant mahogany wood paneling, the luxuriously appointed chairs and couches, and a beautifully finished cherrywood dining table adorned with fresh-cut flowers in crystal vases.

"My understanding is that there were an unusual number of young women in the crowd," Edith Roosevelt said. "They were part of the crush of the crowd, indiscriminately brushing up against young men whom they didn't even know."

"Terrible," Patricia Ellis replied. "People have lost all sense of decorum. I've even heard of women smoking cigarettes in some of the more exclusive private clubs in Manhattan."

"It's that electric ball that fascinates me," the president said, interrupting. "My paper tells me it weighs more than 700 pounds and is festooned with 216 electric light bulbs. Can you imagine that? People cheered madly when it descended down the flagpole. Sounds like Adolph's eager to use it again next year."

"Really?" Ellis said. "I suppose people do love an occasion for a party, and New Year's Eve seems destined to become a big one—more a grand celebration than the simple ringing of church bells we grew up with."

"A *grand* celebration," Roosevelt said with his usual enthusiasm. "It really *is* a grand time to be alive—that's just the right word. Yesterday I finished reading a remarkable piece in the *World*—not one of my usual papers you know, but Archy brought it to my attention. It's titled '1808–1908–2008,' and it talks about the progress we've made in the past hundred years as a country, growing to some 87 million people, and what they think we'll look like a hundred years from now in the year 2008."

"2008—that seems very odd to say, doesn't it?" the president's wife said.

"I'm curious," Ellis said. "Just what do they predict for the future? It seems a fool's exercise to me to make such conjectures."

"You'd be surprised," the president said. "There's science in prediction, and future events can be extrapolated from present experience."

Ellis nodded, knowing that Roosevelt loved discussions like this. As perhaps the most optimistic person to ever occupy the White House, Roosevelt had a popularity rating approaching 90 percent of the adult population of the country—the highest ever recorded for a sitting president. And it was precisely because of his incredible optimism that the people loved him. Even though many of his ideas seemed harebrained when announced, they often turned out to be exactly what the country needed. "As I said, I'm curious."

"Yes, well, here are some of the things they say." Roosevelt retrieved the paper and adjusted his monocle. "They predict the population of the country will be 472 million people in 2008, and there will be gyroscopic railroad trains roaring down the tracks at 200 miles an hour. They even suggest that we may have aeroplanes winging their way through the air."

"I don't know how realistic that is. Since the Wright brothers flew their aeroplane for just twelve seconds, no one has done any better. Twelve seconds isn't much to build a future of manned flight around."

"You're too pessimistic, Jason. Once a thing has been done, it will be done again—and better. My military advisers tell me there will be some genuine progress this year."

"I hope so. Flight would offer so many advantages on so many different fronts."

"Yes. But back to the predictions. They believe in 2008 people will have conquered the motion of the ocean tides to produce electricity, which will replace the need for coal." He looked up from the paper. "You see, of course, that using the oceans for energy means we will never run out of electricity, since the tides are eternal."

"A fantastic idea." Ellis felt cheered by the discussion. As the senior senator from New York, there had been much to fret about in 1907, particularly the spectacular financial panic in October when the whole system had come close to collapse. Having made his fortune in the stock market, Jason Ellis understood these events very well—well enough to have kept his wealth while others were losing theirs. It had been his springboard to the Senate. But having grown up in modest circumstances, he also knew how hard times were for those less fortunate than he and Patricia. Even now many thousands of his constituents were without jobs, and Wall Street was struggling to find its footing after J. P. Morgan had stepped forward as something of a despot to restore order. Morgan's huge infusions of cash into the troubled trusts had soothed the earlier panic, and the Street was trying to figure out what to do next. With the worst of the crisis behind them, people like the famous muckraker Sinclair Lewis were accusing Morgan of precipitating the entire crisis so he could find his way around the new antitrust laws.

If Morgan did cause this panic, Ellis thought, *it got away from him. He ended up losing $25 million. I doubt even J. P. would pay that high a price for one more monopoly.* Ellis stood up and stretched. "Well, I'm sure that the prognosticators are right in saying that the future is likely to be bright. I have a friend over at

Hampton's Magazine who believes that someday people will have their own pocket telephone that will find them wherever they happen to be, and a fellow at the Rockefeller Institute predicts that human organ transplants will become common, which will extend people's lives."

"Oh, for goodness' sake," Ellis's wife, Patricia, said. "That's morbid—and would require the desecration of the human body. I don't think you should even talk about such an awful thing, Jason."

Ellis cast a glance at Roosevelt, who winked at him. "Of course, I shouldn't, my dear. Thank you for correcting me. But the idea of a telephone in every pocket—"

"Is awful to contemplate," Patricia replied. "The world is too noisy as it is. I admit that a telephone in the house is convenient—but for occasional use only. If you had one with you everywhere you went, the world would be so noisy."

"It *is* a noisy world, isn't it?" Ellis agreed. His wife often saw through hyperbole, and he appreciated her for it.

"The future is coming," Roosevelt said, a sudden wistfulness in his voice. "And, unfortunately, I won't be in the White House to experience it. I'm pretty much finished, you know. Just a little over a year to go, and a lame duck at that."

"People hope you will run for a third term, Mr. President. After all, you didn't really have a full first term, coming into the office as you did. And there's nothing in the Constitution to prevent it."

"It's hard to know if I'd have ever been elected directly had McKinley not been assassinated. I've always been popular with the people, but not so much with the Republican Party elite. Even today I frustrate them." Ellis enjoyed the fact that Roosevelt was guileless when talking about himself, accepting his popularity as a simple fact of life.

"But you'd surely be a winner if you ran again. Even the party elders wouldn't walk away from that."

Roosevelt shook his head. "No, I won't do it. George Washington set the precedent: two terms in office, that's all. It isn't healthy to have one man hold power for too long. I'm absolutely committed to letting it go."

"Well," Ellis said, "I am sorry to hear that. But I respect you for it." As the conversation lagged, Ellis glanced down at his newspaper again, but somehow felt he should complete the conversation. "Patricia and I want to thank you again for allowing us to ride with you back to Washington. It really is convenient."

"It's our pleasure," Mrs. Roosevelt said. "You're always good company, and where we both have our homes out on Long Island it only makes sense to travel together. This private train is more than we need, particularly since the children are staying behind at Oyster Bay for a few more days of holiday. And since you represent the same people we do, it cuts down on the expense to the taxpayers." The First Lady paused for a small sip of wine. "Are you looking forward to your trip to Europe, Patricia?"

"Why, yes, I am. We leave in April."

"Nothing like a good congressional junket," Roosevelt said, knowing full well that Ellis would bristle.

"I know presidents and secretaries of state would prefer that the Senate and House stay out of foreign affairs, but we *are* the ones who authorize the money, so it seems we should go see where all that money's going. And it *is* a lot of money."

"And as chairman of the Foreign Relations Committee, you're the right man to go." Roosevelt smiled to show he held no animosity. "But taking William Borah with you is going to be a challenge. He thinks we shouldn't do anything for Europe—or any place else in the world, for that matter."

Ellis nodded. The junior senator from Idaho often had strong opinions, and just as strong a voice for expressing them. "Still," Ellis said, "the committee needs to hear from the critics as well as the supporters, so it'll be fine to have him along." He looked out the window at the corridor of trees marking the railway through Maryland and glanced at his watch, thinking, *Almost there— perhaps another thirty minutes to Union Station.*

"And tell me again what countries you plan to visit?" Edith Roosevelt asked.

Patricia was about to reply when the railcar suddenly and violently jerked, upsetting their drinks and sending a porter sprawling to the floor. Everyone gasped in alarm. Then they steadied themselves in their seats and picked their glasses up from the carpeted floor. Jason rose from his chair to offer the porter a hand in getting up.

Jason Ellis went to the window. "It looks like we've turned onto a siding," he said.

"And we're stopping," his wife added.

"Well, blast it, I'd like to know what train's more important than mine," Roosevelt exclaimed. "We've got to find out what this is all about!" He bolted out of his chair and headed for the door at the front of the railcar, almost knocking the porter down a second time as he brushed past him. Roosevelt arrived at the door just as a Secret Service agent started into the car. Roosevelt put his hands on his hips. "What's going on, John?" Even though the agent was a powerfully built man, he lacked Roosevelt's physical presence and instinctively drew back.

"Trouble at Union Station, sir. We got a yellow light before this siding, so we've stopped to pick up a telegram. It seems there's been an explosion at the entrance to the station, and they're asking all inbound trains to hold up while they sort it out."

"An explosion? What kind of an explosion?" At this point Roosevelt started moving back into the car, beckoning for the agent to follow him.

"What is it, dear—what's happened?" the president's wife asked. Jason and Patricia Ellis were every bit as anxious as she was.

"An explosion at Union Station."

"An explosion," Ellis repeated. "An industrial accident, or—"

Roosevelt turned to the Secret Service agent, who shrugged. "We don't know yet. All that's certain is that an inbound train was involved. It doesn't say if there were injuries, but it's almost certain there are."

"But was it accidental or intentional?" the president demanded.

With something of a trapped look on his face, the agent said, "Let me get off and see what I can find out. In the meantime, I must insist that you stay on board. We're moving our other two agents forward to protect this car."

"I must check on the children," Edith Roosevelt said. "Is there some way I can send a telegram?"

"Yes, ma'am. The next car up has been connected to the telegraph lines at the station where we've stopped. We may even have access to a telephone line."

"Then I must excuse myself." Turning to Patricia Ellis, she added, "Would you like to come with me to see if you can get word to your family that we're all right?"

Patricia nodded. The two women moved quickly toward the front of the car.

With the women gone, the Secret Service agent turned to the

president. "I didn't want to alarm the women, sir, but it seems that the explosion occurred on the very track where we would have been routed. In fact, had we not been delayed in Philadelphia, there's a very good chance that it would have been this train on the spot that was destroyed."

"So this is potentially an assassination attempt," Roosevelt said.

"Perhaps that's premature," Ellis said.

"Perhaps. But these ongoing anarchist attacks across the country suggest it isn't. What better way to get your perverted point of view across than to blow up the president on the first day of the new year?"

Anarchism was a new way of approaching politics—a desire to bring down organized governments, which would be replaced by utopian societies where all property was owned in common and the workingman was supreme. According to the idealistic anarchist philosophers, leaders would emerge naturally without the need for elections, and government would all be local. When nations ceased to exist, the anarchists claimed, the desire for war would disappear, and people would live together in harmony. Or so the theory went. But to destroy the instinct for nationalism, leaders in the anarchist movement believed that world leaders needed to be assassinated and governments terrorized so the workingman would abandon his loyalty to a particular country and join the grand new world where all people were equal and where all men were leaders and followers alike.

Anarchists, Ellis thought, disturbed that this might be another terrorist attack, even as he recognized the logic to what Roosevelt had said. The thought that he and Patricia could have been unintended victims made his blood boil, and he found himself in complete agreement when Roosevelt demanded that the agent find them a motorcar so they could make their way to Union Station. Still fifteen miles outside of Washington, DC, it would take some time. The agent's protests that it would not be wise fell on totally deaf presidential ears. "See that automobile out there? I want you to tell the owner that we need it to get to Washington, DC!" Roosevelt paused. "Hell, why should you tell him. I will! Perhaps he'll even drive us."

"But Mr. President—"

"You stay here and make sure Mrs. Roosevelt and Mrs. Ellis are safe. Senator Ellis and I have work to do!" And with that, the president of the United States was off the train and confronting the astonished owner of a brand-new Buick motorcar—considered one of the finest of the 100 or so small automobile manufacturers trying to develop the new technology.

Mrs. Roosevelt happened to glance out the window of the communications car just in time to see the president wave to her as the Buick drove away in a cloud of dust. "And he's off," was all she had time to say—a phrase that had passed her lips many times before.

CHAPTER 3

YOU SHOULDN'T BE HERE, MR. PRESIDENT!

Washington, DC, Union Station
January 1, 1908

"Turn right onto Massachusetts Avenue!" Theodore Roosevelt demanded. The citizen-turned-presidential-chauffeur had pushed his Buick to its full 34-horsepower capacity in the harried drive into the city. Its beautiful red enamel paint was now caked in mud and debris from sloughing their way through the muddy lanes.

"There it is!" Roosevelt's excitement mounted as the magnificent Union Station depot came into view. "$4 million—that's what it cost to build just the terminal. The entire depot was $25 million; just imagine that, Jason, $25 million! And just three months after opening, this happens!"

"Perhaps we should wait for the Secret Service?" Ellis asked.

"Nonsense—there's no time for that. We're needed now."

What you mean is that you are far too impatient to wait, even if it's dangerous, Ellis thought. *But then you never weigh the cost of danger—climbing sheer cliffs in Rock Creek Park, playing tackle football on the White House lawn.* He shook his head. Roosevelt had an insatiable appetite for action and danger.

"Pull up there!" The president was about to jump from the automobile before it stopped but was prevented by Jason Ellis's firm grasp on his coat and a senatorial warning.

"Hold up for just a few more seconds, Mr. President! You don't want to injure yourself."

Roosevelt turned and laughed. "Thanks, Jason. I'm glad I brought you along. That would make a great story, wouldn't it—'Roosevelt killed jumping from a moving motorcar'!"

Ellis felt too much anxiety about what they were going to discover inside the station to laugh.

"There!" Roosevelt turned to the driver and offered his sincere thanks and congratulations on his fine citizenship. "Tell me your name," Roosevelt said, "so I can pass it on to the press. They'll love this story, and you'll get the credit you deserve."

"John Adams," the fellow said quietly. "No, really," he added when he saw Roosevelt's and Ellis's astonished faces. "The former president is a distant ancestor. My father admired him and his connection to our family, so that's how I got my name. But I'm just a country doctor in Maryland, and nothing like my presidential ancestors."

"The press really *will* love this story, won't they, Jason?" Roosevelt slapped the man on his back and headed into the gleaming new station. Ellis was bemused when a local policeman approached them, waving his arms angrily for them to stay back, only to register the sheer shock of recognition that it was the president of the United States he was waving off. He stepped aside deferentially, apologized, and started walking with them at Roosevelt's invitation.

"Any damage inside the terminal?" Roosevelt asked.

"No, sir. It was all out in the track area. A private railcar was destroyed. But we've mostly cleared the terminal of people while it's being searched for other bombs, just in case. Perhaps you shouldn't go in there?"

"Nonsense. We have to figure out what's happening." Roosevelt and Ellis made their way past the guard into the magnificently ornamented Union Station. Ellis, who had a keen appreciation of architectural innovation, had a brief moment of reverie marveling at the design of the Greek columns supporting the 96-foot high, barrel-vaulted dome, which made it impossible to not look up to where the colorful, coffered-plastered ceiling was decorated in more than 70 pounds of pure gold leaf within egg-and-dart molding. It was particularly dramatic at this hour of the day as the morning sun shone through the skylights. *A truly outstanding work of architecture and a glorious addition to the federal style of buildings that grace Washington*, Ellis thought.

Roosevelt and Ellis made their way from the lobby to the foyer that provided access to the tunnels leading to the tracks, passing the seven-foot-high, ten-ton decorative marble planters. The president was finally being recognized, and as they entered Tunnel 2, a Pinkerton detective came striding toward them. "Mr. President, you really shouldn't be here."

"I'm tired of people telling me where I should and shouldn't be. Whether you think I should be here or not, Andy, is completely immaterial because I *am* here." Then he took a longer look at Andy Pettit. "What happened to you, man? Are you all right?"

Jason Ellis stepped forward and took a close look at Andy Pettit's bloodied face. "Were you out there when this happened?"

Andy pointed to the end of the track. "Let me show you." He strode out of the tunnel into the daylight. "You see that locomotive there? More than a million pounds of iron quite literally saved my life."

"It looks like it committed suicide in the process," Ellis said. "The back end is completely shredded. I've never seen anything like that."

"What happened?" Roosevelt asked.

"I was on the train with Lane Talmadge coming down from New York City. I jumped off while the train was still rolling into the station so I could set up a telephone connection for him. Fortunately, the locomotive was between the blast and me. Even so, the shock wave knocked me off my feet. If I'd been on the railcar when it exploded, I'd be dead and on my way to the morgue."

"Lane was in the railcar?" Ellis looked stricken as he surveyed the wreckage of what had once been the stylish private railcar of his friend and Wall Street associate, Lane Talmadge.

"He was hurt very badly. I don't think he'll make it. His wife was killed, as well as their steward." Pettit put his hand gently on Ellis's wrist. Having been a friend of Jason's most of their lives, he was aware of Ellis's friendship with Talmadge.

Roosevelt shook his head. "You know this Talmadge fellow, Jason?"

Ellis took a long breath to steady his voice. "I do. He's very successful in mergers and acquisitions. An honest man, and a good friend."

Just then a Secret Service agent came running up to the president. "Mr. President—" but before he could say any more, Roosevelt put a hand up. "I'm here, and I'm not leaving. Andy Pettit will act as my bodyguard. What I need you to do is to arrange transportation for Senator Ellis and me to the hospital where they've taken the man who was injured in this blast, a Mr. Lane Talmadge."

"Yes, sir. Right away, Mr. President."

Roosevelt turned to Andy Pettit, whom he knew to be one of the best detectives in the famed Pinkerton Agency. "So tell me what happened, Andy."

"Yes, sir. From what I can tell, a single bomb went off under Track 1, just under the front of Talmadge's private car. I'm not sure it's exactly where the bomber expected the train to stop, but it was certainly positioned close enough to be lethal."

As they talked, a small explosion inside the railcar startled them. The twisted wreckage was still groaning from interior fires that had not yet been put out, and the smell from the burning interior of the car left a stench in the frigid air. *That, and the smell of burnt human flesh*, Ellis thought.

This subdued even Roosevelt. "That's where *my* car would have been, had we arrived on schedule."

"Yes, sir," Andy said. "I can't help but believe that you may have been the intended target."

"Any idea who did this?" Ellis asked.

Pettit shook his head. "It's way too early for that. But I did manage to get a call off to our local Pinkerton group. They'll have people here in a matter of minutes to start an investigation." He looked up at Roosevelt. "I hope you don't mind having a private company look into it. Because I was on hand during the attack, the agency will want to know what happened."

"Not at all. The Secret Service is stretched way too thin for something like this." Roosevelt looked around, trying to take in all that he saw. "Tell me more about Mr. Talmadge."

"Lane's story is much like mine," Ellis said. "He came to New York City with very little money, having grown up in Nebraska or somewhere out west. But he did well as a floor trader, and ultimately started trading for his own account. He's one of the most successful men on Wall Street."

"He and his wife were coming here to visit family," Pettit said. "He wanted me along to keep him connected with his firm while in Washington. He uses Pinkertons to make discreet inquiries when needed."

"Was he worried about something like this?"

"Not that he shared with me. He was using us more for logistics than protection. We're often able to make things happen quickly that otherwise take a long time when left to the bureaucracy."

"And you say he has family here?" Roosevelt asked.

"Joan's parents live in DC," Ellis said. "Her father is James Arens, a Tammany Hall congressman from the Upper East Side of Manhattan."

"Yes, I know Arens." Roosevelt shook his head. "It's even worse when you know some of the people involved, isn't it? They just lost a daughter and probably don't even know it yet."

Roosevelt was thoughtful. "Whoever did this is an anarchist, I'm sure of that. It's not enough that they killed McKinley and the governor of Idaho. Now they're after me, and they killed this man by mistake."

"With all due respect, sir, we don't know that yet. Lane may still be alive. And we don't know that this explosion was from an anarchist's bomb. Although it is the most likely explanation."

Roosevelt walked over and touched the smoldering locomotive. "Well, we should be off. But before we leave, tell me if you've made any kind of initial assessment of this bomber?"

"All I know is that he made some serious mistakes that you'd think an experienced ordnance man would have avoided. For one thing, there was way too much explosive for what he wanted to accomplish. Second, if you really were the intended target, he made the mistake of blowing up the wrong train. He should have known that your private car would have had a unique presidential seal, with flags on the locomotive. And finally"—Pettit hesitated until Roosevelt pressed him—"finally, he left his cap and some tools behind. While his hat is a common enough style, it gives us something to work with. A professional would have never made that mistake."

"So, we're dealing with some kind of lone radical?"

"Maybe," Senator Ellis said, interjecting himself into the conversation, "or perhaps he's just an amateur put up to it by others. Anyone wishing to disrupt the government is well served by an attack on the new Union Station. It's been just a matter of months since you declared it to be a national treasure. What better way to destroy public confidence than to kill the president in his own backyard?" That was a pretty direct statement, but Ellis knew that Roosevelt preferred a direct approach.

Andy Pettit nodded. "That's all very logical, but from my point of view it really is too soon to draw any conclusions. Perhaps Lane Talmadge really was the intended target—a personal vendetta being played out in the public sphere. Anything's possible. Hopefully some group will step forward to claim credit."

"More likely that a dozen of these anarchist groups will step forward—a chance for easy notoriety." Roosevelt did not conceal his contempt.

The young Secret Service agent whom Roosevelt had dispatched earlier approached them. "We have a carriage waiting for you and Senator Ellis, Mr. President."

Roosevelt nodded. "Andy, I want you to find the officials in charge of the terminal and tell them to get this cleaned up as soon as possible."

"But we're treating it as a crime scene—"

"I understand that, but it's vital that we get this wreckage out of here so I can park my railcar on the spot just as soon as possible." When Pettit and Ellis looked surprised, he added, "Can't you see that I need to put my train right here, so people don't lose confidence? This depot is crucial to the success of the city, so we've got to get it functional right away."

Andy Pettit and Jason Ellis nodded in recognition as the political aspect of the situation dawned on them. Roosevelt, the old pro, had gotten there much quicker than they.

"Well, then," Roosevelt said, "let them know that you are speaking for me, and if anyone questions it, call the White House. I'll leave word that you're authorized to act in my behalf."

"Thank you, Mr. President." Andy Pettit turned to Jason Ellis. "If Lane is conscious, will you please extend my regrets for his wife? Tell him I'm sorry . . ." Pettit struggled to control his voice. "Tell him I'm sorry I didn't protect him."

"Of course." Ellis leaned in and gave Pettit a quick hug, even though it made Pettit uncomfortable. "I'm glad that the locomotive was between you and the bomb. I'm not ready to lose the best friend I ever had."

As he moved away from his friends, Jason Ellis thought a silent prayer, just as he often did in times of stress—but it was difficult to know what words to say. *Thank you for saving us!* Of course that was appropriate. *But others have not been saved—please help them, dear Lord—help them to deal with this tragedy.* And then, *Help me know how to help them.* He shook his head. *It was supposed to be us—but they will pay the price. Please, dear God, help them.* It was all he could think to pray.

CHAPTER 4

WHEN BAD NEWS
IS GOOD NEWS

New York City
January 2, 1908

Bank president Maxim Kozlov sat back in his pleated black leather chair and stretched. "I know it's early, but I think we're in for a long day, Tom. There will be a lot of unjustified hysteria about this news of a terrorist attack in Washington." Koslov's speech was a bit slurred, which caused Tom Scanlon, loyal lieutenant to Kozlov, to bite his tongue. He was convinced that Kozlov was the smartest man on Wall Street, but it was clear that his boss had been drinking heavily the night before, and so his head was not yet clear. In Tom's mind, Koslov's consumption of alcohol—and laudanum—was getting out of control.

Koslov yawned and stood up, walking over to check the stock ticker again to see how the market was responding to the terrorist act. While he was up, he freshened his coffee and added a little something from a hip flask.

"I must say that you seem quite sanguine about all this, given the potential threat. It could start another run on the bank!" Scanlon exclaimed.

Kozlov allowed himself a small smile. "I think we're going to be fine, Tom. A piddly-ant bomb in Washington is unlikely to derail the markets."

"Yes, sir," Scanlon said, "but despite what the newspapers are saying about it being a random event, some of the private cables I'm reading suggest that it was originally aimed at Roosevelt's car."

Kozlov nodded. "Of course, *that* would have been terrible for the markets, but maybe not for the country . . ." He quickly corrected himself when he saw the shocked look on Tom Scanlon's face. "You know I don't mean that. It's just that Roosevelt has hardly been a friend of the trusts. I personally will be glad to see him out of office."

"Yes, sir. The fact that he's independently wealthy makes it rather harder to buy his influence, doesn't it?"

"Not for old J. P. Morgan—he just maneuvers us into the biggest financial crisis since the Civil War, then uses it to put pressure on the Secretary of the Treasury to suspend antitrust rules and buys out his competitors for pennies. And Roosevelt, the usually bellicose trustbuster, capitulated instantly when faced with political catastrophe and gave in to Morgan's every demand. So much for high-minded principle." Kozlov took a careful sip of coffee. "Why pay for politicians when you can just as easily blackmail them? And Morgan blithely tells the public that he lost $25 million shoring up weak institutions, when the reality is he consolidated his hold on Wall Street and every industry he plays in. $25 million is a small price to pay for that! As usual, the old codger will come out of it stronger than ever."

"Yes, sir." Scanlon had heard this refrain before. While he was devoted to his boss, he also recognized that his bitterness for

Morgan clouded his judgment. Morgan, the old shark, had forced Kozlov during the October crisis to surrender his highly prized shares in Collier Coal in exchange for cash deposits to keep him from losing his entire stake in First Commerce. Now Morgan and his cronies at the Pennsylvania Railroad were again in control of the coal market—and could charge whatever they wanted.

"Ah, well," Kozlov said, "one can make money even when the markets go down if one is careful."

"That's true," Scanlon said. "I noticed you shorted a number of prominent stocks last week. You ought to be able to close those positions for a handsome profit, given all this market uncertainty."

"I should, indeed!" Kozlov stood up. "In fact, I think I'll do that right now. Send a runner down to the Exchange and tell them to buy shares equal to all our outstanding positions. I have a feeling that this little crisis will blow over quickly. I want to buy while prices are at the bottom."

"Of course, sir, right away."

"I'll tell you what, Tom," Kozlov said as he poured the remainder of his hip flask into his coffee cup. "I owe a debt of gratitude that I could never afford to repay to the fellow who invented short selling." He laughed. "Just think of it. If you think the price of a stock is overvalued, you borrow shares from another investor and sell them. Cash in hand, you pay him a little interest while the contract is open, and then, if the market drops as you expect, you buy replacement shares at the lower price to make good on the ones you borrowed and sold. If the price drops far enough, you're left with a real pile of money."

"But it can go the other way," Scanlon replied. "The upside risk is that you have to buy stocks at a higher price than you sold them at, and then you have potentially unlimited risk."

"You can hedge that, Tom!" Kozlov clearly didn't like anyone casting doubt on the wisdom of his strategies. Scanlon immediately recognized his mistake.

"But in your case, sir, you seem to have a remarkable ability for knowing when bubbles are about to burst."

Kozlov smiled again. "I've done all right, haven't I? Not a lot of losers, and more than my fair share of winners. Somehow things seem to go my way. Something like this bombing comes along, and it all works out. You never know how, but it always works out."

Tom Scanlon excused himself. There were times when he hated himself for staying with Kozlov. Not that he was different from any of the other investment bankers or speculators on Wall Street who were out to make money any way they could. It was just that for Kozlov to profit, some other fellow had to lose the fortune Kozlov gained. And in this case, his profit came from the death of a Wall Street colleague and his wife. "It's a poor thing to earn money on someone else's pain," he said to himself as he crossed the magnificent marble lobby of the First Commerce Trust building to hail a runner. "You there!" he shouted to a slender young man. "Take these buy orders down to the Exchange and see that they get executed immediately. No dallying, or Mr. Kozlov will have it out of your hide."

"Yes, sir," the young man said nervously. "I'll fly like I have the wings of Mercury."

Scanlon eyed the young man carefully. "Of course you will. And if we happen to buy at the low point of the market, we'll give you a little bonus for your good service." That was all the boy needed to literally race out the door. After all, for every $10,000 that Maxim Kozlov made, Scanlon would pay his runner perhaps an additional twenty-five cents—a bonus of double or triple the usual amount a runner could make for a day's labor—and a small price to pay for his best effort.

As Tom Scanlon made his way back across the lobby, he noticed the line for redemptions had grown even longer, and he felt a pang of anxiety as he wondered if the trust really could hold off the frightened depositors. *It seems that each time one of these damned anarchists sets off a bomb, the market collapses in a new panic.* He wished that he had the kind of intuition his boss had so he could make money at times like this. *Still, if the trust goes under, Kozlov will be ruined. And this time, old man Morgan might not step in to save him.* Scanlon sincerely wished there was some kind of medicine he could take for the ulcer that was tearing his stomach apart.

Baltimore
January 5, 1908

"Let's give a cheer for the man who bombed Union Station—a cheer for the cause, and a cheer for anarchy!" Big Jim Fitzsimmons had never been more compelling, and Angel Casimer found himself cheering along with the crowd with all the power his lungs could muster. Which wasn't much, given his remarkably thin frame. Most of the people in this room thought him a no-account loser, if they thought of him at all.

"And yet it is for me that they cheer," he said to himself. There was no danger of being heard in this crowd of dockyard workers struggling to form a union against the shipyard owners and the thugs they'd sent.

"Too bad that the bomb went off before His Majesty Lord Theodore Rex had his mahogany-lined, crystal-encrusted private railcar parked in the right spot just above the explosion. Think of where we'd be had the bomb gone off then!"

Casimer winced at this reference to the fact that he blew up the wrong railcar but was relieved when Fitzsimmons winked at him. No one else knew the wink was for him—most hadn't even seen it—but Casimer knew, and that's all that mattered. It showed that Jim Fitzsimmons, the firebrand union leader and American Bolshevik who'd put him up to the job of bombing Union Station, had forgiven him for killing the wrong man. "After all," Fitzsimmons had said, "Lane Talmadge was a capitalist, which made him an enemy to the unions and to international Bolshevism. So it was a good kill." That gave Casimer some solace for his mistake.

Meanwhile, the crowd cheered wildly in support of Fitzsimmons's rant against Roosevelt until, as the noise started to die down, one young voice called out, "What does that mean, *Theodore Rex*?" The crowd burst out laughing, knowing that he had cheered along with the rest of them though he had no idea for what he was cheering.

Big Jim Fitzsimmons burst into an even wider grin, knowing that he really did have them now. "It means *king* in Latin—and that's what we have—a king! The Germans have their Kaiser, and the Russians have their Tsar! The British have their King Edward, who has grown fat and lazy off the people's toil and off the exploitation of their British colonies, and Spain—well, Spain has the memory of their assassinated king. But sadly, our American king is still alive and well, and his name is Theodore—Theodore Rex! But not forever; one day soon he'll be gone!"

The crowd went crazy, cheering and dancing, and finally singing the songs of solidarity that had been composed to unite labor movements and anarchists all around the world. With hundreds of terrorist attacks in different places around the globe in just the past year alone, it seemed that nothing could stop the momentum—not even the Pinkerton detectives whom steelmaker Andrew Carnegie and other fabulously wealthy industrialists had paid so handsomely to break up their strikes, oftentimes by cracking the strikers' heads.

"The glorious worldwide revolution of the proletariat is gaining ground," Casimer said to the air, "and everyone in Washington is paranoid because of the bomb that I exploded!" Angel Casimer had never felt so important or so alive.

Almost as if he could read Casimer's thoughts, Big Jim shouted to the crowd, "They're frightened of you, right now, because the people of this country are still too hypnotized by the words of men like Carnegie to realize that you are their salvation. They still don't mind that Mr. Vanderbilt owns one out of every twenty dollars in the great United States of America. *One man owns one out of every twenty dollars, and yet they call America a democracy! What king is richer than Vanderbilt?* Not one, I tell you, not one!" He paused to let the crowd boo the capitalists. "And yet our fellow citizens don't seem to care that, along with Vanderbilt, men like Mr. John Pierpont Morgan run the economy. Morgan pulls the strings of banks and investment houses all around the country from his office in his multimillion-dollar mansion on Fifth Avenue in New York City, making tens of millions of dollars at your expense while you work your heart out for less than a dollar a day—*and just how is that fair?*"

The crowd was stirring physically, they were so angry.

"And the people of this great country are still anesthetized by the soothing words of John D. Rockefeller telling them how much better off they will be because he controls all the petroleum and all the pipelines. *But soon they will understand! And when they do, they will thank us, and then they will join us, and then this country will be ours—not the capitalists' and their politicians'—but ours! The country will be ours!"*

So frenzied was the crowd by the hypnotic syncopation of Fitzsimmons's rant that Casimer became concerned for his own safety. As a little man, he could be easily crushed by the crowd that was now surging forward to pull Fitzsimmons down from the stage and onto their shoulders. Gasping for air, he finally bobbed like a cork up onto the shoulders of some of the men who were dancing in the hall. They didn't know why he was up there, but Angel Casimer did.

"It really is for me that you dance!" he cried jubilantly to the sweaty air. "I am the one who did this deed. And I will give you more. I will be the match that lights the fires!"

CHAPTER 5

FREEDOM OF ASSEMBLY

US Capitol, Washington, DC
January 10, 1908

"Senator Ellis, do you believe the president should impose martial law?"

Pushing his way through the crowd of noisy reporters in the downstairs foyer of the Capitol, Senator Jason Ellis paused and turned to the reporter who had shouted that particular question.

"Is that you, James? James Timothy?" He asked this of the crowd, while trying to sort out the faces that now looked at him earnestly, notepads at the ready. From the center of the melee a short, wiry, bespectacled fellow stepped forward and smiled.

"You recognize my voice, Senator? That's enough to make my day."

"I always recognize the voice of the *New York Times*!" He grinned. "Even when it's to respond to a stupendously foolish question like that!" The journalists laughed, knowing full well that Ellis opposed anything even resembling martial law. But he was always good for a quote, and since more than a third of the reporters in the crowd were from New York City, this was a chance for Ellis to reach out to his constituents.

"You can't hurt my feelings, Senator. But I hope you'll give us a serious answer."

Ellis had to be careful. One misstep and he could upset the balance he was trying to strike in the Senate on how to respond to the bombing. But the public deserved an answer, and if done right, he could shape public opinion to get a better deal.

"I *will* answer your question, James, and I *will* do it seriously." He motioned for the crowd to follow him into one of the many small vestibules that provide semi-private spaces in the massive Capitol Building.

Once he got to a place where he could hear his own voice, Ellis said, "Gentlemen, as many of you know, I was in Union Station shortly after the blast, and I was with President Roosevelt at the hospital when Lane Talmadge passed away from his injuries. It was a terrible experience to see an innocent man die because of the fanatical hatred of some group or individual. His children are devastated by the death of both their mother and father, and the demoralizing effect on public confidence has been profound." He halted for a moment to make sure they registered that in their notes.

"But—" James Timothy said.

"But martial law is not the solution." Ellis glanced away from the crowd for a moment, pursing his lips as he formed his response. "It's like this, gentlemen. Anarchist attacks have occurred in just about every world capital, regardless of whether they're ruled by a monarchy, by their military, or by democratically elected representatives. The people who would destroy governments don't give a damn about what *type* of government it is. The difference between America and other types of government is that we have so much more to lose if we give in to fear by sacrificing our hard-earned freedoms on a false altar of safety. We can defeat anarchy, but not by placing armed guards on every street corner and in every public space. We must beat them by continuing to show that our form of government provides its citizens the very type of freedom and opportunity the anarchists want but they're just not smart enough to realize."

Ellis paused for a breath. He liked what he had said but knew it didn't settle the question. "Let me conclude by saying that the right response to this attack is for people to keep going to work, to keep using the trains and subways, and to keep their eyes open for anything suspicious. We don't need martial law—we need to keep our democracy functioning."

"Would you feel the same way if this attack had happened in New York City?"

Ellis shook his head, allowing some anger to creep into his voice. "New York hasn't been immune to these types of attacks—starting with the British Army in the late 1700s. We won that war, didn't we? Since then, we've had mobs, riots, and even our fair share of anarchist attacks, and yet the city just gets angry, dusts itself off, and gets back to business without a fuss. That's what Washington, DC, needs to do right now; step up to the plate and keep swinging." Ellis liked the way that sounded and knew that it would play very well at home, if not quite so well in the DC newspapers.

As soon as he ended his sentence, a dozen questions were shouted out in such a madcap fashion that he couldn't sort any out. Raising his hands, he said loudly, "One more question, gentlemen, then I'm off to debate this very topic with my colleagues." He pointed to a reporter from the *Washington Post*, feeling that he ought to give someone other than a New York reporter a chance.

"Speaking about the ongoing investigation, do you support

the idea of creating a centralized federal investigative bureau to look into this sort of thing?"

"That's hard for me to champion personally since I'm inclined against government becoming too big and too intrusive. But I am open to some kind of federal coordination. Relying solely on states for enforcement can give criminals the ability to slip across state lines and avoid a coordinated prosecution. At the very least, we need a formal framework for sharing information between states. On issues like terrorism, where a single person or group can strike in multiple cities, perhaps we do need a central agency to coordinate information and share it with the relevant states— something like the Federal Agency of Investigation, or FAI, since this town likes acronyms so much. The larger question is if such an agency should have direct authority to act against criminals. Right now, I'm inclined to answer no, but who can say how it will sort itself out? I do agree with at least a coordinating role."

"But is that consistent with your party's platform?" Now the reporters were hot—this would make great copy as the country waffled back and forth over the role the federal government should play in keeping them safe.

Ellis was cautious; he didn't want to obligate himself to a firm position just yet. But then the right words came to his mind, and he smiled. "Let's put it this way, gentlemen. If the ultimate choice is between martial law in Washington, DC, or a federally funded investigative agency, I'll choose the agency any day of the week. Leave the military to international matters and police work to the folks here at home." He breathed a silent sigh of relief to think that he'd managed to find the lesser of what he considered to be two evils. And it would be up to his colleagues to force the choice upon him—at least that was something that he could control, and he'd make sure that's how it appeared to the press.

Baltimore
January 10, 1908

"You didn't have anything to do with this attack on Union Square, did you, Jim?"

Jim Fitzsimmons wasn't surprised by the question from the president of his dockworker's union, but he'd rather not answer it. He preferred to keep out-and-out lies to a minimum. "I wish I had, Ed. We're getting nowhere with this peaceful protest nonsense you seem to champion."

"Nice parry, but you didn't answer the question."

Fitzsimmons scowled. He hated talking with the man who'd beat him out as president of the union. But for now he had to put up with him. "No, Ed, I had nothing to do with it. You won, so we're doing it your way—for now."

"It's just that you use the word *we* a lot in all your speeches, as if the union was responsible for it. I'm not sure we're going to win a lot of friends siding with anarchists. Frankly, I'm a lot more interested in weekends off for our workers than I am in world domination." He fixed a steady gaze on Fitzsimmons. "And I trust the same is true of you."

Fitzsimmons's gaze hardened. "Ed, you know perfectly well I'm in sympathy with the international labor movement, and in many instances that includes anarchists. I've made no bones of the fact I'm a Bolshevik, and the union members knew it when I came within five votes of beating you. So when it comes to anarchists and the international labor unions, I welcome anything they can do to move the cause along, even if it involves violence. As the Russians like to say, 'The enemy of my enemy is my friend.' I'm not saying that's where we should go ourselves, but whatever—and whoever—helps our cause is a friend of mine. I don't want you to go soft on me, Ed."

Ed Smith backed off. "I'm not going soft. There are enough dissensions in our ranks right now to split the union in two, and I don't want to be on the losing side of *that* argument. We've been friends a long time, Jim, and we've made some decent headway in this thing."

Fitzsimmons nodded. "We have, Ed. Which is why you've got to trust me."

Ed Smith rubbed his temples. "I trust you, Jim. But I'm not sure you understand just how high the stakes are. If someone on our leadership team is involved in violence, in an assassination, we'd lose Roosevelt's backing—and the progressive members of his party—and that would sink us." He paused again and stared directly into Jim Fitzsimmons's eyes, which, he suddenly learned, was about as unnerving an experience as a person could have, and said firmly, "So, if you're aware of anyone involved in this sort of thing, you need to bring it to my attention immediately. I'm sure any additional incidents like this will work against our interests, so I hope nothing else happens. Is that fair?" He watched uncomfortably as Fitzsimmons clenched and unclenched his fists. Big Jim Fitzsimmons—all 6'8" and more than 350 pounds of him—could squash him like a bug and with as little regard, and Ed Smith had every reason to believe that he would do it, if provoked.

Finally, Fitzsimmons took a long, deep breath, held it, and then let it out slowly. "I don't know if it's *fair*, Ed, but you're the man they elected to run this thing, so I'll let you know."

His words were strained, and Ed Smith was anything but reassured. The muscles in his legs, which had started shaking, were obviously worried.

CHAPTER 6

DEATH AT THE ORIENTAL GRILL

Washington, DC
January 31, 1908

Senator Jason Ellis looked out the window of the shiny new car that Andy Pettit had used to pick him up at the Capitol Building. "Thanks for the ride, Andy. I hate to be late, and a hansom cab would never have made it in time. Those reporters got hold of me and wouldn't let go." Ellis took a deep breath to slow down his thinking.

"I could see they were hounding you, which is why I barged in. Sounds like things are getting intense. Lots of your colleagues are calling for martial law."

"You heard what I had to say about that?"

Pettit laughed. "I heard. It sounds like this federal investigative agency thing's heating up too. You pivoted to that to get out of the martial law question."

"They'll probably make you the first director of the agency if you want it, Andy. 'Director Andrew Pettit' sounds very impressive." Ellis hesitated. "But *I* want you to agree to work for me. I can put a great deal of resources at your disposal."

Pettit swerved to miss a jaywalker, who cursed at him for driving a "Satan-inspired" automobile that would surely doom civilization. "Why are you so agitated about this, Jason, that you want to open your own detective agency? I understand your role in policy, but this seems a little too personal."

"I wish I could tell you it was for strictly noble reasons. Yes, yes, we have to keep people safe or democracy will fall apart—it could happen, you know. America is still the longest living example of a functioning republic, and we're barely 125 years old. In the scheme of world history, that's hardly more than the blink of an eye."

"I understand that, but you have another reason."

Ellis nodded his head. "I've made a lot of money in what I believe to be honest business ventures. Frankly, I like having money, and I don't want to lose it. These attacks are an attack on capitalism itself, and if they gain traction, they could destroy everything I've worked for. I know you don't worry as much about money as I do, but we were poor—and I didn't like it." He cast a glance at Pettit to see how he responded. Andy was the type of man who was content to earn just enough to eat and find a place to sleep; he'd never really understood Ellis's ambition.

"So, you're willing to spend some of your money to keep the rest of it safe?"

"That's certainly part of it."

Pettit pulled his brand-new cobalt-blue Westcott Runabout automobile to the curb. "I'll think about it. In the meantime, there's lots I can do working as a consultant to the Secret Service."

Ellis stepped down to the running board, since the four-foot wheels put the seats high up from the ground. "Thanks for the ride. I'm attending this for Patricia, and you got me here in the nick of time. You're still coming over for dinner tonight?"

"You're not cooking?"

Ellis laughed. "No, I'm not cooking. It's all done under Patricia's supervision. See you at seven."

The Oriental Grill, Washington, DC
January 31, 1908

"Ah, Mrs. Ellis. Thank you for inviting us to this luncheon today. I've been looking forward to it ever since my husband was elected to the Senate." Patricia Ellis stepped closer to Jeanette Smith, the wife of a newly elected senator from the Midwest.

"I'm very glad you could make it. It was never intended to be an annual event, but somehow it's become one. I know I was very grateful when Jason was first elected to have some of the senior wives take me under their wings as I learned the social landscape of Washington."

"Yes, well, it's very kind of you and Senator Ellis to speak to us today."

Patricia nodded pleasantly, thinking that she could move on to meet some of the other first-timers, but Mrs. Smith leaned in a bit closer. "I'm very curious to know about Mrs. Roosevelt. Is she as grand as she appears?"

"The First Lady?" repeated Patricia. "Why, Edith Roosevelt is just as charming as you'd expect. She's perfectly at ease in high society, and also the mother of six rambunctious children, including her stepdaughter, Alice, whom you know to be *quite* high-spirited. I'm not sure the First Lady is as free to mingle in society as she might otherwise enjoy. In the moments I've shared with her, I find her to be extremely well grounded in the practical matter of running a family—but the task is made more difficult by the intense interest the press has in the Roosevelt children."

"Yes . . ." Jeanette Smith said. She hesitated as if she wanted to say more but recognized that Patricia was trying to end the conversation.

As they stood there, it dawned on Patricia why Mrs. Smith had asked about Edith Roosevelt. "Now that you mention the First Lady, I believe I recall you are to be hostess at a charitable event Mrs. Roosevelt has agreed to attend."

"Yes," Mrs. Smith said, relieved, "and I'm so concerned about how to present her to the other women in the group. This will be the first time I've introduced someone so prominent."

It no longer surprised Patricia to find herself in the role of social advisor, given that her husband was now the senior senator from New York. Even when they first arrived in Washington, her deep ties to New York society meant that she was already experienced in such affairs, while many of the other senators' wives came from less socially sophisticated places west and south of the Hudson River. Since then, Patricia had been drafted as something of a mentor to the other senatorial wives, and this was, in fact, the reason for today's soiree at a fabulous new restaurant that purported to bring the culinary delicacies of the Far East into the heart of Washington. In just two short years it had become a major social hub for political insiders.

"You know," Patricia said with a wink, "I'm happy to help you with this. You're more than equal to an introduction of the First Lady. But I see that my husband just stepped in, and it's my duty to introduce him today. So, if you'll allow me to schedule some time with you privately—say early next week—I'll be glad to help you. Perhaps you can call at our townhouse." She did her best not to smile too broadly as Mrs. Smith thanked her profusely for her help, and then Patricia forced herself out of the conversation, making quick remarks to the other ladies as she passed through the crowd to meet Jason.

"I'm so glad you're here," Patricia said in a way that told Ellis she was ready to get things moving. "The ladies are expecting some good advice on how they can help their husbands' careers. I'll take ten minutes; you take ten minutes."

Jason loved how businesslike Patricia became at these events. Which was appropriate, given that a social gaffe by a politician's wife could sometimes mean the difference between a successful career and one spent in the shadows.

"And don't talk about that awful thing at Union Station, even if the ladies ask about it. This is neither the time nor the place."

Jason nodded. In this he and his wife were in complete agreement. The best thing that could happen now was for the noise around the bombing to just quiet down.

Stepping to the small lectern that had been set up for the occasion, Patricia raised her hands and asked the ladies to please take their seats. It took a few moments for their conversations to close, but they came to order quickly.

"Ladies," she said in a cheerful voice, "I am so pleased that you could join us today. This is one of the events I always look forward to at the beginning of a new year."

Looking up from the table where he was seated, Jason Ellis was still dazzled by her smile, every bit as enchanting at this age as when he'd first spied her across the schoolyard when he was fifteen years old. He'd fallen in love with her then and, in contrast to so many political marriages, had remained so through the twenty-nine years that had passed since that innocent day in 1874. He noted the fact that even though they were joined by a number of wives of senators with far longer tenure, Patricia was the one that everyone looked to for guidance, and Ellis could not have been prouder. Gaining her father's permission to marry her was the greatest accomplishment of his life.

"You are a beautiful woman—" he started to say quietly to himself when he was interrupted by an urgent shout.

"Fire! There's a fire!"

For the briefest moment, Ellis was irritated that someone would interrupt an event like this, but then his brain registered what had been shouted. *Fire!* The hair on the back of his neck stood up, and he instinctively rose to his feet and started racing to the doorway. Patricia paused, and the women in their party turned anxiously to see what he would discover. What he found when he reached the doorway was a terrified waiter racing in their direction, probably to alert them to the danger. But from this vantage point, Ellis needed no warning. It looked as if the entire front of the restaurant had ignited like a torch; the taffeta curtains that framed the entryway were ablaze, the mahogany front desk was in flames, and the maître d' was screaming in agony, his jacket sleeve alight. Terrified patrons first tried to push their way to the front door, then pushed back against each other when the maître d', fully engulfed in flames, rushed toward them screaming in pain. People scattered in terror, their shocked cries adding to the confusion

"For heaven's sake, roll him on the ground!" Ellis shouted at the top of his lungs. "Do something for him right now!" When people hesitated, he forced his way through the crowd and threw the poor man to the ground, kneeling while forcing the man to roll on the carpet until the flames were doused. The feel of the burnt skin on his hands was revolting, but his touch quieted the poor fellow as he gasped for breath, sobbing in pain. Ellis had hoped it would give the man a chance, but he could tell that it was to no avail. The man would die of his burns, of that he was certain.

Standing, he saw the crowd shoving against each other in the opposite direction of the flames, much like the scenes in a moving picture show of cattle stampeding away from a lightning strike. "Calm down!" he shouted, and then, grabbing a waiter by the arm, he asked, "Are there other ways out?"

"Yes, sir, there's a door across from the bathroom—over there," pointing. "Otherwise, only through the kitchen," the man said, his voice ragged. A quick glance in that direction showed that the flames made escape through the kitchen impossible for those in the main dining area.

Ellis stood on a table and shouted "Quiet!" It startled the crowd enough that he could point to the far side hallway while saying, "There's an exit over there—everyone move quickly but carefully. You can all get out without being harmed." The people nearest the hallway looked about, then one of them made his way into the hall and shouted that the door was clear. The crowd moved almost like a single beast in that direction. Ellis would have had them move more deliberately, but it was too late for that.

With that, he raced back to the private room, where the senators' wives had huddled back against the lectern. "Patricia—why aren't you escaping through that door?" His wife moved closer and said, "It's blocked! We've tried opening it, but we can't get it to budge."

Oh dear heaven, he thought. Then his mind cleared, and he shouted to a waiter, "You there, tip that table up and against the doorway between us and the fire." When the man hesitated, Ellis rushed over and started tipping the table himself. The waiter reacted and quickly moved to help him. "We have to keep oxygen from the fire—this will give us an extra few minutes."

"A few minutes for what, sir?"

Ellis pointed toward the large window next to the courtyard. "For us to break out through that window. Will you help me?" The man nodded, and Ellis shouted to the women in the room to turn away from the window while he and the waiter hefted a second table and started swinging it in unison. "One, two," and on "three," they let it crash through the large plate-glass window. The glass shattered, and in just a moment Patricia had wrapped her right hand in a cloth napkin and was busy knocking out the shards that remained attached to the windowsill, while Jason moved to organize the crowd to duck and step through the window.

"Help my wife!" Jason shouted to Jeanette Smith, who quickly followed Patricia's lead. Encouraged by Jason's leadership, the ladies quickly organized themselves. With the table he'd upturned shielding them from the main dining area, he couldn't see if everyone had made it out of the kitchen, but he'd have to leave that up to them.

Meanwhile, the deputized waiter who had taken control of the situation in the main restaurant area had evacuated nearly all the patrons and was even now dragging the unconscious maître d' toward the exit. At least that way the man's family could have a funeral.

Although it had seemed to take forever, it wasn't long until everyone was outside, and Ellis realized that it had really been only a few minutes since the first shout of "fire!" In the distance, he could hear sirens and the sound that draft horses make galloping at full speed on cobblestone.

"Everyone out to the street," he urged, even though many in the crowd had already started through the small wooden doorway that led through the adobe wall of the courtyard onto the avenue. Once on the other side they would be safe. Ellis glanced around and saw a wheelbarrow full of concrete had been tipped over outside the door that the women had tried to open and had hardened there. *Someone needs to explain that!* he said to himself. As the last of his charges made it through the courtyard wall, he started through, turning back to see the restaurant's roof burst into flames and a dark billow of acrid smoke rising into the sky. The upturned table had given them just barely enough time. If they'd still been inside that room, the ceiling would have collapsed on top of them.

Once outside, the two groups who had escaped merged together on the main thoroughfare. Behind them, the fire flared angrily in orange and crimson, and the radiant heat on Jason's face was painful. Touching his right cheek, he realized that his hands and cheek were burned, probably from rolling the maître d' on the carpet. "I hope it's not bad," he said quietly. He was just vain enough to worry that a disfigured senator might not have a shot at reelection.

After closing the door to the courtyard—an automatic response to keep the smoke away from the crowd—Jason turned anxiously until he spied Patricia, who motioned for him to come to her side. She was kneeling by the maître d' and whispering something into his ear. Ellis watched as the man, struggling against the pain, attempted to say something back to her. There was a sharp grimace and gasp, and then the man's face relaxed.

"He's gone," Ellis said, a wave of despair sweeping over him. When Patricia continued to cradle the man's head on her lap, Jason put his hand gently on her shoulder. Looking up, she wiped tears away from her eyes and laid the man's head gently on the ground. Ellis pulled her to her feet and embraced her.

"He has a wife and children," she said quietly. "He asked me to tell them—" She broke off, unable to continue. Jason Ellis pulled her head against his chest as several fire engines swarmed up noisily around them.

I hope this was an accident, he thought to himself.

When an ambulance pulled up, its bells clanging and horses stamping, Patricia motioned to one of the orderlies, who came over immediately. "This man is dead," she said, gesturing to the maître d'. "I know you need to tend to the injured, but out of respect for his family, can you cover him and perhaps move him off the sidewalk?"

"Of course, ma'am. We'll be glad to do that." The orderly glanced at Jason and said, "You've got a nasty burn on your cheek, sir. You'll need to come with us."

Instinctively he put his hand up to his cheek, but pulled it away quickly when he touched what felt like jelly on his cheek. He did his best to muffle a gasp. The excitement finally ebbing, he noticed his hands and cheek were pulsing with pain. Still, he shook his head. "You take care of the others first. I'm sure they need help more than me."

"No," a woman who was standing nearby said, "it was Senator and Mrs. Ellis who saved us. Please take care of them."

The orderly turned and looked at Patricia. She forced a smile. "Perhaps we can hail a passing automobile and get ourselves to the hospital. That way you can take care of those who need an ambulance. We'll be fine."

The man nodded and moved off to help a woman who was choking from the smoke and struggling to get her breath. Stepping forward, Jeanette Smith said to those who had arrived to help: "Thank you, thank you so much." And then she wiped away the tears streaming down her face.

CHAPTER 7

ANDY PETTIT

Washington, DC
February 3, 1908

Andy Pettit kicked a blackened post and surveyed the muddy hulk that had, just a few days earlier, been a popular restaurant. "You're lucky you survived."

Jason Ellis, his hands wrapped, his right cheek bandaged to protect the ointment applied to his blisters, nodded. "Was it an accident or arson?"

"An accident," Pettit replied. "At least that's the official line. They claim a lady's coat caught fire after being placed too close to an electric light bulb in the cloakroom, starting the fire near the entrance."

"Is that possible, Andy? Can an electric light bulb get that hot?"

"If the air around a bulb is constrained, the temperature can climb to more than 300 degrees, so if the people who designed the restaurant were foolish enough to have a wall bulb right next to where they were hanging people's coats, it's possible."

Ellis shook his head. "That just doesn't ring true. The place went up like a torch. We had very little time to react. Look what happened to the fellow who died. It seems to me there had to be some kind of chemical involved. I was there—I saw it!"

"There might have been an accelerant," Andy said. "A highly flammable chemical, maybe applied to a coat? Maybe just spilled on the floor and ignited. That would have increased the rate in which the fuel, in this case the wood and furnishings, was consumed. Had it not been for your quick action getting people out, the fuel would have included the people inside."

"The press is calling me a hero, but had things gone differently—"

"But they didn't. You acted quickly and decisively, and you ended up saving the day. That's always been your strong point. It's why people are calling you a hero. You deserve that."

Ellis shook his head. "Even when we were little, you were the methodical one—figuring out how to track animals and then being patient enough to do so. You'd reason out the answers to an arithmetic problem—and I'd take a wild guess just to get it over with."

"And yet you almost always got the answers right. You have intuition; I have science. Isn't it interesting that we're still the same today as we were then?"

Jason was quiet for a time. "Do *you* believe accelerants were involved? That would make it arson, wouldn't it?"

Andy Pettit made his way through the rubble to what had been the restaurant's front door. The police had cordoned off the site to prevent passersby from getting hurt but had allowed Pettit and Ellis in as a courtesy. "Just don't make any statements to the press" had been the only condition for their gaining access.

"It's like this, Jason. Once a fire takes off, it doesn't care *how* it got started. But if you look how things burned in this part of the restaurant, it's obvious the temperature was much higher at the beginning of the fire than it was where it spread. That's not a usual pattern for an accidental blaze."

Jason sighed. "So, arson." He bit his lower lip as he reflected on the past few days and decided they had been among the most jumbled of his life. He'd taken dozens of calls from well-wishers, reporters—even the White House. No wonder he felt a bit shaky.

"Andy, you know the question I'm going to ask you next—"

"I don't have an answer." Pettit turned and looked directly at Ellis. "Are you aware that the Capitol Hill police found a hand-gun stashed in a lavatory near the Senate chamber?"

Jason Ellis caught his breath. "What are you saying?"

"What were you going to ask me?"

Ellis swallowed the bile that had risen in his throat. "I was going to ask you if this fire was related to the bombing at Union Station."

"As I said, I don't know the answer. What I *do* know is that there have been more than your usual amount of fatal incidents and odd occurrences within a ten-block radius of each other. That's the kind of thing that makes a detective curious."

"I think I need to sit down." Ellis put his hand against the bandage on his cheek, since the blush that had come to his face was painful.

"I'm sorry, Jason. Let's get out of here. Give me your arm until we clear this rubble, and we'll go over to that park and sit down."

To his own surprise, Ellis agreed, allowing Pettit to help him navigate through the fire-scorched debris. He really did feel a little nauseated and was worried that he might throw up right there in public. When they reached the park across from the de-stroyed restaurant, he gratefully sat down on a bench. Andy sat down next to him.

After taking a moment to catch his breath, Jason said quietly, "Tell me what it's like to be a Pinkerton detective."

Pettit was surprised by this unexpected question but realized that his friend was frightened and needed to calm down. So he sat back, his arms outstretched along the back of the bench to show he was relaxed. He'd been in conversations like this before. "Sure. It started with Allen Pinkerton, a Scot who immigrated to Chicago in 1842. He was a barrel maker until he discovered a counterfeiting ring passing phony bills—almost by accident."

"He was a cooper? I didn't know that."

Pettit was glad to divert Ellis's attention. "It's often like that, isn't it? A man with one set of skills he thinks will form the core of his life quite unexpectedly finds something more valuable. Maybe like you switching from banking to politics."

Jason laughed. "A lot of people think that's like changing from a weasel to a snake." Pettit chuckled, and Jason felt the heaviness he'd been feeling start to lift.

"At any rate, Pinkerton, the only one to observe the crime, was hired to find the source of the counterfeiters, which led him to Chicago. He broke the ring by pretending to be interested in passing fake bills himself. It took a lot of guts to go right into the lion's den, where he could easily have been killed. But it was that kind of subterfuge that allowed him to become the world's greatest detective. After working for the city of Chicago for a few years, he opened his own detective agency and built it into the trusted organization that it is today."

"We Never Sleep," Jason said, quoting the Pinkertons' motto. "That famous eye in the Pinkerton logo makes you feel like they know everything about you. It's the most recognized corporate image in America."

"That's how I became a 'private eye,' when I joined the force.

You know, the Pinkertons foiled an assassination attempt on Abraham Lincoln. And we've broken hundreds of cases since then. We're the model for the Secret Service arm of the Treasury Department."

"Which is why it pains me to ask you again."

"Will I leave them to work for you?"

Ellis nodded. "I hate to ask, but I need someone who can find answers. And there's no one I trust to do that more than you."

Andy Pettit sighed. "I'd be happy working for the Pinkertons the rest of my life. I love the excitement, and I love the discipline of the organization. We accept no reward money because we're well paid for what we do, any corruption is immediately dealt with, and so we have a sterling reputation. It's almost not like a job at all."

Ellis decided not to say anything.

"I left them for a while a few years back. I don't know if you were even aware of it."

"Wait, you left the Pinkertons? I *wasn't* aware of it. What happened?"

"When Roosevelt was police commissioner in New York City, there were a series of particularly brutal sexual assaults on Staten Island. The Richmond County sheriff's department was among the most corrupt police organization in the city and were so busy extorting the local business owners they had little time to investigate actual crimes. Commissioner Roosevelt hired me at his personal expense to find out what was going on. I was the lead detective on the case and soon found out why the police were so ineffective—"

"That's right. I remember when the case made the papers—because they were involved."

"It turned out the sheriff was the one guilty of assault. He used his position to thwart any attempt at investigating."

"As I remember it, one of the detectives narrowly missed being assassinated. I didn't realize you were the man in charge."

"His deputies were loyal because the sheriff gave them access to the spoils that come from police working with criminals. Fortunately, there were two deputies who were honest. They gave us the tip that led to his arrest." He shrugged. "After that, I kept working for Roosevelt for a bit."

Pettit stood up and stretched his arms. Jason couldn't help but notice that even now, at forty-five, Andy was still a powerfully built man with a great barrel chest that strained his shirt when he stretched. "So," Andy said, "when Roosevelt left New York, I went back to the Pinkertons. Some thought I'd turned traitor and didn't want me back."

"I talk you into leaving now, it will be the end of your Pinkerton career for good, then?"

Pettit nodded.

"That explains why Roosevelt felt comfortable drafting you into service at Union Station last week." Jason hesitated, then looked intently at Andy. "I wouldn't ask if I didn't need you. But I do. And you don't need to worry about money. When I say *hire* you, it won't be employer/employee. You'll run your own show, hire the men you need to get the job done, and report only to me. I won't tell you how to do your job."

Jason's voice faded. He felt guilty for asking and was about to say so when Andy spoke up. "It's okay, Jason. I made up my mind to join you as soon as I heard about this fire. Something's going on, and I need the freedom to find out what it is. Pinkerton could redeploy me at any time they like, and doing piecework for the

Secret Service isn't going to give me the latitude I need. Working with you is a better choice."

Ellis was smart enough not to ask what Pettit meant by "latitude."

"Good. I'll instruct my man in New York to put you on the payroll and to set up an expense account. Even though I divested myself of my banking business when I was elected, I did keep a small organization to oversee my real estate holdings. It'll be best if you work out of that unit. You tell my assistant what you want for a salary, and he'll pay it. Set things up however you think best."

Pettit shook his head. "I don't think that will work."

"Didn't you just agree?"

"I'm willing to work *with* you, Jason, but not *for* you." He paused to think how to phrase his next words. "We're friends, but no matter how much latitude you give me, I don't want to be in a relationship where you're my boss. It probably sounds stupid, but I've always felt we were equal."

"I agree. And I would view you as my partner."

"But an unequal partnership since you bring all the money to it."

"So how can we make this work?" Jason felt his stomach tighten.

"How about this? I'll start my own agency. If I have a signed commission from you, I'll use that as collateral to get the money I need to open up a storefront, hire the people I need, and then take on other clients when time permits."

Ellis nodded, the relief evident in his face. "I think that's a good solution. I know some folks in New York who'll help make the business part of it happen, if you're open to that." Then he smiled for the first time in three days. "This really takes a load off my shoulders, Andy."

Pettit didn't look at Ellis, but he did nod his head. Both men stood. "All right, then, I'll go to New York tomorrow." Andy turned and looked Jason directly in the eyes, offering his hand. Taking it was the most reassuring thing Jason Ellis had felt in a long time.

"So the official line is the fire was accidental because DC doesn't want anyone to panic thinking this was another act of terror?"

"That's what I understand," Pettit replied.

"But *you* believe it was intentional."

"I'm certain of it. I'll be very surprised if someone doesn't step forward to take credit for it shortly. If you are a terrorist, you want to cause terror."

"Well, if that's the case, let's find them and put them out of business."

CHAPTER 8

THE PATH TO ULTIMATE GLORY

Baltimore
February 4, 1908

"But we *have* to take credit for it! No one knows it was intentional! How can we call attention to our cause if we don't take credit for what we have done?"

Big Jim Fitzsimmons found Angel Casimer's whining almost unbearable. "Because you're an idiot, is why!"

Casimer bolted up from his chair, and Fitzsimmons thought the slight little man might actually try to strike him. "What do you mean, an idiot? How dare you say this to me!"

"Calm down, Angel." Fitzsimmons sat down heavily in his chair and rolled a cigarette. He always appreciated the time it took to roll a cigarette, since he could use it to tamp down his more violent impulses. He had a devoted little fanatic on his hands whose skills and passion he needed, but who would easily put them both in a hangman's noose if he didn't manage him right. He carefully tapped the tobacco into the paper, then slowly rolled the paper and licked the edge to seal it, finally grasping it between his lips. Only then did he lean forward for Casimer to light it, all part of the ritual that he needed to calm himself—and his small friend—down.

"What do you mean by that? 'You are an idiot.'" Casimer demanded, once Fitzsimmons settled back into his chair.

"What I mean, Angel, is that we gain political advantage by hurting politicians and businessmen. But the public sees an attack on women differently from an attack on a senator or congressman. They see that as"—he struggled for the right words— "disrespectful of the fairer sex. Through no fault of your own, it turns out the restaurant you burned down was filled with wives and mothers that day—their meeting was to include a politician, yes, but the *audience* were wives and mothers. It was an unfortunate turn of events, since on a normal day that restaurant would have been filled with bourgeois businessmen and politicians. But you chose the wrong day. Surely you see taking credit for an attack on women would bring fury down upon our cause rather than rallying people to join us."

"But how can a person sort out who will be in a public place when you are attempting to do such a thing?" Casimer replied, his voice filled with indignation.

"You can't. Which is why I don't hold it against you. Again, Angel, you must be reasonable. The authorities have declared this an awful accident that claimed the life of a working man. Letting the press run with that story means you're safe from capture—and available to do something that will gain the attention we seek, rather than being pursued as a fugitive. So, my young Cossack friend, be calm. This wasn't the right moment. We're working for ultimate glory, and there will be other opportunities."

"I am now twice a murderer," Casimer said sullenly. "And nothing to show for it. You . . . how do you say? 'leak' to the *Post* my bombing was the work of 'International Bolsheviks Against Nations Committee,' which no one has heard of, and without the use of my name. In fact, most people say that my attack on the railroad train was a failure, even though I killed a great capitalist, and so it has all been for nothing . . ." His voice trailed off in anger and despair.

"It was not a failure, Angel. It put all the fools in the government on notice that we're here. Even now they're considering legislation to impose martial law in the District of Columbia—just think of the disruption you've caused." He paused. "And the time will come for your name to be known. I promise that it will come. But you must be patient until we bring about a truly spectacular display of power. Your role will one day be revealed—but it will be because of many such events like these that you'll become legendary, not one isolated attack in a restaurant. Then you'll have one final, glorious opportunity that will cause your name to be known for generations. Be patient, my devoted friend, be patient."

Angel Casimer bit his lip so hard that Fitzsimmons expected blood to drip down the man's chin. "But where next?" he whined. "What can I do that I can take credit for?"

"It must be outside of DC. You must go somewhere else so that the whole country becomes involved, so that people feel terror everywhere." The tone of Fitzsimmons's voice had grown decidedly more optimistic. "I will go to our benefactor. He's the one to choose the place, since he's the one who puts up the money."

"But where?" pleaded Casimer.

Fitzsimmons tilted his head back and took a long draw on the cigarette. Holding the cloud of smoke in his lungs for maximum effect, he then let it out slowly. When he had fully exhaled, he turned to Casimer and smiled. "I do have an idea, Angel. I will suggest it to our leader. I think he—and you—will like it."

New York City
February 4, 1908

"Mr. Maxim Kozlov is waiting, sir."

J. Pierpont Morgan looked up from his paper. The rosacea that had discolored his face and the resulting rhinophyma that deformed his nose gave him a particularly fierce look, one which Morgan almost delighted in confronting people with. If they recoiled from his distorted face, he had little time for them. The naturally assertive ones seemed not to notice. Regardless, as the center of the financial universe, Morgan could not care any less what people thought of his physical appearance.

"Show him in."

Morgan remained seated as the Russian émigré entered the room. "Be seated, Maxim." Morgan did not look up for a few moments, which is why he missed the look of pique that crossed Kozlov's narrow face. Morgan was a physically imposing figure, particularly in comparison to Kozlov's athletically slender physique, so when Morgan looked up he already enjoyed a natural advantage.

"A little trouble at First Commerce?" Morgan asked.

"Nothing we couldn't handle. Since the market adjustments of last year we've improved our capital ratio and were able to fund all requests for redemption."

"I'm glad. Not everyone could do that. I hope that your deposits have returned?"

"Nearly all. The slight shortfall is more than made up by some profits we enjoyed on our market activity."

Morgan sat back in his chair. "Yes, I heard. Not that I'm opposed to making money during a run, but it appears unseemly to make a habit of it. Jay Gould has tried to build his empire on such tactics, but all it ever accomplishes is disarray in the markets." It was well-known that J. P. Morgan disliked nothing more in the world than a disorderly financial market. While Rockefeller, Gould, and Carnegie had made their fortunes by creating—and then exploiting—market turmoil, Morgan's immense fortune was built on stability. Only occasionally did he yield to the temptation to plunder one of his properties at the expense of the other shareholders.

"You asked me here?" Kozlov said. Few in the financial world would try to force the direction of a conversation with Pierpont Morgan, but Kozlov was an anomaly. Morgan had long ago judged that some kind of deep anger fueled Kozlov's intensity. Not that it mattered; whatever drove a man to success was fine with Morgan so long as he was reliable.

"I did. I have a number of items to discuss with you, Kozlov, not least of which is your interest in the Reading Steel enterprise. I've taken a position in steel and have a proposition for you to consider."

Kozlov nodded. "I'm open to discussing steel. For me it's a sideline, and I haven't the capital to fully exploit all the opportunities out there."

"Good. The second thing I want to discuss with you comes out of your own life experience. You may not have an opinion, or you may not choose to share it with me. But I would like your insights if you do."

Kozlov raised his right eyebrow. "And what could possibly come out of my humble beginnings that could interest such a man of privilege?"

Morgan smiled. Not many men had seen that before. "Why, it's just that very sort of attitude I wish to discuss. Obviously you see me as one born to privilege who's capitalized on my father's earlier success in finance. And yet you do not view that positively."

"No insult is intended."

"None taken. It really doesn't matter what you and I think of each other. What matters is that there's a disturbing trend among so-called anarchists to spread destruction in a seemingly random pattern around the world. Two congressmen killed in the past five years, President McKinley murdered eight years ago, and the former governor of Idaho murdered by an anarchist in front of his own home just two years ago. Even King Edward, while Prince of Wales, narrowly avoided assassination. And now our colleague Lane Talmadge. There has never been anything like it."

"And what do these events have to do with me?" Kozlov's gray eyes had the appearance of glinting steel.

"They have *everything* to do with you and me. You had a run on your bank as a result of this incident in Washington, DC, apparently caused by some fringe Bolshevik element. Now a restaurant burns down, which everyone believes was related to the earlier event, even though the authorities deny it. We still haven't recovered from that dip. Every time one of these attacks happens, our financial institutions are put at risk. I'm sure that despite gaining depositors back, you must find yourself constrained by all the capital you have to hold in reserve?"

"It *has* restricted my options," Kozlov replied, his demeanor growing less dark. "But what can I possibly do about it?"

"Obviously you can't do anything about it. What you can do, because of your experience living overseas, is tell me what organizations you believe are behind this. I want to know from your perspective if this international effort is truly organized—or if these events are rogue actors capitalizing on each other's exploits around the globe. We need to find a way to prepare the markets for unknown events, even intentional events like these, so that the financial system isn't held hostage to political machinations."

"I have not lived overseas for years. I know nothing of international conspiracies." There was a ferocity in his voice that would have intimidated lesser men than Morgan. "Besides, it seems to me that business institutions are held in just as much contempt as are governments—perhaps more. In fact, our Mr. Roosevelt seems to be enormously popular, while those of us on Wall Street are viewed with suspicion and scorn."

"And yet it's the political leaders who continue to be attacked," Morgan said. "Certainly you have European connections for your financial operations. Do you still have any connections in Russia, or was that too long ago?"

Kozlov decided that he hated Morgan. J. P. Morgan was, financially speaking, the United States' equivalent of the tsar, and Kozlov had no love for the tsar.

"Are you investigating my native country?"

"No, I have very few connections there. That's why I invited you." Having to reveal this hole in his network was clearly irritating to Morgan.

"Ah. Now I understand." Kozlov nodded thoughtfully. "I do come from a dark place."

It seemed to Morgan that Kozlov was relieved by this revelation for some reason, probably because it gave Kozlov a small bit of advantage.

"Well," Kozlov said, "perhaps I can be of service. My ability to speak Russian does bring me occasional lines of business from that sad part of the world. It's proved helpful to me to act as an intermediary for those in the United States who would do business with Russians, and to Russians who would like to do business here. That is one of the roles I play that has helped First Commerce survive the turmoil of the past ten years."

"A very wise use of your talents," Pierpont Morgan replied. "So, you'll help me find out to what degree Russian people may be involved in anarchist attacks here and abroad? I want to know if anyone in that part of the world has connections to what is happening here. I need to understand the attitude of workers there, of people in finance, and of the government. This Bolshevik claim about the Union Station bombing must have some Russian connection—"

"Or it was a convenient name to give the public to conceal the identity of the real conspirators. I have never heard of the International Bolsheviks Against Nations Committee, and I doubt that anyone else has either."

Morgan nodded. "Exactly—but how can we know for sure? Of course, I worked for my father's brokerage house in London, so I have my own contacts there. And in France. But I need to understand the situation in as much of the world as I can. So perhaps you can shed a little light on the eastern European states?"

Kozlov swallowed. There was great risk in having a man like J. P. Morgan poke around in Russian affairs, including his own. But it was better that Morgan learned what he needed from Kozlov rather than someone else. And the chance to be drawn into Morgan's circle held many advantages. "I will try to help you, as a token of appreciation for the support you provided in 1907. But it's difficult. People there are suspicious. It will take time."

Pierpont Morgan stood up. "You owe me nothing for 1907—saving First Commerce Trust was good business." Walking around his desk he asked, "Would you care for a drink, Maxim?"

"Not today, thank you. But I will be in touch."

CHAPTER 9

CHAOS IN HARTFORD!

Hartford, CT
February 10, 1908

"Union Life Insurance Company unfair to workers!"

Chants like that were rare in Hartford, Connecticut, the very buttoned-down insurance capital of the world. Now the labor movement had found its way to the massive bronze doors of the forty-year-old Union Life Insurance Company, formed directly after the Civil War to capitalize on the goodwill associated with the word *union*. Of course, a strike against an insurance company was far different from one against a large industrial concern, such as Carnegie Steel. The workers were almost all white-collared young clerks keeping track of the vast tides of money flowing back and forth between the company and its clients. Their hands were soft as opposed to their brawny brothers, and the threat of violence was much lower. But their passion was no less than that of others in the cause, and they were resolved to organize against the tyranny of the men on the thirteenth floor—the wealthy executives versus the rank and file who struggled to get by.

"No more twelve-hour workdays! We must unionize!"

That was the main issue. While the capitalists at the top had grown rich from the massive industrialization of the past fifty years, workers still labored in spartan conditions with long hours that left them little time to spend with their families. And while the work that clerks did was certainly easier on the body than working in a mill or railroad, the tedium of the job was every bit as destructive to the mind.

"Eight-hour days, thirty minutes for lunch! We demand to organize!"

It was here that Angel Casimer had made his final preparations. After his previous failed attempts at lighting the fuse of anarchy, he was finally allowed to strike in a place where his action would have immediate effect.

It's not right what the capitalists do to people like us. He repeated this old phrase in his mind, the same phrase he'd heard his father repeat. It had become his own mantra. His father's voice continued in his mind: *America was supposed to be the land of opportunity, a place where we could make our way into a better life. Instead, we come to work for bosses who care nothing for us and who discard us the moment we are of no value to them.* Casimer had to put down the rifle that he had been cleaning to calm his hands, now trembling in anger at memories from his childhood.

"I remember what they did to you, Father," he spoke aloud. The remembered indignity of the textile mill owner physically throwing his father into the street after the elder Casimer had accidentally broken his arm in one of the company's machines made Angel's face burn with indignation.

"I went into the US Army to support the family when my father could no longer work. I served in the same Spanish-American War that made Theodore Roosevelt famous, but he was treated as a hero while my fellow soldiers treated me with contempt for my accent!" Casimer's voice quivered with rage. He had gone through this routine so many times in his mind that it repeated itself over and over like one of the fancy new newsreels that played at the local cinemas. No matter how many times you watched it, the wording never changed.

Angel Casimer forced himself to concentrate. Just three days earlier there had been a knock at his door, which he opened to find no one there, only an envelope at the threshold. Picking it up, he opened it to find $100 inside and a note: "Go to Union Life in Hartford, Connecticut, and assassinate . . ." Thinking back on it, he wondered again who'd provided the money for his train ticket from Baltimore to Hartford. He'd memorized the name of the man he was supposed to kill. Fitzsimmons claimed to know nothing about the envelope but encouraged Casimer to act on it. The rest of the message read, "Tell no one your name—you have more work yet to do." That requirement had galled him and almost made him refuse. But Fitzsimmons had persuaded him to find his way north. Here on the fifth day of the clerical workers' strike, he was perched above the city square, eager to act.

"Whoever sent you this envelope is shrewd," Fitzsimmons said. "He realizes that with no attribution, the terror will increase. Everyone will be a suspect. No one will know if it's a stranger or their neighbor next door, and it will seem like the whole world is ready to blow up."

Casimer had protested, but to no avail. Fussing again with his Winchester rifle, the old mental script started to play again in his mind. "Where are you *really* from?" his army comrades used to ask. "You smell like bratwurst and sausage," they said, even though he ate the same food they did. "You'll amount to nothing, Casimer!" the corporal who commanded his unit used to say multiple times per day.

"Nothing? We'll see who is nothing!" He spat on the roof and focused his gaze on the main entrance to the Union Life home office. Small and wiry, he'd struggled with the physical demands of the army—but not when it came to weapons. He had an uncanny ability with a rifle and had soon been made a sniper. When he demonstrated he was also fearless around explosives, he was trained in ordnance. The army had taught him all he needed to know as an anarchist. "It will be me who stands up to those who treat us 'lesser people' with contempt. *I* will be the one to light the match."

As he inserted another shell into the rifle's magazine, the commotion in the plaza grew louder. Rising to his knees, he stuck his head carefully above the façade of the building he had chosen to shoot from and watched as a band of Pinkertons moved between the crowd and the building. Finally, one raised his arm to quiet the crowd. Casimer strained to hear what the man shouted at them, and then smiled as he heard the words he'd been straining to hear. Really, the only word he needed was "Smithson," the name of the president of Union Life—and the name from his anonymous letter.

Levering a cartridge into the chamber, he waited until the massive brass doors swung open and a heavyset, well-dressed man emerged at the top of the steps. Casimer moved his index finger onto the trigger, but decided to wait a few moments to allow Smithson to start his speech. *It will be more shocking for him to die in the middle of a sentence.* Straining to hear, he heard Smithson rebuke the workers for their ingratitude while simultaneously promising to address many of the concerns they had. Smithson ridiculously said he could meet their demands if they gave up the idea of forming a union, but then he said they'd all be fired if they insisted on organizing. Casimer felt an inhuman scream rise up from his throat and felt himself rising to his feet while carefully aiming at the man saying such outrageous things.

"Death to all capitalists!" he shouted just before he pulled the trigger. He had the satisfaction of seeing Smithson look up to lock eyes with him—and then relished the greater spectacle of Smithson's chest exploding and blood spattering into the crowd. As if in slow motion, Smithson's body fell back against the brass doors and marble steps of the great Union Life Insurance Company. "A new claim for you to settle!" he shouted, thinking gleefully that there would be no workers to process the claim. Then, as the crowd started to turn toward his position, he aimed his rifle at the ground at the back of the crowd and quickly fired several more rounds, forcing the people to back away. It was thrilling to see people scatter because of his actions, and he felt a wave of euphoria rush over him.

Throw the grenade, Angel! You must act according to your plan. He reached into his satchel and tossed a grenade over the wall to create more panic. The confusion the explosion wrought gave him time to race to the fire escape at the back of the building. He descended quickly and ran to the young horse he'd purchased earlier that week. He swung into the saddle and thought to himself, *Today the workers of Hartford know the cause for which I stand, but soon the whole world will know! My time has come!* He rode off, confident that no one could follow, and completely unaware how badly his confidence was misplaced.

Washington, DC
February 10, 1908

"It seems to me there will be eight candidates by the time we reach the convention," Theodore Roosevelt said. "Taft, Cannon, Foraker, Hughes, Knox, La Follette, and Shaw."

"That's seven," Jason Ellis said.

"There will be a handful of votes cast for Vice President Fairbanks, even though my endorsing Taft pretty well sinks any of his hopes."

"Do you think any of the rest pose a serious threat to Taft?"

The president took a long drink of water. "I don't believe so. Probably the biggest threat to his nomination is that damn Speaker Cannon. He's done his best to be a thorn in my side." Despite himself, Ellis couldn't help but smile. The action caused him to wince. His cheek was healing nicely from the burn, but he still felt a tightness when he smiled.

"And just what are you smiling about?" Roosevelt demanded.

"Sorry, Mr. President. His name brought to mind a quote he made a while back. He can be very colorful."

"It's that obnoxious quote he made about me, isn't it?"

"He's made more than one, sir."

Roosevelt narrowed his gaze. "Yes, he has. So, which one makes you grin?"

Ellis wished he'd kept his thoughts to himself. "'Theodore Roosevelt has no more use for the Constitution than a tomcat has for a marriage license.'" Ellis couldn't help but smile again.

"Oh, that's a good quote, all right. It's why the papers call him 'Uncle Joe' and treat him like a country rube. But he's about the shrewdest man to ever hold the position of Speaker. He's done as much damage to my programs as any Democrat could hope to do. With Republican friends like him, I don't need enemies."

Ellis nodded. The Republican Party had to sort out its feelings about progressivism versus their more traditional conservative values on fiscal policy. Roosevelt's "Square Deal" played well with the crowds, but not with the barons of industry.

"You know I'll be in something of a bind," Ellis said, "if they follow through and nominate Governor Hughes. Since he's New York's favorite-son candidate, I'll probably have to vote for him on the first ballot as a show of unity."

"I won't vote for him, even though I was governor of New York." Roosevelt was firm. But then he softened. "But you do what you must, Jason. I doubt I'll have any trouble getting Taft through the nomination if you can join us after the first round."

The door opened, and Roosevelt's personal secretary walked in. "Excuse me, sir. You have an urgent telegram from Hartford, Connecticut."

Roosevelt reached out and took the telegram. "Will you excuse me a moment, Jason?"

"Certainly." Ellis went back to the schedule he'd been working on, trying to balance the speakers at the convention to keep political egos properly fed and nourished. But his concentration was quickly interrupted by Roosevelt.

"Blast! There's been an assassination in Hartford. The president of a life insurance company was just shot and killed during a union organizing rally. Don't these idiots realize that it wrecks their cause to do these terrible things?"

"A life insurance company? What's that got to do with unions and anarchists?"

"Apparently the company's clerks were trying to organize. At any rate, a man by the name of Smithson was killed."

"Jefferson Smithson?" Ellis asked.

Roosevelt glanced down at the telegram. "Yes, do you know him?"

"If he's with the Union Life Insurance Company, I do. I was on the board of directors for Union Life and chair of the committee that recruited Jeff Smithson. He's a very good man, the father of five children. This is an awful thing!" Ellis felt a deep pain in his stomach as he processed this news.

"I'm sorry for the loss of this man's life," Roosevelt said. "I'll send the family my personal condolences. Perhaps you could represent us at his funeral?"

Ellis hesitated. A funeral would be the perfect place for yet another attack. But his momentary fear was quickly replaced with anger and resolve. "Yes, I'm sure I can."

The swoop of emotions caused Ellis to feel lightheaded, and he felt detached from the conversation, almost as if he were observing it from outside his body. *Two of my associates killed by assassins!* He once again resorted to a quick mental prayer, *"Dear Father—why is this happening? What am I to make of all this? Please guide me . . ."*

"Well," Roosevelt said, "so much for planning the convention. I'll have to find out what's behind this murder in Hartford. We've got to find out who did this. And forthwith, at that!"

Casimer's head was alive with exhilaration as he drove his horse at full gallop down an obscure country lane he'd mapped out well in advance of his attack on Smithson. *It isn't murder when you are fighting a war, no matter what they say,* he thought to himself. *I was considered patriotic when I killed Spaniards in Cuba, so why not so when I kill one of the generals of capitalism?* The vast difference between a war legally authorized by one nation against another and a guerilla attack on an unarmed man in a public square seemed not to enter Casimer's thinking.

And there will be more opportunities to serve in this battle. Big Jim keeps promising me that! As Casimer daydreamed, he heard the unique whine of a bullet passing close to one ear. And a fraction of a second later, the report of a weapon from behind him. He let out an involuntary shout of alarm while casting a glance over his shoulder. His plan for disrupting the crowd had been so perfect he should have enjoyed a commanding lead over anyone pursuing him, but as he looked back in the distance, he saw two men in black topcoats pursuing him furiously on horseback.

The Pinkertons! How can they be after me so quickly? He spurred his horse and leaned down as close to the animal's body as possible, hoping to reduce his silhouette to the men firing at him.

It is much easier to fire forward than over your shoulder, he said to himself, his mind racing furiously through potential solutions to this unanticipated problem. *That gives them the advantage. But I've got a lead on them, and it's just two miles to the train!* He had planned to catch a southbound train at an obscure siding, and then to lose himself in the crowd when it arrived in New York City. He checked behind again. The Pinkertons were gaining.

He spurred his horse even harder, the chance to catch the train he'd been hoping for now an evaporated dream. *Curse it— why the Pinkertons?* He knew their reputation for never sleeping. *But they must sleep the same as any other man, mustn't they?* It was a ridiculous thought, but that's what came to his agitated mind, the image of the famous never-sleeping eye taunted him. *I will have to sleep sometime. I am just a man.* He leaned closer to the horse. *But at this moment, I must escape. That is all I can think about. I must find a way to escape.* It was proving more difficult than he had planned.

If you hope to get out of this alive, you have to confuse them. You must do something they will not suspect. You must get off the road. Just thinking it sounded stupid. *Confuse the Pinkertons—fat chance of that!* But as the absurdity of it settled into his brain, a wild thought came to his mind. *It probably won't work, but it will scare them out of their wits.*

With that he charged full speed into a tiny break in the thick bank of trees. His horse tried to slow, but he applied the whip and hoped he wouldn't be torn from the saddle by a tree branch.

CHAPTER 10

PURSUIT

New York City
February 10, 1908

"The market's already reacted, though the news has been on the ticker for just a few minutes." Tom Scanlon sounded incredulous. He looked down nervously at the strand of paper tape in his hands to confirm the bad news. But all the ticker could show were changes in the price of a sampling of stocks, not the specific information he really wanted. News of the assassination in Hartford had been phoned to them by a friendly correspondent at the *Wall Street Journal*, which should have given them an advantage, but the news was spreading quickly. It would be just a matter of minutes until special editions of all the major newspapers started to reach the street with the ominous headline, "Assassination in Hartford!"

"When will this madness stop?" Scanlon asked Maxim Kozlov.

For his part, Kozlov was unmoved. "This will have little effect in the long run. The natural market recovery we are in will easily overcome this setback, just as happened after the bombing in Washington." He drew on his cigar. "But it is going to have an adverse effect on Jason Ellis's portfolio. Have they suspended trading in Union Life stock?" Kozlov's voice was cool and steady.

"Not yet, sir. It's dropping like a rock off the roof of a building. It just came over the wire. Ellis is likely to be angry, even if we sell out his position."

"It's hardly our fault that he forced us into keeping a portion of his investment in Union Life as a condition of setting up his personal trust. If he wants his money in a blind trust, then he should trust those of us who can see. He used to sit on Union Life's board, so that was a purely sentimental decision. He even resigned when he was elected to the Senate—he's such a prude about conflicts of interest. No other senator seems to worry about being on a corporate payroll."

Scanlon was struck again at how quickly Kozlov could contradict his own thinking: first criticizing Ellis for holding onto Union Life stock and immediately criticizing him for not keeping a lucrative position on their board. He should know that if Ellis had given up the stock, he wouldn't be eligible to sit on the board. Scanlon shook his head. Regardless of Kozlov's opinions, Scanlon admired Ellis for his scruples.

"Yes, sir. Do you want me to send him some notice about it?"

"No. I'll send a personal note. I borrowed some of his stock earlier this month. I'd been studying the financial situation of Union Life and decided it was likely to drop in value. I'll replace it once trading opens again. Besides, he may be all right in the long run, since this is being treated as an attack by the clerical workers union, which makes it easier for Union Life to throw the union out." Kozlov pondered for a moment and then smiled. "An ironic twist of the word, isn't it? The lowercase 'union' fanatics attempt to destroy the uppercase 'Union' insurance company by assassinating their leader, only to find that it ultimately boosts the value of the stock and destroys the unionization drive." He chuckled and settled back down in his chair.

Scanlon hesitated before replying, "Bad news for Mr. Smithson, though, despite your prediction it'll be good news for the markets in the long run. All a bit cynical, isn't it?"

Kozlov looked up from his desk with a curious look in his eye. "Sometimes I think you're too soft for this business, Tom. Mr. Smithson is of no concern to us or to our clients. His murder, on the other hand, is of great concern. We need to extract as much value from it as possible for our clients. I feel no guilt about an event beyond my control having a positive outcome—and smashing the union is just such a positive outcome."

"Yes, sir." Scanlon felt the hair on the back of his neck stand up. "Is that all, then?" He tried to conceal the indignation in his voice but wasn't sure he'd pulled it off. Fortunately, Kozlov waved him off without a comment.

Rural Connecticut
February 10, 1908

As Angel Casimer forced his horse, heaving and lathered, through the maze of thick hardwood forest, he could hear the Pinkertons' horses crashing in pursuit behind him. He knew the trail of smashed branches and undergrowth he was leaving would make it easy for them to follow. But what they didn't know was that this was his backup plan. He'd noticed as he'd scouted his escape route that there was a stream between the road and the railroad siding. And the streambed had a slightly submerged sandbar downstream from where he'd intersect it. Forcing his horse into the water and turning downstream, he was confident he could round a bend before they spied him. By the time they arrived at the stream, they'd have to pause to figure out which direction he'd headed, and even if they chose correctly, they'd have to figure out where he'd left the streambed. Going downstream would make it harder to follow him, since any mud or debris he stirred up would follow him and obscure his trail.

And then I will break out and into the clear! As the undergrowth thinned, he dropped against the horse and whispered, "You can do this!" Responding to centuries of domesticity bred into its genes, the animal reacted to his encouragement and lunged forward. As they reached the streambed, Casimer grabbed hold of its mane as the horse literally leaped out into the water, a great wave splashing up as the startled animal recoiled. "Now go!" he shouted, urging the horse to turn to the right and swim. Leaning down again, he whispered, "As fast as you can!" He touched the horse gently in the underbelly with his feet to urge its very best performance, and it quickly responded. "Another twenty seconds, and we will be home free, my friend." He hoped desperately the lead he had was enough to round the bend before the Pinkertons could see him.

If his memory was right, the stream was deep for a stretch, but there was a shallow ledge on the southern bank around the corner. *Ten, nine, eight . . .* He listened but did not hear the Pinkertons in the water yet. *Four, three, two . . .* and with that, Casimer's horse rounded the bend, and Angel quickly guided it to a spot just shy of the southern bank, where it found solid footing. In a matter of moments they were splashing at almost a full gallop along the submerged ledge until, after turning around a second bend, he turned out from the streambed and on to hard-packed gravel.

The horse didn't want to go there, the rock shifting under its feet, but Casimer forced it, and soon they were up on solid ground, having left very little evidence where they'd exited. He figured it would take the Pinkertons at least a few minutes to realize that the submersed shelf even existed, which would give him just the time he needed to complete his plan.

In the far distance, he heard a gunshot, muted by the trees between them, which told him one of the Pinkertons had reached the stream and was signaling to the other. He smiled with the realization he would likely escape, after all. *The railroad should be just up there where the sun is shining through.* It seemed miraculous how clearly he could recall the details of his scouting trip, but his senses were alive with excitement, and his brain was functioning with greater clarity than ever before. He loved the exhilaration of overcoming obstacles.

I think I will make it, he thought, happily, but perhaps a moment too quickly, for just as victory was in sight, he felt his poor horse slacken its pace. He dug his heels in, forcing the animal ahead until they broke out next to the railroad tracks, and then allowed it to rest for a few minutes. After confirming the location in his mind, he nudged the horse just inside the tree line so the engineer and fireman wouldn't see him when the southbound train went by. "Just a little bit longer, and you will be done with me," he said quietly to the horse. He felt it panting heavily beneath him, and he reached down and petted its neck to help it calm down. "You have done very well, my young friend, very well indeed."

A few minutes later, just as he expected, a southbound freight train loomed into view, and he waited anxiously until the engine passed by. When the moment was right, he urged his horse one last time, quickly matching the speed of the train until he was galloping dead even with the last car. He edged the horse ever closer to the railcar until he was able to grab hold of a ladder rung and pull himself off the saddle and onto the side of the freight car.

Relieved of his weight, the horse started to pull away from the tracks. Unfortunately for the horse, it was not quite soon enough, for just as soon as Casimer's feet were safely on the lowest rung of the ladder, he whipped out his pistol and shot the horse dead, and it tumbled into a heap on the track, just as Casimer had hoped it would.

Yes. That will tie up the next train coming up the track. The Pinkertons couldn't possibly catch him by horse now, as the freight train continued to pick up speed. His lead was simply too great. And with a dead horse to deal with, they couldn't hope to catch him before he'd jumped back into the wilderness. While they could eventually send a telegram ahead, it would only be after they'd gotten to the next station on the line. Angel would disappear back into the forest long before then, and with a million acres of forest to hide in, he wouldn't possibly be found. Once on foot, he would disappear into the underbrush and make his way back to Maryland. *A mighty blow on behalf of the union cause—and an escape from the Pinkertons. Someday there will be a "Ballad of Angel Casimer" that we will sing.* He leaned against the back wall of the railcar, wedging himself between the ladder and the body of the car, and glowed with pride. *Not many men can say such a thing!* He had never felt more alive. Inhaling deeply, he replayed the thrill of the chase over in his mind. *I escaped the Pinkertons!*

But, as is usual, the moment was short-lived. As the adrenaline drained from his system, he sighed. *But I have killed a man who has never done me any harm.* It irritated him that his conscience chose to speak at such a moment. *You would rob me of my glory,* he told himself. *You are a thief, and I will not listen to you.* But he couldn't stop the thoughts coming, and he was quickly overcome by a wave of despair. Feeling sullen and depressed, and with at least another twenty minutes before he'd need to jump from the train, he climbed to the top of the car, where he could lie on the roof to catch his breath.

As he pulled himself onto the roof, he noticed a pain in his arm. Looking down, he saw evidence a bullet had grazed his arm. In the heat of the chase, he hadn't noticed it, but now it was throbbing painfully. He knew he needed to attend to it right away. *Do not let your conscience rob you of this great victory, Angel! You will be famous . . .*

Washington, DC
February 10, 1908

"He escaped?" Jason Ellis asked, an air of resignation in his voice.

"Yes. How did you know that?" the president asked.

"I could see it in your eyes." Senator Ellis took a deep breath and let it out slowly. Roosevelt crumpled the telegram and threw it into the wastebasket. "It's the same person—the man who blew up the train and burned down the restaurant."

"You can't know that, Jason. These incidents are nothing alike."

Ellis nodded. Roosevelt was right, of course. But somehow the senator knew that it was the same man. He didn't know how he knew, but he knew it nonetheless.

"You should go home and pick up Patricia, Jason. We really can't miss the banquet tonight. We're just three months from the convention, and we must put forth a good face. The Democrats will nail us to the wall about our failure to stop this crime spree."

Ellis tried to smile but couldn't pull it off. "Of course, sir. I'll see you in two hours, then."

As Roosevelt reached the door to his study, he turned and called after the senator. "And Jason, I want you to meet with Andy Pettit tomorrow morning. It's urgent he start finding the threads that connect these events."

"I thought you didn't agree that there's a connection."

"I don't have enough information to agree *or* disagree. But I know you well enough to know your hunches are often accurate."

"I'll meet with Andy. But you saw him just a few days ago. May I ask what he shared with you then?"

"Some new information about the Union Station bombing suggests a link to international sources. I think it warrants an investigation that may involve you." Roosevelt paused and stroked his chin—a penchant of his. "Instead of meeting with Pettit by yourself, perhaps you could bring him over to the White House. Now that I think of it, I have something special in mind for the two of you—something that needs the Senate's prestige but Andy Pettit's investigative wiles. Any chance you can make it tomorrow morning?"

Jason Ellis nodded. "We'll be there at nine o'clock, sir." He was still too heartsick about Jeff Smithson's assassin's escape to even be curious about what Roosevelt was planning.

CHAPTER 11

BOGEYMEN AND MIRACLES

New York City
February 11, 1908

"You seem distracted today, sir."

"I suppose I am," Maxim Kozlov said, scowling. He bit his lower lip, which was not common, and Tom Scanlon wondered about it.

"Trouble with the work Mr. Morgan asked you to complete?"

"What do you know about what J. P. Morgan wants?" Kozlov demanded sharply, breaking the nib of his fountain pen as he looked up. "Damn you! Look what you made me do!" He stood in a fury and reached for a blotter to sop up the ink that had flooded onto the document he'd been working on.

"Here, let me do that," Tom Scanlon said quickly. "I meant no harm." Scanlon moved immediately toward the desk to clean up the mess, and, as he did so, Kozlov took note of how pale Scanlon was. Kozlov stood aside and allowed Scanlon to deal with the ink, getting his hands covered in the stuff as he did so.

"Tom, what do you know about J. P.?"

Scanlon looked at him, stricken. "Only what you told me the other morning, sir. You said Mr. Morgan had taken you into his confidence and asked you to provide details about something he was working on. It seemed at the time it pleased you, so I was just following up to make conversation. I'm very sorry . . ."

Kozlov walked over to the liquor cabinet, purposely taking his time to steady his breathing. "I'd forgotten I'd told you that."

Tom Scanlon noted that Kozlov's hands were trembling as he poured a shot of whiskey and then downed it in a single gulp. Kozlov turned to Scanlon and did his best to act nonplussed. "It's rather confidential, and I prefer no one else know I'm working with Mr. Morgan right now." He attempted a smile. "Some things are better kept secret."

"Yes, sir. Of course. Rest assured I've told no one, and I'll never mention it to you again." Scanlon's mouth was dry; he wasn't used to seeing his boss nervous.

"Actually, perhaps it's all right that you know. I need someone to conduct some discreet inquiries, and you've done that well for me in the past. Perhaps you'd be open to some new inquiries? You'd be well compensated, of course."

Scanlon flushed. "Of course, sir. I'll be glad to do whatever you ask." He found himself simultaneously intrigued, flattered, and frightened. He knew—as well as anyone could know—the darkness that always seemed to surround Maxim Kozlov. Scanlon was one of the few employees trusted enough to know Kozlov operated certain trust accounts under assumed names, the true identity of their beneficiaries known only to Kozlov himself. Without knowing who the men were behind these accounts, Tom did know that the men who showed up for an occasional withdrawal were not the sort of people Tom would like as friends. And the after-hours errands Kozlov had Tom perform all up and down the East Coast were always shrouded in mystery.

"There, sir," Scanlon said, stepping back from the desk. "I'll have the mail clerks bring up a new desk pad immediately. Again, I'm sorry."

Kozlov stiffened. "Say nothing more about it. Now, will you check the price of Union Life Insurance? I understand it's been rallying since the assassination."

"Quite a shock, isn't it? Almost an emotional reaction from the Street to bolster one of their own. Or someone's trying to make a market in the stock and will be rewarded by the rally."

"Yes," Kozlov said darkly. "Such a rally does not usually happen naturally. I would very much like to know who has intervened."

It was only then Scanlon remembered that Kozlov had shorted the stock, which accounted for his pique. He could lose a great deal of money if the stock continued to rise. *Perhaps that is why your mood's so foul today.* Inexplicably, the hair on the back of Scanlon's neck stood up. "I'll see what I can find out about it." He took Kozlov's silence as an endorsement and quickly excused himself.

Rural Connecticut
February 11, 1908

Angel Casimer furiously wiped a tear from his face. "Curse this sprained ankle!" He hobbled painfully through the underbrush, doing his best to conceal his tracks. "But I lost them, I am sure of that. A bad ankle is a small price to pay." Encouraging words, and very much needed as Casimer searched for a spot to lie down for the night. "Tomorrow I will find a way to bathe and to wash my clothes so I can catch a train in Binghamton without raising suspicions. I am sure they will still be looking for me." Talking to yourself in the middle of an empty forest isn't by itself a sign of mental instability, but the exhausted desperation in Casimer's voice suggested that he needed rest, both physically and emotionally—and soon.

"Ah, here is a spot. Hiding in this overgrowth just above the creek will make me invisible." He winced in pain with each step, using a leafy broken branch to obscure the last twenty yards of the path. "You were a fool to jump as you did—you should have bent your knees to tuck and roll as you were trained, rather than trying to stay upright and running. The train was going too fast. You are such an idiot, and now you have this ankle to show for it!" The bullet graze on his arm felt even more painful than it had on the train. "You have to take some time to clean and wrap that, Angel!"

Once he was quite sure he'd erased his path, he stepped into the creek and sloshed upstream another thirty yards to a spot he had identified earlier. Even if an animal—or a Pinkerton—were somehow following his smell, it would be lost in the stream, and his sleeping spot would give him plenty of time to hear them. "Which proves that you are not an idiot. No fool in the world could escape from Pinkerton detectives, and right under their very noses. No, you are a great soldier, Angel Casimer, 'a guerilla warrior in an important cause,' as Big Jim likes to say." Casimer curled up against the damp and moss-covered ground, hidden by the foliage above him, and rubbed his tired eyes. He was asleep as soon as his eyelids closed.

Washington, DC
February 11, 1908

When in Washington, Jason Ellis lived in a comfortable townhouse in the prestigious Stanton Park neighborhood of the Capitol Hill district. It was an easy walk from there to the Capitol Building as well as to Union Station to catch a train to his estate, "Ellis Shores," on Long Island, which he'd purchased at the height of his investment banking career.

Walking home on a late night, Senator Ellis mentally rehearsed his work that day on the Senate Banking Committee. They had been discussing what was now being called the Bureau of Investigation, which draft legislation tasked with "investigating crimes against the United States." With such a broad mandate, members of the subcommittee were working to define a much narrower range of crimes that would fall under its jurisdiction. Ellis resented that organized criminal conspiracies were driving Congress to take such a step.

It was past 11:00 p.m., he was tired, and he was wary about Patricia's reaction to what President Roosevelt had discussed with him and Andy Pettit earlier that morning. Which is why he first failed to notice the sound of footsteps behind him. His conscious mind was racing through the testimony they'd heard, the posturing from both sides, a rebuttal he wished he'd voiced—too much in turmoil to pay attention to the walk home. But the hair on the back of his neck somehow paid attention, and as he turned right off A Street NE onto 7th Street NE, he felt a chill run up his spine. Though some locales had begun to switch their streetlights from gas to electric, Stanton Park still relied on the feeble flickering glow of gas, providing little illumination past a small circle cast on each corner. Ellis's conscious mind finally registered what sounded like footfalls at a distance behind him.

Probably nothing, he said to himself. *Or it's another overly devoted public servant on his way home.* Most had no idea the long hours that members of Congress and their staff worked, often arriving early in the morning and leaving late at night. He picked up his pace to provide a little distance, not wanting to seem paranoid by turning to look behind him. "You know people with dogs have to walk them, even at a late hour," he said under his breath, wishing *he* had a great big German shepherd type of dog with him.

For a few moments he heard nothing, enough of a relief that he slowed down a trifle and chastised himself for worrying. But just as before, he again heard the sound of someone behind him matching his speed exactly.

At this point, he was halfway through the block that would carry him into the intersection of 7th Street NE and East Capitol Street NE, where he was sure the lighting would be stronger. *If I speed up again I can lose this person until I get to the light. The Capitol Hill police often send someone around up until midnight, so once I reach the light there won't be a problem,* he thought while speeding up. He hoped his prediction about the police was right, but was not at all sure that Congress hadn't reduced the police's budget earlier that year because of the slowdown in revenue caused by the 1907 Panic. "I'm sure I didn't vote for *that,*" Ellis said under his breath, trying to calm down his pounding heart with a little humor.

Okay, what's happening? Jason was in the habit of analyzing every situation, so he forced himself to ask if what he was hearing was imaginary or real.

It's real. He was certain now. And that was enough to make his thighs tingle, a sure sign he was frightened. *I've got to turn around and see who's there. Who cares if I startle them?* But his walking pace at this point was just short of a military double-time, and if he slowed down to make the turn, the person following could easily close the distance.

Just half a block to the streetlights—one on each corner. No one would think to attack under their full glare. He wished he could believe himself, but his breathing was now so quick he was getting lightheaded. He unconsciously reached inside his coat pocket, and finding it empty, thought to himself, *No, I'm not carrying a gun. I don't do that anymore, but maybe I should.* He realized the steps were getting closer. *I've got to make a dash for it.*

He leaned forward and broke into a run. The feet behind him kept up. *You're nearly there! Keep going!* His heart was pounding, his lungs were burning, and he realized he was in terrible physical condition. *It's getting close!* He was concentrating so hard he let out a yelp when the person behind him shouted, "Senator Ellis! Senator Ellis!"

He stumbled and almost fell as he tried to register what was happening.

"Senator Ellis, it's me, Matthew!"

"Matthew!" he gasped as he slowed down, stopped and turned. A young man emerged from the darkness. "Matthew? Matthew Porter? Is that you?"

"Yes, sir. I've been trying to catch you. You left your briefcase and the papers in it you need for your meeting with the attorney general tomorrow morning. I didn't think you'd want to have to come back by the office to pick it up." Ellis was at least partially relieved to hear Matthew breathing hard, too. He'd given the young fellow a run for his money.

"Oh, for heaven's sake," Ellis said. "I'm sorry you had to do that. I picked up my umbrella because it looked like it might rain, then forgot the briefcase."

"Boy, you don't waste any time getting home, do you, sir?" Matthew's chest was heaving in and out.

Ellis was grateful for the odd color from the gas lights since they likely masked how red his face had become. "I guess I was in a bigger hurry than I thought. Why didn't you just call out? I would have come back to meet you."

"I should have, but I didn't want to startle anyone in the neighborhood. I thought I could just catch you and explain it quietly."

"Ah." Now Ellis really was embarrassed. "It took me a long time to hear you, and when I did I assumed you were someone else on his way home. I guess I didn't want to be passed in the dark."

"I hope I didn't frighten you, sir."

"Frighten me? No, no. Not at all. It was very kind of you to trouble yourself this late at night." Ellis hoped the tremble in his voice wasn't noticeable.

"You're welcome, sir. I know you and the party have been working very hard on this project."

"Yes, yes we have. I guess it's left me tired and a bit off my game." Ellis reached out and took his leather briefcase from the young man. "Matthew, since it's so late, why don't you come in at noon tomorrow? I'll call Mr. Anderson and let him know it's all right."

Matthew's eyes widened. "Noon? Really? You really don't mind?"

"Not at all. You deserve a break. We don't have a committee meeting tomorrow, so I'm sure it's all right."

"Thank you, sir. I'll see you tomorrow afternoon, then. My wife will be very pleased."

Ellis smiled. "Mine too. Now be off." Matthew shook his hand and then disappeared into the gloom.

"Ah, Matthew. I don't even know where you live." Ellis walked on pensively. He'd almost shot a man once based on a misunderstanding much like the one this night, and had decided then his gun-carrying days were over. *And yet tonight I reached for a nonexistent gun.* He made the final turn onto the street where he lived. *You've got to figure this thing out, Jason Ellis, or it will destroy you—or someone innocent like Matthew.* As he put his hand on the front door's doorknob, he felt his heart truly calm down for the first time since he'd heard footsteps behind him, and he took a long, deep breath so he could talk with an even voice to Patricia when he went inside. *I wonder if I'll ever be able to take that walk again without feeling anxious?* It was a question he dreaded.

CHAPTER 12

THREADS

Washington, DC
February 12, 1908

"Whoever the assassin is, he's either incredibly skilled or unbelievably lucky," Andy Pettit said.

"Because?"

"Because he finally got it right, but he shouldn't have."

Jason Ellis shook his head. "I have no idea what that means, Andy."

Andy Pettit sighed. "That's because it was a stupid thing to say—idle words from a frustrated detective who hasn't found the person responsible for all this mayhem." Pettit stood up and walked over to the window in Ellis's office. "Remarkable view, Jason. A magnificent view of the new Library of Congress and the Old Brick Capitol."

"I think the Library of Congress building is nothing more than an expensive new eyesore and the Old Brick Capitol is a relic that should be torn down and replaced with something that befits such a great location on Capitol Hill. It was a prison during the Civil War, for crying out loud."

"Ah. And I was just thinking it's nice you have an office with windows."

Jason Ellis opened his mouth to reply, then closed it. "Sorry. You were just making conversation."

"No, please go on. I love hearing your thoughts on architecture."

"You'd love for me to focus on the problem at hand." Now it was Ellis who got up and walked to a window. "Andy, I've been debating whether to ask you a question that on the surface seems incredibly foolish. But it bothers me."

"What is it? In an investigation no question is foolish. I promise you that."

Ellis inhaled and laid a hand on the wall next to the window, bowing his head.

Pettit noticed that Ellis shook his head ever so slightly from side to side.

"Really, Jason—if there's something troubling you, it likely has significance."

Ellis pulled back from the window and turned to face Pettit. "Well, it seems so indirect as to have no logical bearing. But here goes. I was in Manhattan tending to some business in the financial district when Jeff Smithson was killed, nowhere near Hartford. It was almost ironic—J. P. Morgan was talking to me about what a row he is in over all these assassinations around the world at the very moment one was taking place here in the United States. When we heard about Hartford, he went apoplectic. He's convinced that the anarchists, Marxists, and Bolsheviks are all out to bring down the entire financial system—which, ever the narcissist, he interprets as a personal attack. Leave it to

Pierpont to make something as terrible as an assassination in Hartford somehow related to him. But now he wants Congress to clamp down hard and use our investigative powers to find out what's behind all this. As if we *have* any investigative powers."

"You have me. And the Secret Service. It seems like the Treasury Department should be interested in Mr. Morgan's concerns. Why not initiate investigations there?"

"That's the whole problem, isn't it? Treasury would love to add on a whole new bureau dedicated to prosecuting financial crimes. But this problem is of a very different character. Assassinations are a political tool, not a financial one. So now Morgan will add his weight to the congressional debate we're having about creating a new federal police force with professional detectives. Can you imagine where that will lead?"

"Speaking as a professional detective, it may lead to a better career path—"

"I'm being serious, Andy. And it *could* work against you; if we do create a new federal bureau, who'll need independent contractors like you?" He shook his head. "The problem is that whatever this new police force is, it will have to decide between two very different courses of action. It will have to abide by the letter of the law, which means that it'll be ineffective if deception and infiltration are required. Or it will become a law unto itself, which can easily lead to lawlessness on the part of its agents, but with the full force, power, prestige, and treasure of the federal government behind them. Who in the political class can hold such an agency accountable if the agency can hide behind a veil of 'national security?' For that matter, who in the country would be safe from such an agency if it had the power to investigate even members of Congress or the administration?"

Pettit opened his mouth to say something, then closed it. He tried a second time. Finally, he said, "It's going to be a tough decision, isn't it? As a detective—and not a smart guy this time—it seems perfectly logical we should increase our investigative powers. But there are risks to it, aren't there?"

Ellis sighed. "Yes, there are, but I guess it really doesn't matter. It's inevitable that we'll pass a bill, most likely this year. My job is to try to figure out how to empower this new agency with enough flexibility to get the job done, but with enough restraints that it won't become a law unto itself. I'm not sure it's possible to pull that off." He stood up and stretched. "But now it's me who's gotten us off the subject, isn't it?"

"Ah, yes. You were telling me that you were in New York City when the assassination took place in Hartford."

"That's it! So I was nowhere near the crime when it happened, as I was in the earlier attacks."

"True. But it sounds like there's an 'except' in your voice."

"Well, that's why it seems so foolish. I seriously doubt it means anything, but as it turns out, I'm the one who got Jeff Smithson his job as president of Union Life. I was on the board of directors, and also head of the search committee. I'd known Jeff as a very competent insurance man at New York Life in Manhattan, and I knew he was open to a change. I'm the one who invited him to apply—and now he's dead, his wife's a widow, and his children are orphans. Yet again, I have a connection, indirect as it is."

Pettit mulled this over in his mind for a few moments, twirling a yellow pencil in his right hand as he did so. After closing his eyes for a few moments, he asked, "Do you understand the difference between correlation and causation, Jason?"

"I don't think I've ever thought about it. Why?"

"Correlation means that two things are related. Causation

means that one thing causes the other. You are clearly correlated to all three of these incidents—"

"But it doesn't mean I *caused* them." Ellis nodded, feeling a little foolish.

"Don't be so quick to judge. Correlation is always the first step to finding causation. We try to uncover every possible detail associated with these attacks without worrying about cause or effect. Then we start working out any correlation between the three events, assuming there are links. Only then can we narrow the field to discover causes. Right now, you're the only connection I've found between these three actual incidents. Another correlation: a gun was found—but not used—here in the Capitol Building, in the bathroom nearest your office. It's certainly possible that your association with all these things may be purely coincidental: you happened to be a passenger on the president's train when he was the real target; as a substitute speaker, you happened to be in the restaurant when it caught fire; and as a prominent businessman you happen to have a professional relationship with the assassinated insurance company president. With that said, it's also very unusual for one person to have this many close connections to events such as these."

"So, perhaps—"

Pettit tilted his head to the right. "Perhaps you've given me something useful; only time will tell. In the meantime, I advise you to pay attention to what's happening around you. It's difficult to do, because there is a strong temptation to overreact and see phantoms where only shadows lie, or to become so lost in your work that you miss even obvious clues."

"You want me to start looking for suspicious people? I promise you that I've been doing that already!"

Pettit smiled. "I just want you to be aware of what's happening;

that's all. When you enter a room, take a moment to glance around. See what's there and compare it, if you can, to the previous time you were in that room. Notice who comes to the hearings you hold and the restaurants where you eat. Most likely everything will be in order, and you should dismiss mild suspicions immediately so you don't become paranoid. But if something's different in a disconcerting way—well, let me know. Leave it to me to determine if it's significant. Is that fair?"

Ellis inhaled deeply and released slowly. "I'm afraid you may be a little late with your warning about paranoia. Since the restaurant incident I've had trouble sleeping. I dream of bombs and fires and bullets." He again held his breath a moment to steady himself. "I feel a lot better having shared these thoughts with you. You've managed to make my concern feel valid and yet less threatening. Thank you."

Andy nodded and then glanced at his pocket watch. "It's time for us to head over to the White House to see what's on the president's mind today. Then I'd like to go to New York City. Would you mind providing me with a list of the people you met with while you were there?"

"New York City? I can't imagine that it has anything at all to do with these events. It's just where I happened to be when Jeff Smithson was shot."

"I don't see any connection either—and that's why I'd like to check things out. Do you have any objection?"

Ellis looked at him from the corner of his eye for a moment. "No, I have no objections. You have the necessary resources to get there?"

"You've made certain of that, Jason. Your open-ended expense account gives me everything I need. Whether or not the trip will produce anything of significance, I won't know until I'm done.

But it really doesn't matter, if neither of us have any expectations of success before I make it. Expect nothing and find nothing; your thoughts are confirmed. Expect nothing but find something; you have an unexpected reward."

"All right, then, I'll write the list on the way. Meanwhile, what's a 'smart guy'? You said something earlier about you not being one? I've never heard that phrase."

Pettit laughed. "It's new; it means a sarcastic know-it-all. I'm guilty of that sometimes."

"Ah. I think we can both be accused of that." Ellis smiled. "'Smart guy' is a very good phrase. As it turns out, I work in a chamber full of them."

CHAPTER 13

JUST A LITTLE DISTANCE . . .

Baltimore
February 14, 1908

"Who goes there? I have a gun!" Big Jim Fitzsimmons slouched in his chair, cocking his Colt, and waited intently for a sound he could aim at.

"It's me, Mr. Fitzsimmons! Don't shoot!" Angel Casimer's voice trembled in the darkness.

"Oh, for crying out loud!" Fitzsimmons eased the hammer back, lowered the gun, and tried to peer into the darkness. "You should know better than to sneak up on me when I'm working late. You're lucky I didn't shoot you!" The only light in the room was a gas lamp in the center of Fitzsimmons's cluttered desk, which left the front entrance of the union hall, some thirty feet distant, almost completely obscured in darkness.

"I am sorry. May I come in?"

The irony of hearing Casimer, a remorseless murderer, acting frightened in his presence was not lost on Fitzsimmons, and he realized more than ever that he had to keep the psychological advantage with this unstable young man. Fitzsimmons put his gun down on the desk, the muzzle pointed to the side but within easy reach if he should need it, and motioned for Casimer to come into the light. As he started, though, Fitzsimmons held up his hand. "Just a moment." Big Jim got up and went over to an open window between his desk and the entrance and pulled down its blind. "There—now you can come." Fitzsimmons sat back down behind his heavy oaken desk and placed his hands in front of him.

Angel Casimer moved forward haltingly, wincing in pain with each step. His right hand clutched his upper left arm near the dirty bandage wrapped around his bullet wound.

"Good Lord, man, you look awful! What happened to you?" Fitzsimmons motioned for Casimer to sit on the high-back chair on the opposite side of the desk, and Casimer sank down onto it.

"It is a long way from Hartford to Baltimore taking local trains and switching between railroad lines regularly so no one will get a good look at you. Even worse when you have been nicked by a bullet and had to jump from a moving train." He looked at his ankle and was irritated when Fitzsimmons didn't offer any sympathy.

"Well, the good news is that the pencil drawing they made of the Hartford assassin doesn't look anything like you. That probably helped. I worried they'd make you out when you stupidly stood up and shouted as you shot that jackass Jefferson Smithson."

"What do you mean stupidly? How else would they know why he was being killed? I had to shout that it was for the cause!" Casimer's eyes, which moments before had been passive and hollow, were now filled with fire, and for the first time Fitzsimmons felt the fury that drove the man.

Raising both his hands, his palms facing Casimer, Fitzsimmons backed down. "I didn't mean that. You did what you had to do." He took a slow breath to keep his voice even.

"You *should* be sorry! I am the one who has been hunted and shot at and—"

"And I should show proper respect for what you've been through." Fitzsimmons stood up and extended his hand. "You've done a great service to our cause."

"Then why did you say that thing?"

When Casimer failed to take his outstretched hand, Fitzsimmons sat down heavily. He'd never had trouble cowing Casimer before, and he found his new assertiveness disturbing. "It's just that I'd expected you would shout, as you did, but perhaps without showing so much of yourself. It was very brave, but it could have turned out badly if anyone had been able to identify you, or even worse, shoot back. I'd hate for you to get hurt or captured, that's all."

"You do not care about me. You would simply hate to lose your assassin. But you were not there. You did not have to hear the drivel the man was saying, telling his workers they would be fired if they choose to join the union. All they desired was fair treatment, and he was threatening them. You would have done the same if you had been there to hear such arrogance."

Fitzsimmons knew very well he would *not* have done the same thing, but kept that thought to himself. "Yes, well, you pulled it off, Angel, and you managed to escape, even though Smithson had hired the Pinkertons to intimidate his employees. Were they much trouble?" Fitzsimmons judged that it might be helpful to let Casimer talk to draw off some of his emotion.

"It was," Casimer said, puffing up, "a miracle that I escaped. I do not believe a lesser man could have done it. No one escapes from the mighty Pinkertons—but I did!"

"All that army training you received in Cuba was helpful?"

"I could teach the army a few things!"

"Ah—I'm sure you could." Fitzsimmons felt contempt in his stomach. Casimer's sense of self-importance had grown a thousandfold since the last time they met.

"You carried off the task successfully, and now you've made it back to us." Despite his best effort, he wasn't able to say the last part of that sentence as casually as he would have liked.

"Your voice tells me you are not really glad to see me." The fire in Casimer's eyes glowed again.

"Of course I'm glad to see you. You're a hero returning home."

"But?"

Fitzsimmons took a deep breath. "But there's a nationwide manhunt for you. Roosevelt himself has taken an interest in the case, and senators are calling for a national investigative agency with the manpower to effectively find escaped criminals."

"I am a criminal only in their minds. I am a friend to the people."

"Yes, you are, Angel Casimer. A great hero."

"So when will you tell the world who I am, so I get the credit that I deserve? How can people follow someone they do not even know?"

"It wasn't my decision to withhold it this time. Since I assume it was our sponsor who reached out to you, I can only conclude he has good reasons for wanting you to keep it quiet. But I'm sure that the time for telling the world about you is very soon." When Casimer started to protest, as Fitzsimmons knew he would, Big Jim raised his hands. "I mean it, Angel. I'm sure he's been preparing you for something truly heroic in scale—something that will put you in the history books forever. Such things must not be rushed. When that moment comes, all you've done up to this point will be revealed, and your deeds will become a legend to our friends around the world."

"You say that, but nothing ever happens. No one even knows that it was me who did those other things in Washington."

"Yes, and I know it's frustrating. But something's coming that will put your name on par with John Wilkes Booth."

"The president!" exclaimed Casimer, excitement creeping into his voice for the first time. "I know I failed at Union Station—"

"Don't worry about that. What you did turned out fine in the end. The railroads are having trouble convincing passengers Union Station is safe, so you've injured the great capitalist machine after all. Even better than that, the Secret Service is beside itself any time Roosevelt's train leaves or arrives." He laughed. "In fact, they're so paranoid they're talking about building a spur to the White House so they can more easily guard the track. Can you imagine that—a rail line leading right to the White House!" He laughed so hard that he had to wipe his brow.

"And how does that serve our cause?"

Fitzsimmons's eyes widened as he realized Casimer didn't see the humor in it. *A completely humorless man—and stupid at that!* He opened and closed his mouth as he tried to form a rational response. A joke is never funny if it has to be explained. "You see, Angel, this is exactly what you hoped for when you started with us. The more your activities isolate the political class from the people, the more the people will distrust them. There has to be a bond of familiarity between politicians and the people, or the people will tire of their self-serving acts. When the threat of terror becomes so pervasive that the president's own people talk seriously about closing off the White House to the public, then the president will be seen for what he is—a self-serving despot whose only goal is to feed his own ego while hiding from the people. The reason Roosevelt is so popular is that he relishes the crowd— being with the people. Take that away from him, and he loses power. And because of what you did at Union Station, you've moved things in that direction. It may not seem like much, but I assure you it is. You've done just as much to serve the cause of social unrest as if you had killed him. More, in fact, since his inability to find you makes him look weak and contemptible. Believe me, he hates you for that, even though he doesn't yet know who you are. So don't despair!"

"Am I now to kill Roosevelt? And if I am not, how can I possibly become as famous as Booth, who killed Lincoln?"

"I think it's time I told you about it." Fitzsimmons swallowed hard. He'd only received the final orders earlier that week and knew that putting such information in Angel Casimer's unstable mind carried great risk. But even greater was the risk that if he kept Casimer in the dark, the man would go berserk and do something that revealed them all—and that wouldn't be good. There were people Fitzsimmons had to protect, himself most of all.

"And just who is this 'sponsor' that you speak of? Why do I not know his name? He must know mine."

"He knows your name, all right, Angel. He's the one who gives us the money for the explosives and guns and your travel arrangements."

"But who is he to decide which targets we choose? You must tell me about him. How do I know I can trust him?"

Fitzsimmons laughed. "The truth is, my dear small friend, I don't know who he is either. Almost a year ago I received a note in the mail saying that if I wanted to advance the cause of workers everywhere, I would go to a park in the Canton neighborhood at one a.m. and stand under a specific tree. I was curious, so I went."

"What happened?"

"Nothing. Nothing happened at all. I waited twenty minutes and left in disgust."

Casimer shook his head, as if to clear it. "But then how did you meet this sponsor?"

"Two weeks later, another letter arrived. The letter said a man had observed me at the park, which proved I was interested. He waited to see if anyone else came, which, of course, they did not. That told him I was trustworthy, so he offered to meet again, along with a promise I would be handsomely compensated for my trouble."

"And where did you meet this time?"

"In a dark corner of a bad café in the same neighborhood. He was wearing a hat, dark glasses, and a scarf, and he spoke in a deep voice that was difficult to understand. He told me he was interested in seeing the workers of the world stand up for their rights, and that he could provide the means for provoking public outrage. That's how it began."

"But his name—you must have asked his name."

"He told me it was no concern of mine—that if anything went wrong, I must not be in a position to compromise the movement. He made me feel there's much more going on, that you and I are but small pieces of a much larger machine. I didn't press him, so he didn't tell me. I haven't seen him since, nor do I know his name. He now sends a nervous little courier who seems to know nothing."

"But what about me? How does he know about me?"

Fitzsimmons pursed his lips and smiled. "I have no idea about that, Angel. He somehow knew your name, and said I should seek you out. He left two one-hundred-dollar bills on the table and told me to keep fifty for me or the union, and to give you the rest to cover your living expenses and the supplies you'd need. And that was the end of our first interview."

"He has been testing me since then to see if I will do as he asks?"

"Exactly! That's *exactly* what he's been doing. Which is why you must trust him. So far everything has worked to our advantage."

Casimer shook his head. "I do not like not knowing. One day I will be apprehended, and it is I who will be executed. I should know for whom I work!"

"It is for the movement that you work, Angel—for the movement. There's a great brotherhood of the working class, of which you are an important member. You want the world to know who you are: they will! We will plan so that after you carry out this last great scheme, you can go into hiding under a new name, perhaps even move to another country. But the name *Angel Casimer* will be in all the newspapers, and workers around the world will celebrate what you have done." Fitzsimmons's confidence had returned, and his voice had grown in both pitch and volume as he painted a glorious picture for his young apprentice. He was pleased when Casimer nodded thoughtfully.

"All right, then, I will do as you ask. I will give this man another chance. But we must go public the next time, or else—"

"You will not need to do anything. Next time is the event of which you have dreamed."

"Then tell me about it. Tell me now!"

Fitzsimmons smiled and was pleased when Casimer attempted to smile back. "Come close, Angel. I have dark things to tell you. And then you must disappear for a time so that you will not be captured before the great event takes place. Can you do that, Angel? Can you wait until the moment arrives?"

CHAPTER 14

THE MARXIST RUSSIAN SOCIAL-DEMOCRATIC WORKERS' PARTY

New York City
February 25, 1908

"Yes, I know I lost money, but it's insignificant compared to what I've already raised," Maxim Koslov said. "You must understand how these things work! Capitalism both destroys and creates. You cannot win every time." He looked steadily into the eyes of his Russian overseer.

"But you were so sure of this." Koslov did his best to conceal his contempt for the mercenaries questioning him—a party functionary and his two thugs—who had no idea how capital markets work or how a man like Ellis could unwittingly unravel his plans.

"It is that accursed senator, Jason Ellis," he said. "If things had progressed as they should have, I would have made a great deal of money—enough to fund your activities for six or seven months."

"But *how* did this Mr. Ellis foil your plans?"

Koslov shook his head, exasperated he would have to try to explain. But he was spared that exercise when one of the thugs spoke up.

"Should we have this Ellis killed?"

"What?" Kozlov looked up sharply. "No, of course not. Particularly now. Doing so would give his investigator friend the information he needs to connect this all to me. And then you would lose me, your most valuable source of funds. No, you must not do anything to Mr. Ellis, do you understand?" He was glad that the men nodded, but not at all sure they meant it. Their answer to anything was broken legs or dead bodies. *Perhaps someday you can kill Jason Ellis and his beautiful wife, but not now. Certainly not now!*

"So, what are you going to do? We need money, and you made commitments—"

"I know I made commitments. You do not have to remind me of my commitments. It was I who came to you, not the other way around. If I did not believe in the movement, I could easily live a life of luxury and ease unlike anyone lives in Russia, except for the tsar. In fact, I could live better than the tsar! But I risk all of that for the movement—and now you threaten me!"

The men he was talking to were unmoved by this. "It is true that you came to us, and our leaders are grateful. But now you are one of us, and there is no going back on that. What *might* have been your life is now pure fantasy. You are part of a great cause, and you must do your part. Surely you see our position?"

"Yes, of course. I am not wavering. It is just that you and the rest of the party think operations like this are ordinary and easy. They are not. It is difficult to make a great deal of money, even in America. If it were not, everyone would be rich."

"Compared to Russia, everyone *is* rich."

Kozlov nodded. He relished the role of being one of the leading fundraisers for international Bolshevism, but he hated whom he had to deal with to funnel the money to the right places. "Yes,

Americans are rich, all of them—but not millions of dollars rich. I have given more than a million dollars to the party! And I do it by acting as a capitalist myself—by going into the enemy camp and playing their evil game against them. You see the price I pay!" He had raised his voice, hoping to put them on the defensive.

"Calm down, Maxim. We just need to know what is next. We have many operations dependent on your money."

"But what you do not seem to understand is that I cannot control all the variables. You must not think I can come out ahead every time—it just doesn't work like that. Instead, you must judge me on all I do, not individual projects."

"But it was our money you risked and lost on this project. That is why it is our concern."

Kozlov flared. "It was money I gave you that was put at risk!"

"But once you gave it to us, it was ours. In the glorious world for which we fight, there is no 'my money' and 'your money.' It is all *our* money, and so you must be careful not to waste it. That is all." The man smiled, and Kozlov felt his stomach churn.

"Of course. I am sorry this turned out badly. But the next event I have planned will raise more than all I have raised so far, or anyone else for that matter. It will create profits so vast that our comrades can plan disruptions even more massive than the 1905 revolution!" Kozlov paused, happy for just a moment to think what he could do with the money he would make. "Yes, far greater than the 1905 revolution."

"That would be good." The man smiled. "When will this great event take place?"

Kozlov settled back in his chair. "In June. It will take place in June."

"That is good—just three months from now. We will need

more money in June." The man's smile faded. "We *must* have the money in June, my dear Maxim. In June! Do you understand?"

"Yes," Kozlov said, his voice again dark, "I understand."

"I am glad. Now you must go back to your *humble* abode at the Waldorf-Astoria hotel."

"I live at the Waldorf-Astoria because it is what is expected of a man like me. Must we go through this again? If you want to take money from the capitalists, you must act as a capitalist. You must gain their confidence, live as they live, and do as they do. It is already difficult because I am Russian. They still view me with suspicion."

"Except, perhaps, Mr. J. Pierpont Morgan?" The man had a feigned look of curiosity on his face.

Kozlov rolled his eyes. "You want to know about me and Pierpont Morgan?" Then his eyes narrowed. "Which means that you have been following me."

"You are an important asset to us. We do not want anything to happen to you—"

"You don't want me to turn on you." Kozlov turned away, so angry his hands were trembling. When he turned back, his voice was steady and firm. "Now you listen to me. It is lucky for the party that Pierpont Morgan called me. It allows me to infiltrate his network. I can manage what he hears and sees. Acting with discretion, I can protect our interests here *and* in Europe. So, you will *not* follow me anymore, and you *will* trust me to do what's right for the party. Otherwise, you can save yourself a lot of trouble and kill me now. When I am dead, you can trust me, but you will *not* have any more money to send back to Russia. This is your choice—kill me this moment while my bodyguards are out, or leave me alone until June. If you do anything else, I will have *you* killed! That is something I can afford."

"Maxim, be reasonable—"

"I will *not* be reasonable. You are powerful men. You kill and murder. But I have my own allies, and I have enough money that I can have you taken out of the way. You will not come to me in my own office with threats. You are in America, not Russia. Either leave me alone, or it's over. My part in this comes to an end. I will not live with outside eyes prying into my every action. I cannot do what I must do if there are eyes on me, because my capitalist enemies—and there are many of them—will see your men, and they will know I am up to something more than running a bank. If that happens, we are finished."

The fellow's nostrils flared, and for a moment Kozlov thought he might just go ahead and kill him. *In so many ways that would be a relief!* But then the man leaned back in his chair.

"All right then, Maxim. We will not follow you. But you must not leave New York City without letting us know. You know how to reach me."

Kozlov nodded.

"Then we will not meet again until June, unless you need our help." He smiled. "You may need our help, do you think?"

"If I do, I will get in touch."

Washington, DC
February 26, 1908

"Russia? The president wants us to go to *Russia*? We were planning on Europe, but Russia? Whatever for?" Patricia was astonished.

Jason Ellis looked into the deep blue eyes that were part of his wife's charm. If he saw alarm in her eyes, he'd call Roosevelt immediately and tell him they couldn't go. But what he saw told him that the trip would take place. Her feigned indignation couldn't conceal her delighted curiosity.

Jason wasn't ready to answer her question directly, so he fell back on an old political trick and diverted the conversation. "St. Petersburg, to be precise. We'll also get to London, as we planned. But with Russia added, we'll be on a very tight schedule. Just six weeks total. And we won't be able to take the children."

"Oh? Why not? With the convention in Chicago in June, the children will think we've abandoned them completely."

"They'll be all right." He hesitated. "We *could* bring them with us to Chicago to make up for this. I think it would be good for them."

"Perhaps," Patricia said, "we could spend a week or two of vacation at Mackinac Island with Great-Aunt Cathy following the convention. I used to love to go there as a child."

"Perfect!" Jason said, relieved that she was open to the idea. And now that she was, he decided he could answer her initial question. "There are really two reasons Roosevelt wants us to go to Russia. First—and this must remain confidential—the investigation of the Union Station bombing turned up remnants of a unique blasting cap that is used widely in the Baltic States, but almost never here in America. That suggests that the bomber is connected to that section of the world. These suspicions are confirmed by several eyewitness accounts that place a young man of Eastern European descent coming out of the tunnel closest to where the detonator was used. Then, as more information came in from Hartford, the description of the shooter was similar. Andy Pettit is interested in trying to see how all of that fits together and to see if it's reasonable to believe there's a European connection to these attacks."

Patricia frowned and stood still.

"When Andy briefed Roosevelt, the president decided he needed someone to meet with officials in London and Russia and learn what they know about the international Bolshevik movement and any connections it may have to groups here in the US. When I said we'd already been planning to go to Europe, he immediately summoned the ambassadors from the countries he wants us to visit and arranged to make our trip an official delegation. You and I will provide the façade of a state-sponsored goodwill tour while Andy Pettit and two fellows from the Secret Service meet with their counterparts in each country. Treasury will want to see if there are any unusual money transfers, although that's difficult to pin down. Meanwhile, you and I get to meet with the prime minister of England and perhaps even the tsar."

"Not that handsome King Edward?" Patricia feigned hurt, finally relaxing.

"Afraid not. Apparently he's out of London just now. But our ambassador to the Court of St. James is working furiously to see if we can perhaps meet with the Prince of Wales, who appears to be a very decent sort of fellow. It will still be an interesting visit."

"Oh, Jason, this really is impossible. You should have the common sense to know a visit like this takes months of preparation. There are protocols to be observed when in the presence of British royalty or even the Russian tsar! And clothes—I need a new wardrobe. I just don't see how we can get this right."

"You are, of course, correct in everything you say. But the need is urgent, and I think it's best we go." He reached out and took her arm. "We'll be all right. The State Department has people trained specifically for this type of situation, and we'll have protocol officers traveling with us the whole time. They'll teach me what I need to know on the way over and will be at our sides as we meet with these dignitaries. You will act gracefully, regardless of the coaching. Remember, we'll only be there as window dressing for the real purpose of the trip, so all we need to do is act interested. And in the end, the British are still our great allies, and Russia must be courteous if for no other reason than appreciation of President Roosevelt's role in brokering the Portsmouth Treaty to conclude the Russo-Japanese War. It's not likely either country will allow us to be embarrassed, and we won't go out of our way to try to embarrass ourselves."

Patricia considered that. "What was the second reason the president wants us to go?"

"I think he wants us out of the country for our own safety. Both Andy and the Secret Service are troubled that I know—or knew—people involved in each of these events."

"And you're troubled too." When Ellis looked startled, she added, "Listen, my dear, we've known each other for more than thirty years; we've been married for nearly twenty-five. I know when you're concerned. The extra men you've hired to help here at the house, the guards that follow the children. We all know you're worried."

"I'd hoped it wasn't that obvious. Since you are such a skilled detective, you should work for Andy."

"Perhaps I should." She smiled. "I think there are things a woman could learn that even the very best of male detectives could never find."

Ellis stepped forward and embraced her. "So you'll go with me?"

She kissed his cheek. "I suppose. I'm sure I'll find it an awful burden to meet the Prince of Wales and the tsar. But my true motivation is that the idea of sending a handsome and charming man like my husband to Europe by himself is pure folly—those grande dames of European society would consider you too great a prize, and they'd use all their tricks to seduce you. I go as your chaperone."

Ellis laughed. "You flatter me, and I love it." He drew her into an even closer embrace. "You needn't worry. I am and always will be a one-woman man. But the fact that you pretend you're jealous is great comfort to my ego."

"You went to the funeral?"

Jason Ellis set the cup of coffee he'd been nursing down on the table. So far, he and Andy had shared pleasantries and ordered from the menu. Now it was time to consolidate their notes.

"It was a very sad affair. What can you say to a widow and her orphans in such a circumstance? If a man dies in an accident, you speak of tragedy. If a person dies from a disease, you speak of God's will. But to be murdered in broad daylight for doing exactly what you're supposed to be doing—what can you say to that? Trying to express condolences to his widow was one of the hardest things I've ever had to do."

"I know this will sound callous, but I don't mean it that way. Since Smithson worked for a life insurance company, I assume his widow and children are provided for?"

"Not because Jeff Smithson had thought to buy a policy himself, unfortunately. But Union Life has accepted responsibility and so will provide a settlement that will take care of the family. I made sure of that before I left Hartford."

"He didn't buy his own life insurance? How is that possible?"

Ellis smiled, ruefully. "It's an old cliché—attorneys die without wills, doctors live unhealthy lives, and apparently life insurance salesmen fail to buy the products they sell to others." He looked up. "And investment bankers often act stupidly when it comes to their own portfolios."

"How did that play out? I understand you had a sizeable position in Union Life."

"It would have been a disaster if I hadn't gotten back into the market. The problem was that I did something I would never allow a client to do—I kept stock in Union Life for sentimental reasons."

"Pretend I know nothing about dealing in stocks and bonds—because I don't—and help me understand what happened."

Ellis laughed. "It's like this. You buy stock, which represents an ownership interest in a company. If you're a small investor, you're likely to see the price of your stock manipulated by people who buy and sell stocks for a living. The value of the stock often has little to do with the real underlying value of the company; rather, it reflects what the market thinks is going to happen."

"And who is 'the market' everyone speaks about? I don't usually think of a market as having a mind, and yet the newspapers always say something like 'The stock market declined today on fears that North African pirates are going to invade America' . . ."

Ellis smiled again. "Those of us on Wall Street often do speak of the market as if it were a person, don't we? 'The market' is simply the collective thinking of everyone who trades in securities. Which means that it's extremely emotional and sometimes irrational. When enough people think things are going well for the economy, the value of stocks goes up, even the value of companies that aren't well managed. If something awful happens that threatens confidence, like the Union Station bombing or the Hartford assassination, then most everyone panics and wants to retrieve any value they think their positions hold, so they start selling at a discount. In such a case even healthy and well managed companies lose value, not because things *will* go badly for them, but because people think things *may* go badly for their own portfolio."

"And Union Life Insurance?"

"Yes, Union Life Insurance. Normally, a cataclysmic event like an assassination would send the stock price tumbling, since investors would be afraid that there might be more attacks against company officers, in which case buyers of life insurance would become spooked that the company could get into financial trouble without good leadership, and so they'd stop buying policies from Union Life. That is how the trouble begins. What normally occurs in a situation like this is a cascade of negative news which leads to a dramatic drop in share price."

"But not this time?"

"It started out that way. When news of Jeff's murder reached the Street, all trading in the stock was temporarily suspended. But they can only do that for a very short time. When it opened back up, the market was flooded with sell orders, which sent the price of the stock into deeply negative territory."

"Which meant that a sizeable part of your portfolio was going down the drain?"

Ellis nodded. "Yes, Andy, that's what it means—and thank you for stating it so delicately."

"I'm just an investigator; facts hold little emotion for me."

"Well, it *is* emotional when it's your own money." Ellis took a long sip of coffee.

"What did you do?"

"I called up some of my investor friends, and we intervened in the market." When he saw Pettit's puzzled look, he continued, "We started buying Union Life stock—as much as people wanted to sell. As the market continued down, we bought more and more shares, at an ever-lower price. Of course, you can only do that until you run out of money, and in this case it reached a point where I thought I'd be all tapped out. In fact, a few of my friends were ready to throw in the towel and stop buying. That would have been a disaster."

"Because if they had stopped buying—"

"The company may very well have failed, and we would have lost a lot of money. If the market price had dropped too low, the state of Connecticut would have been forced to step in to take control of the company, and then the stock would have never recovered. We would have lost everything."

"So you stood to lose not only your original investment, but all the extra money you put in as well?"

Ellis nodded. "You see why it's emotional?"

"Whew! It takes a lot of guts to play on Wall Street. Sounds like a mean game."

"And everyone thinks we're just greedy hacks who somehow make dollars materialize out of nothing. The truth is that we take on incredible risk to get the economy growing." Ellis paused. "Sorry about that. I'll get off my soapbox. We do get paid well when things go right. Which in this case they finally did. When enough investors saw that a strong cohort were continuing to buy, the panic subsided, and people decided that maybe they'd made a mistake. Almost as quickly as the market dropped in value, it started to rebound. Literally within an hour the price of stock had come back up to its earlier selling price." Ellis shrugged. "I actually made a lot of money on the shares I bought at the bottom of the market when the share price rose."

"And that happened because . . . ?" Pettit asked, exasperated.

"It happened because people react in something of a herd

mentality. When the stampede starts, everyone joins. But once the cowboys take control of the cows, everything settles down. Remember that nothing about Union Life had changed, except that it was time to find a new leader. The sales force was still present, the financial reserves were untouched, and the employees were still there to process the business. They were a strong company before this happened, and they're still a strong company. Once people realized it was still sound, its stock returned to its natural value on the market."

"But it did that only because you and your friends worked to steady the market by buying shares when they were down?"

"Well, that and the fact that some whispers found their way into market publications that the assassination had killed both Jeff Smithson *and* the unionization drive. The clerical employees at Union Life don't have the stomach for violent confrontations. With the union out, the company looked stronger than before."

Pettit shook his head. "And those rumors got started by . . . Maybe it's best if I don't know."

"Just because they're rumors doesn't mean they're not true. Sometimes rumors cause things to *become* true."

"I guess I'm more comfortable cracking bad guys on the head than playing this game. So in the end, everyone was happy."

"Not everyone. People who sold their shares of stock at the bottom were clearly unhappy because they allowed their fears to convince them to sell at a loss. And the short sellers were unhappy because most of them failed to sell out at the bottom, so their hoped-for profits never emerged. The market turned around too fast for them to get out."

"Short sellers?"

"It's too much to explain in detail. Just know that guys like Maxim Kozlov make a lot of their money by betting *against* companies rather than *for* them. They borrow other people's stock, sell it at the current market price when they think it's high, and then they buy replacement shares at a discount if the share price goes down. In this case, Kozlov had done that with some of my shares. He borrowed them from me when they were trading at five dollars per share, sold them for cash, and then could have replaced them by buying discounted shares at as low as a dollar per share. If he had pulled that off, he would have made four dollars on every share he borrowed, and I'd be left with the loss. He would have made a fortune."

"But that didn't happen."

Ellis shook his head. "No. Like I said, the market rebounded too quickly because of our intervention. I'm sure Kozlov wanted to kick himself for not buying replacement shares at three or four dollars. As it was, by the time he figured out that the market drop was going to last less than a day, he had to buy shares back at six-fifty, so he lost a lot of money on the deal."

"I've heard of Kozlov. He's Russian, isn't he?"

Ellis nodded. "A real anomaly in our world. He came to America with what appeared to be nothing, but somehow found an initial stake that allowed him to start trading. He has a real knack for it, and was soon doing some big deals. I have a portion of my money with him in a mostly blind trust . . ."

"A blind trust?"

"A trust that is managed for me without my knowledge. The idea is that as a senator I can influence the market value of companies by the committees I serve on and the legislation that we pass. So, by putting my money in a blind trust no one can accuse me of taking advantage of people, since I don't know if the companies I'm dealing with in Congress are in my stock portfolio or not."

"Do all senators do that?"

Ellis shook his head. "No. Many of them take advantage of the insider's game and make a great deal of money at the expense of other investors, including their own constituents. I think it's a rotten way to do business, so I don't do it."

"Does this Kozlov fellow do a lot of short selling?"

"I don't know. Probably not more than anyone else. It's really quite common. You take a look at a variety of companies and figure out which ones are going to have trouble. If you can figure it out before the other guy, you borrow his stock and sell it. The other fellow's no worse off for it, since he always gets his stock back, plus some interest earnings from the guy who borrowed it from him. It's the short seller who takes the risk; if the price of the stock rises, the short seller has to buy at a higher price than he paid. The risk can be steep."

"So Kozlov's quite a risk-taker."

"We're all risk-takers. If you're on Wall Street, you learn a variety of ways to manage risk, but you can never eliminate it. That's why both the profits and the losses can be so large."

"What do you know about Kozlov?"

Ellis set his glass down. "Forget Kozlov, Andy. I just used him as an example because I knew he was short in Union Life. It could be anybody on Wall Street."

"But Russian? Does he still have connections to the old country?"

"I don't know—how would I know? He runs an investment bank. A good one. He knows J. P. Morgan. That's all that those who work, or used to work, on Wall Street need to know."

Pettit chewed on his lip.

"Honestly? Why is this an issue, Andy? Pretend I said J. P. Morgan instead of Kozlov."

Pettit nodded. "I'm sure you're right. It's just that some of my Pinkerton friends have done some work for Kozlov. He can play rough with people. I'm sure it's just coincidence you chose him for your example, and I know a little something about him. That's all. Coincidence." Pettit had a faraway look as he chewed on the pencil he always carried.

"I wish I could see what you are thinking, but I guess that's why I've hired your firm. You'll let me know if this means anything?"

CHAPTER 15

NEXT STEPS

Baltimore
March 9, 1908

"So, we meet again, Mister . . . ? I guess I don't know your name." Big Jim Fitzsimmons squinted in the dim lighting. The man, whom he'd met on just three other occasions, had managed to conceal himself in the shadows so that the most Fitzsimmons could make out was that he was slender, well dressed, and must have dark hair. The only other thing he knew was that the little man was not from Baltimore, as evidenced by the way he talked. Though the fellow tried to disguise his voice by speaking much deeper than natural, his accent was all wrong to be from anywhere near Baltimore.

"I've been told to tell you this is the last envelope you will receive, but that it should be more than enough to complete your task."

"Why the last?"

"I know nothing about the task or why you receive these letters. I am aware that the man who sends them will not be available for a while. Beyond that, I have no knowledge of why he's interested in you. If there's anything you need to know, you'll have to look inside. There's nothing more I can tell you."

Fitzsimmons felt like a chump when, after glancing down at the letter for just the shortest possible moment, he looked up to find that the slippery little fellow was gone. "A damn cipher, if you ask me." Fitzsimmons slipped the thick envelope into his trouser pocket and made his way across the park to where his buggy was waiting. "There'd better be a *lot* of money in this envelope. This operation is going to be expensive."

Long Island, NY
March 14, 1908

"It's days like this that make me feel less anxious about giving up the presidency," Theodore Roosevelt said as he and Jason Ellis walked briskly along the narrow beach that fronted the Ellises' tasteful but relatively modest Long Island estate. "I love this place almost as much as I love politics."

"Almost as much?"

Roosevelt laughed. "Yes, almost."

Ellis struggled to keep up with Roosevelt, even though they were nearly the same age.

"You leave tomorrow?" Roosevelt started to say just as Ellis asked, "What do you think you will do to occupy your time when you leave the White House?"

"What was that?" asked Roosevelt.

"No, you go first."

"I just said, 'You leave tomorrow?' It was a question I really didn't need to ask. I just hoped for an update on your plans."

"First to London, a brief stop in Tallinn, Estonia, and then on to St. Petersburg. We've never been to the latter two, and Patricia is excited."

"I wish I were going," Roosevelt said. "I've not been to Russia, either. Now, you were going to ask me a question?"

"It's not really important. I asked what plans you have for when you leave the White House. Just trying to make conversation."

"You'll be discreet?"

"Have I ever given you any reason to distrust me?"

"Sorry. I didn't mean it like that, Jason. It's just that everything I do is under scrutiny."

"Of course. If you don't want to tell me, it's okay."

"Africa. I think I'm going to Africa. I've had some discussions with Andrew Carnegie, who's indicated a willingness to finance a safari. And the board of directors of both the Smithsonian and the American Museum of Natural History here in New York are anxious to enhance their collection of rare animals and other specimens from Africa. The Smithsonian's lead scientist, R. J. Cunninghame, would be a natural to lead the expedition."

"It sounds like the perfect job for you. Although I hope you won't think me too rude to point out you're not as young as you were when you were a cowboy in the Dakotas or a dashing young colonel charging up San Juan Hill."

"I'm only forty-nine years old—hardly over the hill."

"Yes, sir. I can see real advantage to such a trip."

"Mostly it gets me out of the country. The last thing Howard Taft needs is a former president looking over his shoulder and second-guessing his decisions. And the last thing I need is to be constantly frustrated when he does things differently than I would."

"When you put it that way, are you sure this safari isn't Taft's idea?"

The president laughed. "Is Andy ready to go?" Roosevelt asked, changing the subject back to the European trip. "It's important he be there."

"Yes, sir. Andy's coming. He's developed some interesting leads in the case, so he'll be in a good position to ask questions."

"What have you and Andy come up with now that you're his client?"

"Well, we've got a much better description of the Hartford assassin. The Pinkertons who chased after him have found the farmer who sold him the horse he used in his escape. The farmer gave them a good description, and the new sketch going out to all the post offices and other public buildings is accurate. We'll have a lot more eyes looking out for the fellow."

"Still no group has claimed credit for it?"

"No, sir. Even though most of the people at the scene thought they heard the assassin yell something pro-union, he was too far away for people to hear clearly. And the union representing the clerical workers specifically disavowed any knowledge of the attack. But it pretty well put an end to the unionization drive against Union Life. So even if the fellow was pro-union, he was probably acting on his own. Most union agitators think it's been a negative for them overall."

"Business leaders think I'm *pro*-union, but all I really am for is getting a square deal for the working man. I detest things like strikes and protests and the violence that goes along with them."

"If it's any consolation, most of the union people I talk to think you're anti-union."

Roosevelt laughed. "Well, that's just how I like it. Keep 'em guessing." He grew serious. "I was anti-union early in my political career, but that has softened as I've learned of the often deplorable conditions that working families live in. It's understandable that both sides see in me what they want to see." He shook his head at this uncharacteristic introspection. "But what about future attacks?"

"I think we have to expect it. The assassin's still out there, though probably lying low for a while. Pettit has engaged his own detectives as well as several of his Pinkerton friends all up and down the East Coast to try to find anyone who recognizes the assassin from the new poster. I think it's just a matter of time until we know who he is, and then we can discover who else he knows and where he's been seen. Hopefully, we can grab him before another incident. But there are an awful lot of 'if-thens' in all of that."

Roosevelt nodded. "Well, we've reached the end of the property. Care to keep going, or do you want to turn back?"

"I want to get home in time to help Patricia get the children ready for our leaving. She just got back from visiting our married daughter in Vermont, so it's hectic at our house right now. Her sister's staying with the younger children."

"Let's go back, then. I appreciate you walking with me. I'll head back to Oyster Point directly." Roosevelt headed away from the surf, which was a relief to Ellis since the ground was firmer there and would be easier to walk on.

"I know I've made you put this trip together on short notice, Jason, but I still need you back in time for Chicago. When will you arrive at the convention?"

"Me? I'll arrive the Sunday before and take out a suite at the Drake. I plan to do a lot of business besides nominating a candidate. A convention's a great place for horse trading. Deals can be made there that are harder to get done in Washington. What about you?"

"For me it's all about the nomination. If I'm to have a legacy, it will be up to the next president, so getting the right man nominated is paramount."

CHAPTER *16*

ONLY THE LITTLE PEOPLE DIE

Baltimore
March 17, 1908

"So the good senator's going to Europe." Big Jim Fitzsimmons set the newspaper down. This was the time of day he loved the best: early in the morning before work started, the only time he could nurse a cup of coffee while reading the newspaper. "Most people think we union men are overgrown troglodytes who don't even know how to read a newspaper. Wouldn't they be surprised to know I graduated from Princeton?" He smiled and took another long sip of coffee, savoring the bitter taste in his mouth. "And graduated fortieth out of a hundred and fifty at that."

He recalled the heated arguments he'd had with some of his professors and many of his fellow students. To Fitzsimmons, it had always been clear that the wealth of the nation was created by workers—people like his father—and yet their share of the total national wealth was paltry in comparison to their numbers. "The five great barons of industry—Morgan, Carnegie, Vanderbilt, Gould, and Rockefeller—they're the reason we're all successful, according to all of those arrogant idiots who have never held a hammer in their pampered hands. Well, I'd like to see how much oil Rockefeller could drill without the men who work for him, or how much steel Carnegie could refine with his own hands. The titans of industry live in well-manicured mansions, far removed from the blast furnaces that scorch a man's skin and fill his lungs with coke dust." He shook his head. "In the end it's only the little people who die." Fitzsimmons was always surprised at how wonderfully the bitterness came through in his voice.

Another reason he liked this time of day is that he could talk to himself, and his arguments always formed more clearly when he could hear them out loud. "Why is it that such intelligent men refuse to see that if the workers are given ownership of these great enterprises, they will work with greater purpose to succeed? Why do they refuse to see that the greatness of a nation is sharing its wealth with everyone so that every man prospers? In the long run the Rockefellers and Carnegies will remain wealthy—perhaps even more so than now, since they will sell their organizational skills to the enterprises and prosper from the royalties they receive in designing new processes. It's innovation they should be rewarded for, not ownership!" He shook his head. "That's good, Fitzsimmons, that's very good. You need to put that out there, somehow."

He picked up his cup of coffee again and started reading about an idiot representative from Iowa who'd spoken at the Press Club the day before, extolling once again the virtues of individual property ownership and how men like Roosevelt were taking the country down a dangerous path to socialism. Fitzsimmons shook his head. "How can men like this get elected when they're too stupid to see that the path to social equality is inevitable? Socialism will prevail, and we'll all be better for it. One hundred years from now people will marvel that there once was something as foolish as private ownership of industry."

He glanced back down at the paper. "And now the ever-so-popular Senator Ellis is going to England and Russia on a goodwill mission, and perhaps to check in with the equally stupid political leaders in those countries to see how they manage their anarchists and agitators." He laughed. "Well, good senator, my guess is that you will find that they all have an Angel Casimer— or two or three—just as malleable and fanatical as mine. *That's* how they manage it, and *that's* how their kings, princes, and labor barons get themselves murdered on such a regular basis. Perhaps we should murder you, Senator Ellis, and then you might understand." He sighed and pointed his fat index finger at Ellis's photo in the newspaper. "But even then you'll wind up in capitalist heaven, where every man is fabulously wealthy just like you. At least that seems to be the religion you believe in."

Big Jim paused. "Heaven, where everyone's wealthy? Now there's a good thought. Isn't it in the Bible that Jesus promised, 'In my Father's house are many mansions, I go there to prepare a place for you'?" Fitzsimmons smiled. "So even Jesus was a socialist, and heaven is a place where all men have mansions. And right after his death his apostles set up a society where all of the people who joined with them held everything in common. Was that not socialism?" He nodded at this new thought, fully aware he'd find many ways to work this into his speeches in the future. "Remarkable! If I can add the persuasive power of religion to my workers' sermons, think of the new audience I can attract and the zeal it will inspire . . ." The thought of this prospect was thrilling. "My mother always thought I should be a preacher. Perhaps now I will be!" That prompted a good laugh, but the moment passed quickly.

He stood up and moved around the room restlessly, thinking about the trip that Jason Ellis was taking. Few people would attach any significance to the fact, barely mentioned in the newspaper account, that the detective Andy Pettit was accompanying him on the delegation, but Fitzsimmons knew better. "He's going to try to find the connections between terrorist acts here and their counterparts in Europe and Russia." The problem was that Fitzsimmons didn't know if there *were* any connections. He'd made it very clear to the few Bolsheviks he knew in America that he was sympathetic to their cause in Europe and had even donated some union money to their work. It was dangerous for him because most in his union didn't want to be connected to the Bolsheviks, but for him it was a matter of principle.

"Still," he said restlessly, "I wonder if there's a connection between this sponsor of ours and the party there?" He squinted his eyes. "I wonder if there's a connection to our Angel that I don't know about, but our sponsor does." He decided it was surprising how little he knew about Angel Casimer. Even though he was of Eastern European descent, his family coming from someplace like Lithuania or Estonia, he knew Angel had been born in America. So how could someone so naïve possibly have connections overseas?

"The greater risk is that our sponsor is connected to Europe and that conniving Pettit will find a connection." Perhaps the only person in the world whom Fitzsimmons hated more than Roosevelt was Allen Pinkerton, since it was his detectives the moguls hired to beat up his men whenever a strike was called. They were ruthless, even though they were laborers themselves. He often dismissed them as "fool-tools of the capitalists" when giving a speech. Still, his abundant stomach was unsettled by the thought of Andy Pettit prying around for connections. "I've often wondered if the money I receive comes from Europe; but how could I possibly know? That pitiful creature with a phony voice in a darkened restaurant simply shows up with envelopes filled with money and directions, and I do the bidding of whoever it is that sends the envelope." He corrected himself. "Casimer does their bidding. I haven't killed anyone. I haven't set off any bombs."

He gazed out the window, then impulsively turned and went to his small liquor cabinet, taking a quick swig from a bottle of Irish whiskey. He almost never drank in the morning and was shocked to find himself doing so now. "The mysterious men with the cash could deal directly with Angel, but they want me to take the fall if something goes wrong. The trick is to help Casimer do all that he wants to do without getting implicated myself. I'm no good to the movement dead, and if they figure out I'm part of this, I'll certainly be executed." The image of a fat man dangling from a hangman's noose came into his head, and he shuddered at the thought that his substantial weight could break the rope before he was dead, which would force them to do it again. He looked down to see that his hand was trembling. "Casimer will make a great martyr—it's what he wants. But how do I keep the Pinkertons from connecting him to me? When the movement finally succeeds, they'll need me to be their leader."

He paced even more restlessly. "The problem is the little fool will tell them everything once he's captured. He's such a braggart he can't help himself. What do I do about that?"

He sat back down heavily in the chair and pondered. "The only possible choice is that they mustn't capture him alive. They must find him, they must know his name—he deserves that—but they cannot find him alive." Fitzsimmons drummed his fingers on the arm of the chair. "Angel must die directly after the assassination." He took another gulp of the burning liquid in the glass and was pleased to find that his stomach had settled down.

CHAPTER 17

TO ENGLAND ON THE HAMBURG-AMERIKA LINE

Atlantic Ocean
March 25, 1908

"Your first time to England?"

Ellis turned to look at the handsome fellow with a slight trace of a German accent who had just addressed his wife. The smartly dressed man was standing at the railing of the ship close to Patricia, while Ellis was a few feet away chatting with Senator William Borah of Idaho. The fact that the man had the impudence to talk to his wife was somehow irritating, so before Patricia could reply, Ellis walked toward them and responded. "My wife and I have been there a few times. We enjoy the shows at the West End of London. Our last trip, we went to a show with H. H. and Margot Asquith." Ellis, his hackles up, had a suspicion that this man was the type who made it their profession to travel the seas in tuxedos and coattails to win the affection of wealthy women who would, for a time, become their sponsors.

"Ah," the man said. "The Chancellor of the Exchequer. I see."

"I think you'll find, if you read the *Times* regularly, that H. H. is now the prime minister," Jason said.

The man nodded, unabashed, and cast a wily glance at Patricia.

"I'm sure I don't know how to say this delicately," the man said, "but I understand Mr. Asquith has something of a reputation with the ladies."

Ellis frowned. Even though it was true, it wasn't something to be said in front of a married woman. The English undersecretary of state, Winston Churchill, had told Ellis on their last visit that his wife, Clementine, had complained Asquith was a "groper" who liked to peer down the top of ladies' dresses. And now the man was prime minister of England!

"I beg your pardon," Ellis said to the German, "but I hardly think that's an appropriate way to talk with people you've never met." He extended his arm to Patricia so they could walk away. She winked at him as he did, pleased at this sign of jealousy on his part.

"Of course not," the man replied quickly. "It was very rude of me, wasn't it? I'm sure I forgot myself. Perhaps it is a Continental failing when speaking with Americans."

Ellis grimaced, irritated that he had to moderate his natural reactions. The Europeans liked to poke fun at the Americans for their prudishness, and this was one of those occasions. But by doing so, the man had forced the Ellises to pause, and now it would be impossible to not make introductions. Which is why he was astounded when Patricia found a way to embarrass the man.

"The only thing that surprises me," she said with a purr, "is that a German would take an interest in such things. I suppose we in America often think that everything in Deutschland is about factory lines and efficiency, perhaps even when it comes to matters of love and affection. Is that a misunderstanding on our part?"

Ellis laughed out loud at this remarkable retort and was pleased to see the man momentarily nonplussed. Then the fellow relaxed and smiled, acknowledging that he'd been bested.

"Ah, my dear lady, you are clever. Please forgive my impertinence and allow me to introduce myself."

"Of course," Patricia said smoothly.

"I am Kurt von Oetle, a minor count from the district of Hanover—a far more romantic region than most of my country."

Ellis smiled at his good-natured reply, even as he recognized the name; Count von Oetle was far from a minor political figure, and it was now highly improbable that he'd started a conversation without recognizing the Ellises. The subterfuge was his way of letting them know Kaiser Wilhelm II of the House of von Hohenzollern was interested in their travels. Von Oetle was a well-known confidant of the Kaiser.

"And we are Mr. and Mrs. Jason Ellis of Long Island, New York. My wife's name is Patricia."

The fellow tipped his head back slightly. "Ah, so you are the famous Senator Jason Ellis of New York? I had hoped to meet you on this journey." He frowned, "But it is my understanding that you plan to visit England and Russia on your excursion—but not Germany?"

And now it was out there.

"We made inquiries with your beautiful country but were not able to put anything together, I'm afraid. It's certainly our loss."

"What?" von Oetle feigned a sense of indignation that sounded almost sincere. "But that certainly won't do. You plan to meet the prime minister of England and members of the Russian court, but not Kaiser Wilhelm? We must see this oversight is changed."

Ellis took a long breath to calm himself. An hour on the boat, and he was already facing his first diplomatic challenge. "Naturally we had hoped to meet Kaiser Wilhelm and had even put in a request to do so, but we were told that he would be on holiday on his cruise ship. We wouldn't want to interrupt that."

"Ah, I am afraid our bureaucrats have failed to understand the importance of this excursion of yours. Please be assured that Wilhelm would feel that he had done our American friends a great injustice if he were to miss such an opportunity. I am sure of that. Perhaps you could modify your itinerary to accommodate at least a few days in Germany if I can arrange it?" Though von Oetle had posed it as a question, Jason seemed to hear more of a command than an honest inquiry.

"That would be wonderful, but only if it wouldn't be too much of an imposition on you. I can say with absolute certainty that nothing would please President Roosevelt more than to have our small delegation meet with members of your government. And it would be such a great personal honor for Patricia and me to meet your king. But it seems too much to hope for."

Von Oetle nodded knowingly. "Why don't you let me see what I can do, Senator Ellis? I am sure His Majesty would never forgive me for not making arrangements when I tell him how perfectly charming you and your beautiful wife are. With whom should I communicate any details?"

"Please speak directly with me. Since you say such a thing can be arranged, I want no misunderstandings. I am confident that there is nothing more important to be accomplished on our visit than this."

"Then it is settled!" von Oetle said with obvious satisfaction.

King Edward was off on a state visit to Scotland, it would be impossible for the Ellises to meet with him, and so a meeting with the king of Germany would trump anything else the British could do. "Now, I embarrassed myself earlier. Perhaps you will allow me to save face by inviting you to join me at the captain's table for dinner tonight. I know he will have you there in your own right, but it would be a tragedy not to sit together on our first night at sea. And then, if I promise to watch myself, perhaps Mrs. Ellis would honor me with a dance."

"As long as Senator Ellis gets a dance with your wife, I'm sure that would be lovely." Once again, Patricia said just the right thing.

"Oh, I am afraid she is not with me on this visit. I was in America doing those very boring German things you spoke of— arranging business meetings and trying my best to steal manufacturing secrets that have made America the leading economic force in this modern world of ours. We Germans are working so very hard to keep up." He smiled a devilish smile. "But you will still allow me at least one dance."

"I'd be delighted." Patricia flashed him one of her best smiles, which the count acknowledged with a slight bow.

"Perfect! Until this evening, then." He stared directly into Jason Ellis's eyes, and for just a moment the count's eyes went cold—so cold it sent a chill up Ellis's spine. But it was so brief that before Ellis could react to the change, the artificial warmth returned and Count von Oetle snapped his heels smartly together and gave them a final smile before turning on his heel and disappearing into the crowd.

As they watched him leave, Patricia finally broke the silence. "Well," she said, "that was rather amazing."

"You're the amazing one. Without you I would have embarrassed myself in front of the count."

"You did fine, my dear. The Germans are clearly irritated we didn't press them harder, and now they're pleased they've found a way to top the British. In the end it should strengthen your hand in both countries—perhaps even with Tsar Nicholas, since he won't want to be outdone by his cousin Willy in Germany."

Ellis laughed. "We're each going to gain twenty pounds on this infernal journey, aren't we? Each of these countries will compete to fete us with the kind of lavish European dinners that always give me heartburn and add to my belly." He paused for a moment and looked over the railing at the shoreline off the port bow. "But you did well. We're now well placed in each of the three countries, and if I can just keep my wits about me, we may do some good."

Before Patricia could respond, Andy Pettit came ambling up. "You know who that was you were talking to, right?" he asked casually.

"We found out. Count von Oetle of Hanover."

"One of the Kaiser's henchmen. He charms the elite of foreign nations while driving a ruthless armament program in Germany. The Hanoverians are well-known for their connections to England, which von Oetle uses to his advantage. But at heart he's a diehard German whose family supported the first Kaiser Wilhelm when he moved to unify Germany in the 1870s. And the count is playing a similar role for Wilhelm II."

"As it turns out, he's going to arrange a visit with the Kaiser for us. I hope that will give you an opportunity to find out something about the anarchists in Germany."

"There aren't many of them, at least publicly. The Germans aren't nearly so patient with their troublemakers as we are in America. Still, there's always something to learn, so I'm glad to open additional lines." He shuffled one of his feet. "Be sure to say hello to Wilhelm for me. I think we're related through a distant ancestor."

"You're German?" Ellis said. "That explains a lot, doesn't it?"

Andy Pettit smiled as he shook his head.

Marlborough House, London
March 28, 1908

"It's true," Patricia said.

"What's true?"

"What Clementine Churchill had to say about Mr. Asquith."

Ellis pretended to cough to conceal his smile. They were, after all, standing in a formal reception line at Marlborough House, the London home of the Prince of Wales. "Well, then, I'm just glad you're not sitting on a couch next to him." Patricia laughed, and at least a few people glanced their way. Although he should be offended to think the prime minister of England would ogle his wife, he was also flattered. "You *are* the most beautiful woman in the room," he said quietly, "so I can't really blame him."

Patricia squeezed his hand.

Having arrived at the front of the line, he attempted to hand his card to the protocol officer who introduced each guest to the Prince and Princess of Wales. In this case, the fellow deftly diverted the card back and announced solemnly, "The Honorable Senator and Mrs. Ellis from the State of New York, the United States of America," indicating their preference at the event. Their announcement without a card was a signal of their status.

Stepping directly in front of Prince George and his wife, Ellis bowed while Patricia did a small curtsy.

"Senator Ellis, what a distinct pleasure. And your wife is so lovely."

"Thank you, sir. The pleasure is ours. I bring the personal greeting of President and Mrs. Roosevelt, as well as that of my colleagues in the Senate. Thank you for receiving us."

"Of course. England has no better friend than the United States. I hope you are both finding a warm reception here."

"Very cordial. Your ministers have treated us with the greatest courtesy. On a personal note, perhaps you'll allow me to say that I've read about your interest in the Royal Philatelic Collection. I confess a weakness for rare stamps myself."

"Ah," the prince said, "a fellow philatelist. For me, I'm afraid it is very much like an obsession. Hopefully you are not quite so deeply affected."

Ellis smiled. "Someday, sir, I hope to retire to my Long Island home and pass many a comfortable day scouring the catalogues for those rare gems of forgotten stamps that do so much to enhance one's collection. Unfortunately, that still seems a long way in the future."

"And do you share your husband's interest?" Princess Mary asked. From the tone in her voice, it was apparent that she did not.

"I'm afraid I do not. My duties as a mother and in society make the more reflective pursuits well beyond my reach."

"Then it sounds as if we all have a great deal in common," the prince said. "Perhaps you could make time in your schedule to have a private dinner with us?" The oldest son of the urbane and polished King Edward, Prince George was far less assuming than his father, well-known for preferring the life of a quiet country gentleman to the social activities of his playboy father. And yet, he was still well-liked by his countrymen.

"It would be a pleasure," Ellis said easily. "I would love to see a portion of your collection, if that's not too much to ask."

Prince George nodded.

"It's settled, then," the prince said. "I look forward to seeing you again before you depart for Germany. I understand that you are to meet my cousin Wilhelm as well as Nicky in Russia?"

Ellis wasn't surprised that the prince had been advised about the nature of their trip, including an up-to-the-minute briefing on their itinerary. "I certainly hope so, sir. Germany has become such an economic powerhouse I'm sure I have much to learn from the Kaiser. And then, if things work out, we will be honored to meet your cousin Nicholas on the final leg of our journey."

"Yes, well, I suspect you'll find you don't have to do much of the talking when you encounter Wilhelm." The prince smiled at the discomfiture this produced in Ellis. As it turns out, the prince's jab at Wilhelm was a dramatic understatement; just a few months earlier in an interview with an English magazine, the gregarious leader of Germany had intended to improve Anglo-German relationships but had instead managed to offend nearly every nation in the world in one way or another. At one point he said the "English were mad, mad, mad as a March hare!" which offended all of Britain. His emotional outbursts were so dramatic that many in Germany were calling for his abdication.

As Ellis struggled to form a response to the prince's joke, George took him off the hook. "But I'm sure you'll find Nicky far more discreet. I hope you'll bear my good wishes to each of them."

"Of course." Ellis discreetly clenched then unclenched his hand to steady himself. The thought that a country boy from up-state New York was having this discussion with English royalty was astonishing.

Prince George turned to his protocol officer and nodded, which meant that it would all be arranged.

"Well, until then, I hope you enjoy your evening." And with that, they were dismissed and free to circulate in the crowd, the people in line behind them irritated by how much time had been devoted to the American interlopers.

"It seems that His Royal Highness has taken a liking to you." Ellis turned at the sound of the prime minister's voice.

"It certainly is easy to like him, isn't it, Mr. Asquith?"

"Indeed. He will be an even-tempered king when the time comes."

Faint praise for a future monarch, Ellis thought. Asquith moved easily in this crowd, having spent a lifetime climbing to "the top of the greasy maypole," as a previous prime minister, Benjamin Disraeli, had said of the role of prime minister.

After Patricia left to chat with Mrs. Asquith, Ellis stepped closer to the prime minister. "Not to mix too much business with pleasure, sir, but perhaps you're aware that one of the purposes of our trip is to share information on the terrorist attacks that have been occurring in our countries. I know it's an unpleasant subject at an event like this, but I have a personal friend of the president in my delegation who specializes in such matters. Do you suppose he can arrange to meet with Scotland Yard for such a discussion? It's quite important to President Roosevelt." Ellis understood that this was a violation of protocol, but to this point in their trip the English diplomatic officers had shrugged them off, and Andy Pettit was growing frustrated.

Asquith sighed. "It *is* an unpleasant topic, isn't it? And my understanding is that both you and Mrs. Ellis were placed in harm's way during one of the incidents."

"The restaurant fire? The nature of the fire still isn't certain, although I personally believe it was, indeed, an act of anarchists."

"Yes, well, we do have our concerns here as well." Asquith straightened up. "And naturally we want to be as helpful as we can. But such discussions must be discreet. One wouldn't want members of the opposition party to think that we are somehow conspiring against them, would we?"

"Of course not. Which is why I was hoping that perhaps you could introduce me to some of the influential people on that side of the aisle for some rather frank discussions. Of course, it would only work if you were our moderator."

Asquith nodded. "Very shrewd, Senator. I can see why you succeed in American politics." He cleared his throat. "Why don't you call on me at Number 10 tomorrow morning at eleven, and we'll see who we can have there. Bring your man and whomever else you think should be part of the discussion. Perhaps you'll join us for luncheon afterward? And then we'll see that your fellow has the chance to meet with his counterparts at Scotland Yard."

"Why, thank you, Prime Minister. That is everything we could hope for."

Asquith nodded and then spoke in an even more subdued voice. "The only thing that I ask of you, Senator Ellis, is that you keep all this off your public itinerary. I'm sure you have reporters trailing you about, so if you don't mind, I'll send an auto that can bring you to and from the meeting without attracting any attention."

"Certainly."

"And," Asquith cleared his throat, "just one more thing. Perhaps you will keep these discussions confidential when you have dinner with the Prince and Princess of Wales—Marlborough House may not be the most appropriate place to talk of such things." He cleared his throat. "Sometimes it's better not to give the people you plan to talk about any new ideas."

Ellis tensed as he realized the implication. "I certainly wouldn't want to put the prince in any kind of jeopardy." The fact that King Edward had been the intended victim of an anarchist's attack while still the Prince of Wales was brought back forcefully to his mind, and he instantly saw what a propaganda opportunity it would be to launch an attack against both the current Prince of Wales and a US senator at the same time.

Asquith nodded. "Good, then we understand each other. And I'm sure your man will also understand?"

"Far better than I. He's the ultimate professional, and you can rely on his discretion."

London
March 28, 1908

"So," Pettit said, "you managed to arrange the meetings after all." He'd come to the Ellises' room for a nightcap and to find out what had occurred at the prince's reception.

"Yes, and I was surprised at the reason for their reticence up to this point."

"Which is?"

"Which is they're worried the terrorists will use our visit as a chance to launch an attack against me and the Prince of Wales or other government officials."

"What?" Patricia said. "Who told you that?"

Jason poured Andy two fingers of scotch, neat. "The prime minister himself."

Patricia sat down on the crushed velvet chair in their suite at the Savoy, the most elegant hotel in London. "Do you think they're serious in that?"

"Asquith certainly seemed to be serious. The only way I was able to provoke him to meet tomorrow was to tell him that it was very important to the president. Otherwise, I think they would have put us off until past time to leave."

"Oh, dear. And I was having such a wonderful time here. Now I'll worry about one or both of us being blown up." The distress in Patricia's voice pierced Ellis's heart.

"While I'm sure it's a credible concern, I wouldn't worry too much," Andy Pettit said, quickly downing the scotch. "The British are discreet in the way they protect their officials, and from what I've observed you're under constant protection."

"Really?" Patricia asked. "I haven't seen anything to suggest that. It seems we come and go with nothing more than a driver and a political attaché."

"And that's exactly what I mean. The fact that *you* don't notice it means that few others will. But I assure you a small brigade of detectives has been watching our every move, perhaps both as spies and protectors."

"But mostly protectors," Ellis said, who had loosened his tie and cummerbund. The tuxedo short coat was King Edward's invention. As he'd grown in girth with the passing years, he had come to prefer less formal and more comfortable attire, now known as appropriate evening dress for all but the most formal occasions.

"I have a headache," Jason said to no one in particular; it was undoubtedly caused by all the polite banter he'd had to endure, "but I do take comfort that I've seen some of the detectives you mention, although I'm sure not all." He leaned his head back against his chair and closed his eyes. "One thing's for sure."

"And what's that, my dear?"

"We must go about our business here regardless of the threat. You should enjoy your visit to the Tower of London tomorrow to view the crown jewels, while Andy and I go to our meetings. The only way the anarchists can win is if they inhibit our governments from doing what's in the best interests of our people."

"Well said," Pettit said.

"Which means the only thing left," Patricia added, "is to figure out what I should wear to our dinner with the Yorks at Marlborough House. I must be careful to dress equal to, but not in something that will out-glitter what I wear when we meet the Kaiser." When Ellis raised an eyebrow, she smiled. "Yes, dear. *Your* only choice is tails or a tuxedo coat, and the protocol officers tell you which is required for a specific event. But *I* have to worry about gowns and jewels and hairstyles, all with the knowledge that both the Germans and the British are paying close attention to make sure they're not slighted."

Andy Pettit placed his elbows on his knees and rested his head. "It's just ridiculous," he said. "And what's all this about York and Wales, and who knows what else?"

"The Prince of Wales is also the Duke of York. His wife is both a princess and a duchess. It signifies both their property interests *and* their place in the royal succession. It means a great deal to the British, I'm sure."

"Well, it's still a load of"—Andy glanced at Patricia—"manure." He scowled, and Patricia laughed.

"It's at times like this that I want to go back to upstate New York and become a gentleman farmer," Ellis said.

"Or an even more avid stamp collector?" Patricia asked.

That had the desired effect, and Jason Ellis laughed. He loved that Patricia always seemed to know when his mood needed lightening.

CHAPTER *18*

MEATPACKER TO THE WORLD—AND HOST TO THE REPUBLICAN CONVENTION

Chicago
April 2, 1908

"Now, listen carefully, Angel, because it's crucial you get this right," Big Jim Fitzsimmons said.

"I am listening," Angel Casimer said sullenly.

"Don't be like that, Angel. It's only for a few months that you won't use your real name. On the day of the attack, your true identity will be revealed. But in the meantime, we need you to establish yourself at work and in this neighborhood as an ordinary, unremarkable fellow. You can't do anything that will cause people to be suspicious. So you'll be Willy Stebbins of New York, temporarily relocated to Chicago on assignment from your employer, the Crustas Line, who handle freight coming into the shipping bays in Chicago. We've arranged your employment history so it looks as if you've been employed by Crustas for five years and have an excellent work record."

"But I'm too small to lift and carry heavy freight."

"Which is why you've been assigned to expedited courier shipments. You'll handle small packages with the highest delivery priority. It's work any member of our union would be proud to perform, and it'll pay you enough to live comfortably while you prepare for the great convention. Many parcels will be delivered to the convention, and that will give you access to their facilities. Your face will become familiar to the security guards, and that will lull them into a false sense of security. You'll have time to familiarize yourself with all the entrances and exits to the Coliseum, and that will help you to be in the right place at the right time to make your grand gesture to the world."

"I have already made three successful *gestures*, but no one knows—"

Fitzsimmons sighed and stood up to go over to the window. He'd made his way to Chicago on the pretext that he needed time to organize demonstrations against the Republican convention when it convened. While this was true, it also made it easier to conceal the true motive for his trip—setting Angel Casimer up for the sensational blow he'd strike when the moment was ripe. Fitzsimmons looked out the windows of the once elegant but now shabby townhouse that was the increasingly brooding Casimer's new residence.

"Chicago's the right place for this to happen," he said thoughtfully. "Brash and noisy, the people here will understand why we strike. It was wrong to make you act in Washington and Hartford—the workers there are cowed by their bosses and dulled by their prosperity. But here, the movement is gritty and driving. This is the right place for you to strike."

Thinking all this was mostly just his own musings, he was surprised to hear Casimer splutter in the background. When Fitzsimmons turned to look at his troubled young protégé, he found that he was sobbing. "Oh, dear Lord," he said as he moved to pull the young man's head against his ample belly. "It's all right, Angel. All you've done will find completion here."

"It is the right place?" Casimer managed to choke out the question.

"It is." Fitzsimmons patted Angel's shoulders. The toll of murder weighed on this little man in what had to be a fatal devolution of his mind. "Hang on, my dear friend, hang on. It won't be long now." In some corner of his mind, Fitzsimmons managed to hate himself for what he was doing—both to Casimer and to the two future conventioneers who would die at Casimer's hands. Fitzsimmons knew his own mother would be ashamed. "But it's for the cause, our great international cause." He was not reassured and was startled to think that he, too, felt some of the emotion that Angel so foolishly exhibited.

Washington, DC
April 2, 1908

"Senator Ellis met with success in England?" Edith Roosevelt asked.

Theodore Roosevelt turned to his wife. "He did, indeed. The cables I've received from our embassy there said that he got on famously with the Prince of Wales. They had a private dinner that lasted well past ten. That's highly unusual for the prince."

"I'm sure it was interesting for Patricia."

"Like you, a perfect wife for a politician: smart, witty, and discreet."

"Better than me, I think. I'm a family woman. Patricia understands society far better than I do."

Roosevelt reached over and patted her knee. "You *are* society, my dear. You have no need to understand it, since society must make way for you."

She took his hand in hers. "I hope they're all right. Somehow I feel they're in great danger on this trip. I can't tell you why, but perhaps they shouldn't have gone."

"But of course they should have gone." Had it been anyone else, his indignation would have burst out in a tirade, but he was patient with his wife. "One faces dangers every day—crossing a street when traffic is heavy, going hunting on safari, or slipping on a bar of soap in the bathroom. Danger should never stop one from living his life."

With anyone else, Edith Roosevelt would have felt insulted by this response, but she knew that her husband believed every word he said—and that he meant it with no guile. "You're right. I'm sure they'll be fine. And if not, the world will go on." She patted his hand. "It always does, doesn't it?"

New York City
April 2, 1908

"It's best for it to happen in Germany, I tell you. We took your advice and canceled an attack in England." Koslov's Russian handler bristled at the way Koslov was lecturing him.

"You cancelled a *catastrophe* in England." Maxim Kozlov made no attempt to conceal the irritation in his voice. Shaking his head while pacing the small room, he added, "Do you not pay *any* attention to the political climate in the places you act? Random violence creates fear, not unity. The attack on King Edward in Belgium in 1900 by our anarchist brother Jean-Baptiste Sipido made the working men in England indignant, if not sympathetic, when the bullet grazed his hand—it wasn't inspiration for our cause. If the people who planned that attack had even half a brain, they would have realized that in England you can kill *political* leaders with little—or even positive—consequence. But *not* the royal family—attack the king or queen or the princes, and you strike at the heart of every Englishman. Now you propose to blow up Senator Ellis while conversing with the emperor of Germany? It's pure madness. The Prussian Guard would travel the entire world to hunt down everyone involved—and in the process drive our great movement to extinction." He paused long enough to pour himself a drink.

"But the people are calling for Wilhelm's abdication!"

"The *people* love Wilhelm for standing up for the coal miners. They love him for standing up to the British. Perhaps the German *ruling* class is aghast at his erratic behavior and want his abdication, but the people *we* want to join *our* movement see him as their ally and protector."

"You will end up telling us to do nothing!" The man whom Kozlov hated so much, the man who reported to his European masters, pounded his fist on the table.

"So very mature of you to pound the table." Scorn dripped from Kozlov's voice. "But you'll listen to me, and then you and comrade Lenin will do what you want to do. But at the very least you'll listen to me."

The fellow sat down with a scowl. "I am tired of listening and not doing. Perhaps you are friends with Senator Ellis, which makes you unwilling to see him harmed—"

"You dare accuse me of doing *nothing*?" Kozlov stormed across the room and shook his finger in the man's face. "Do you think that the assassination in Hartford happened by happenstance? Do you think the bombing in Washington, DC, materialized out of thin air? And do you think the restaurant fire was an accident?"

Kozlov's face flushed, and the fellow braced to be hit, a result that would not be entirely unwelcome since he could kill Kozlov in response. *You, comrade Kozlov, are rich, but you are also pompous. You think you are so much smarter than us, but it is your kind who will be brought low when the revolution comes.*

For a moment it looked like Kozlov really would strike a blow, but he forced himself to step back. When he saw the look on the man's face, he realized that he'd said too much, and needed to regain his self-control. "You must listen to me. Russia is ready to light the fuse. I have been there. I have friends there. The people hate the tsar—they've wrested concession after concession from him, and yet he continues to think he can dominate them. He is willfully blind to their suffering. While Kaiser Wilhelm provides benefits to his people—such as lifetime pensions when they retire—the tsar is indignant when his people plead for bread. Do you not see that *this* is where we should strike? As for Jason Ellis, you're free to do with him whatever you want. He is no friend of mine and is exactly the type of man who should be destroyed."

The fellow stood up. "You are passionate, my friend. I give you that. But you are also right that it is up to Lenin to decide. He is in Austria; he is exiled from Russia. He knows what is best. All we need from you is an assurance that the man you've planted in the American delegation will strike whenever he is told to. You must make sure that he will not hesitate nor act on his own."

Kozlov took a deep breath, and then turned to look directly at his antagonist. "Perhaps you need to worry about such things in Europe, but I assure you that in America my people are completely under my control. He will strike when I tell him." Kozlov waited just a moment for his words to soak in. "And as for me, I will wait on comrade Lenin. He has earned my loyalty. That is all you need to know."

CHAPTER *19*

AT SEA WITH WILHELM II

Baltic Sea off Kiel, Germany
April 3, 1908

"So, my good senator, what do you think of my yacht? Is it not a great vessel worthy of the German people?"

It took all of Jason Ellis's concentrated effort to reply to the Kaiser of Prussia, the emperor of united Germany, without throwing up. "I think the *Meteor* is a wonderful boat," he said weakly. Having experienced seasickness before, he knew his skin was green from nausea, but it would not be manly to admit to it. And manly was, after all, the coin of the realm in Germany, a nation that had embraced the idea of survival of the fittest as none other in the world. The magnificent passion of the four operas forming *Der Ring des Nibelungen* by Richard Wagner had set the German heart aflame and had become the unofficial anthem of the new German state. Wilhelm I, the grandfather of the current Kaiser, had created it in 1871 by consolidating the north Germanic duchies.

Born with a deformed hand through a midwife's error,

Wilhelm II had pressed himself mercilessly to live up to the German ideal of strength and vigor. His mother, the daughter and namesake of England's Queen Victoria, taught him the social graces, but his mercurial temperament often triumphed over his training. At this stage, nothing was more important to Wilhelm than his navy, which he had created primarily to challenge Britain's primacy of the seas. But since there was no war to showcase his great coal-powered dreadnoughts, he had to be content as the patron of his royal yacht club based out of Kiel.

"Something tells me," Wilhelm said in a conspiratorial tone, "that your wife enjoys yachting more than you do."

Patricia smiled as she leaned against the mainstay of the *Meteor.* "My husband has always been troubled by an inner-ear disorder. But he's a brave fellow, knowing that I really do love yachting and wanted to enjoy this day with you. For my part, I particularly enjoy sailing as opposed to powered crafts since it is so smooth and quiet. What can equal the feel of the air around one's face, the snap of the sails to the wind, and the sensation of pure, effortless speed through the water that one experiences on a grand ship such as this?"

"Why, my dear Mrs. Ellis, you are a poet. You have captured perfectly how I feel when I am at sea. It is the one place in the world where the troubles of state do not intrude, and I can be at one with myself and nature."

"Yachting off Long Island, where we live, is a very popular sport," Ellis said. "Perhaps you should try the waters there someday." *And sailing inside the Long Island Sound isn't nearly as turbulent as these waters. I might stand a chance there.*

"I'd like that. But not with the *Meteor.* The truth is, it is something of a disappointment to me. Which is why I've commissioned a new yacht that will do much better in competition. For some reason the *Meteor* doesn't do as well as expected. Germany is quite accustomed to winning the Blue Riband in the luxury steamship realm, you know, so it only makes sense that a German yacht should win in yachting competitions as well. And yet my Uncle Edward's *Britannia* consistently does better in time trials." He took a sip on his drink. "And that is unacceptable."

Wilhelm's uncle was King Edward VII of England, and *Britannia* was his pride and joy.

"And when will this new craft be ready?" Patricia asked, her enthusiasm spontaneous and authentic.

"About a year from now. I plan to name her the *Germania*, so it is essential that she be the best in the world. And you, Mrs. Senator Ellis, must come sail on her. I will spare no expense, you know."

Of course not, thought Jason Ellis while quietly counting the cost that these spoiled royals spent on themselves to feed their vanity. *Britannia* and *Germania! This intense rivalry between Germany and England will have awful consequences if it continues to grow. Family jealousy is one thing, but when the families employ armies and navies, it gets a bit ridiculous.* He'd reached this conclusion after spending many hours with Wilhelm and his entourage over the past few days. On the one hand it was obvious that Wilhelm had great respect for the English—his spoken English was flawless, his voice almost identical to his cousin George's. But his talk of the British king rambled between abject admiration and extreme contempt. In the end, Ellis had decided that it would be difficult to serve as one of Wilhelm's ministers because of his mercurial temperament. He was glad to be an American.

"We will hit calm waters inside the breakwater very quickly, Senator, and then your headache will disappear. The best thing for seasickness is to eat a hearty meal, so I have instructed my staff to having something substantial waiting for us."

Both Wilhelm and Patricia laughed as Ellis's eyes widened. "Perhaps a warm drink before I try anything substantial?"

"That's just what you'd think would be right, isn't it? But I assure you the answer is to eat well and put something solid in your stomach. Trust me on this, good senator, and you will be amazed."

Since there was nothing else he could do, Ellis nodded and said, "Of course. I'll be interested to see how it works."

It was another thirty minutes before the *Meteor* slipped easily and silently into her slip, and with a great deal of royal flourish, the emperor helped Patricia down the gangplank, leaving Ellis to his own devices. Wilhelm's wife, Empress Augusta Victoria, was in Russia visiting relatives there.

"Now we will help you feel better," said Wilhelm cheerfully. Ellis had decided that despite the Kaiser's bluster and vanity, he quite liked him for his good-natured enthusiasm. While Wilhelm was outwardly a braggart, Ellis suspected that there were dark moments in the man's life, and he felt a little sorry for him that he could be in so prominent a position, fame and fortune assured, and yet still suffer from envy.

It was at this moment that two things happened. First, he caught sight of Andy Pettit, who'd stayed on shore to meet with some local union men, and second, he saw the colorful tent that had been erected for their luncheon. He was pleased to see that, given the number of tables inside, the lunch was to be a small, private affair, unlike all the other grand banquets they had encountered. Up until this point, most of their meetings had been staged events that the emperor saw as an opportunity to show off his American guests to as many people as possible, including an obedient German press corps.

"You will sit by my side at the table," he heard Wilhelm say to Patricia. Because of the lingering effects of motion sickness, Jason had a hard time fully processing everything he heard. Being nauseous always seemed to take most of his concentration while his brain struggled to find equilibrium. Conversations at times like this felt otherworldly to him.

Perhaps it was because of his altered state of mind that he didn't immediately recoil when he saw a server pick up a round object from behind one of the silver chafing dishes, hold it against the flame under the chafing dish, and then arch back to throw it. In his somewhat addled state he thought how odd that was, but nonetheless heard himself shouting to Patricia and to Wilhelm to get down while simultaneously diving in their direction. Behind him he felt Andy Pettit turn and shout, and he somehow managed to catch a glimpse of Pettit drawing a revolver from his breeches. A split second later, Ellis fell against Wilhelm and Patricia, knocking them both to the ground. He rolled as he fell and saw a lick of flame shoot out from Andy's weapon, and he instinctively recoiled from the retort. Once on the ground, he had no idea what was going on above him, but he did hear a commotion from the direction of where he'd seen the man with the round object.

"Cover yourself!" he heard Pettit shout, and then felt the crushing weight of Andy Pettit falling on top of him. He waited for what he now realized would be a blast and was sickened when he heard the muffled sound of a small explosion.

"Stay down, Patricia!" he said furiously, hoping that there weren't others acting in collusion, yet feeling this might be the end. "What is it?" he asked Andy Pettit, a perfectly stupid question, since it was obviously a bomb, but then a person doesn't really think about what he's saying at times like this.

Rather than answer, Andy stirred and got up to his knees to look over the buffet they'd dived behind. "I think it's all right," Andy said as he stood. Reaching down to help Jason, he said quietly, "One of the Kaiser's bodyguards threw himself on top of the bomb—and you don't want to see what happened."

Ellis tried to stand up but found himself unable to do so. He turned to Patricia to warn her, but she'd heard Andy as clearly as he. As he tried to stand a second time, he felt a hand push him down and looked up to see that they were now surrounded by fierce, armed members of Wilhelm's personal guard, and for just a moment Ellis wondered if they were going to shoot him. After all, it's very much against protocol to knock a monarch to the ground.

"Are you all right, Herr Senator?" he heard Wilhelm ask in perfect English. In the confusion of the moment Wilhelm had mixed the language of his titles. Ellis rolled onto his back and looked up at the Kaiser, now standing directly above him. *If there's anything less dignified than this, I can't imagine what it is,* he thought miserably. *Seasick with a monarch who loves the ocean, and now lying in a clump on the ground, sick to my stomach, and hardly able to get up.* For just a moment he hoped this was a bizarre dream, but he realized that even in his worst nightmares he couldn't have come up with the look of terror he'd seen on Patricia's face.

"I'm all right," he said, extending a hand to Andy, who apparently now had permission to help him up. "I'm sorry I had to push you, Your Majesty, but—"

"Nonsense. You did what you had to. It appears that you, in concert with Mr. Pettit and my bodyguard, have saved my life."

Wilhelm acted as if he wanted to say more, but the men who surrounded him would have none of it. "I must leave—you will be escorted back to your lodgings. Perhaps you will come by the Wilhelmina Palace before you leave."

Before Ellis could even reply, the emperor was rushed off by his men, leaving a much smaller cohort to deal with the two dead bodies and the Americans who had been part of the drama.

"You must go—right now!" the Kaiser's guard demanded.

"Of course. But—"

"Right now!"

One of the men put his arm on Ellis's and pulled him toward the waiting Daimler-Mercedes automobile. "I can do this on my own," said Ellis, roughly pushing the man's arm away. No matter the circumstance, he was a United States senator, and he would not be treated like a child.

As they reached the car, he, Patricia, and Pettit were helped roughly inside, and then the door of the smartly styled limousine was closed firmly behind them. Since the driver was seated in a separate seat in front of the enclosed carriage, assuring their privacy, Andy Pettit felt at liberty to speak quietly to Ellis.

"I know you are not feeling well—"

"But?"

"But . . ." he hesitated, while glancing nervously at Patricia.

"Tell us," Patricia said. "We need to know what's happening."

Pettit took a deep breath. "You should know that the man who threw the bomb was aiming for you, not Wilhelm."

"*What?*" Ellis couldn't be sure he was hearing anything correctly, given the speed of events and the haze he'd been in when they started.

"Wilhelm may also have been a target, but he was definitely going for you. Don't say anything to anyone else, though. It's better if Wilhelm thinks he was the intended target. I saw exactly where he was aiming as I fired my pistol, and it was at you. If the Kaiser had been hurt, it would have been as collateral damage, not as the primary target."

Both Jason and Patricia were left speechless as this new information sank in. Finally, clearing his throat, Ellis said, "Okay, now, tell me again exactly what you think happened. So far, nothing makes any sense."

Andy Pettit nodded. "I just said the man was trying to kill *you*. I don't know why, and I don't know who put him up to it, but you must know that somehow you've become a target."

"Oh, Jason," Patricia said, "what have we done in coming here?"

"I don't know. I just don't know."

CHAPTER 20

A DARKER SIDE

Berlin
April 5, 1908

"Why do you keep looking out the window?" Jason Ellis was at the fireplace adding another log to the fire in an effort to get rid of the chill that still clung to the room even at eight in the morning. This was probably the twentieth time he'd seen Andy Pettit pull the curtain back in the drawing room of the Ellises' hotel. The window looked down on the famous Brandenburg Gate marking one of the four entrances into the ancient walled city of Berlin.

Without answering, Andy said suddenly, "You'll have to excuse me. I have something urgent. I'll be back shortly."

"But where are you going—"

It did no good to ask, since Pettit had already bolted through the door, slamming it behind him.

"Don't go to the window, Jason."

"What?"

"I know you want to look out the window to see whatever Andy was looking at, but it's probably dangerous. Don't!"

Ellis paced nervously. "Of course not. It's foolish. I wouldn't have any idea what he was looking for, anyway." He went over to one of the upholstered silk ottomans and sat down, picking up a copy of an English-language newspaper. After fidgeting through a couple of pages, with no idea of what he was reading, he finally stood up and moved toward the window. "This is ridiculous! I will not be told I cannot look out a window." He glanced at Patricia. "I'll be discreet."

Patricia shook her head and scowled but said nothing.

Inching his way to the same window Andy had been looking through, he slowly pulled back a corner of the curtain and looked down on the plaza. It was surprising how many automobiles were in the great plaza—certainly more than made their way up and down the streets of Washington, DC. But perhaps it was normal, given the Germans' love of technology. It was, after all, Gottlieb Daimler who'd first successfully used an internal combustion engine to move a wheeled device, which resembled a bicycle with four wheels. Experts agreed it was the first successful marriage of a gasoline-powered engine and a wheeled contrivance. Shortly afterward, he'd joined with Karl Benz in creating an automobile factory that was now world-renowned for the quality of the machines they made.

"So what do you see?"

"Nothing out of the ordinary. People and horses and . . ."

"And?"

"And Andy Pettit talking to a man wearing black." He strained to see who the fellow was, but the distance was too great. He was able to pick Andy out of the crowd only because of Andy's height and the unusual hat he favored. Both were standing near the edge of the curb. "It looks like they're arguing."

This aroused Patricia's interest enough that she came over to join him at the window. "I don't think they're arguing. But Andy does seem quite intense." They continued to study the scene for a few moments, wondering who in this country Andy had been wanting to see.

"Well, I'm sure it's none of our business," Patricia said, "and if it is, he will tell us—" Before she could turn from the window, both she and Jason gasped.

"Dear heaven! What just happened?"

"That man . . . he just fell in front of that automobile!"

As Jason and Patricia watched, a crowd began rushing to the scene. The driver of the car had stopped and was bending down to the man who lay sprawled motionless in the street.

"Where's Andy?" Ellis phrased it as a question, but it was really more of a plea.

"Jason?"

He turned and looked at Patricia, her eyes wide.

"Jason, did Andy push that man?"

"What?" He shook his head. "Of course not." He bit his lip. "He couldn't have. He wouldn't." His voice was shaking and, his legs feeling like jelly, he motioned to the couch. They made their way over. "I'm sure he didn't. I wasn't paying close attention. They were standing very near the curb. It's very possible that the automobile clipped the man as it went by."

"Clipped?"

"Yes, the side edge of the automobile must have struck the man." He exhaled sharply. "That must have been what happened."

Patricia was glum. "It certainly didn't look that way to me."

Just then there was a knock on the door, and Andy Pettit

came in, carefully closing the door behind him. Instinctively both the Ellises stood up.

"Andy!" Jason was surprised at both the pitch and intensity of his voice.

"There's been an accident," Andy said. "I need to send a cable."

"A cable?"

"Yes. And it would be better if I sent it in your name. Is that all right?"

Jason forced himself to sit back down, taking Patricia with him by putting his arm around her as he did so. He took a deep breath. Then, trying to keep his voice as steady as possible, he said, "Andy, we were watching from the window. The man hit by the car was talking to you when the accident happened . . ." He allowed his voice to trail off, hoping that Andy would enlighten them.

"Yes, that's true."

Ellis felt his heart pounding in his chest, but he still wasn't ready to ask the question pressing on his mind. Instead, he asked, "Does the telegram have anything to do with this 'accident'?"

If Andy noticed Jason's change in inflection on the word *accident*, he gave no clue that he did. "Only indirectly. Now, do I have permission? I really need to go."

Ellis felt Patricia's grasp on his right leg tighten, and he knew that he had to ask. It would sound natural now and would only be more awkward if asked later.

"Andy, before I say yes, I have to ask you a troubling question." He stood up and walked over to the fireplace, used a poker to stir the fire, then turned to look at Andy. "Did you push that man?"

Andy's face, which always looked a little flushed, seemed to glow even brighter. Ellis couldn't tell if he was angry or embarrassed. But the change was noticeable. His attitude was hostile enough that Ellis instinctively drew back, even though it was unlikely he could protect himself from an angry Andy Pettit. He braced for whatever was coming.

Andy did take a couple of steps toward Jason and then paused. Jason watched as he slowly took off his hat, took a deep breath, and placed the hat on the coffee table. Jason was surprised when he asked, "Mind if I sit down?"

Perhaps he expected Andy's voice to tremble, as his would have done in the same circumstance, but it didn't. Jason motioned to the side chair opposite the ottoman, and then, only after Andy sat down, did he return to Patricia and sit down himself. He wanted to break the silence that ensued but decided that if he were ever to get the truth, he would have to wait until Andy was ready to tell him.

Finally, Andy sighed and said, "Let me ask *you* a question."

"All right."

"Did you know Cooper, the blond fellow in your detail, before he was assigned to travel with us?"

"Cooper? No. He was a last-minute addition from the State Department. Why?"

"That's who just died."

"He died! Oh, no!" Patricia exclaimed.

"He's dead. There's no question about that."

"Cooper? But what were you talking about?" Jason had thought he could never feel more nauseous than when he'd been at sea with the Kaiser, but he realized he was wrong.

Andy looked up at them slowly. "I was asking him who paid him to hire the server to throw the bomb that nearly killed you."

Jason's face paled. "What are you talking about?"

Pettit scowled and turned his head away.

"Andy, whatever you know, you've got to tell us. We're here in Europe to *uncover* secrets, not create new ones."

Pettit looked back at him. "All right, I'll tell you. I've been suspicious of this guy for some time. All the other men on the detail have been forthcoming with me, but Cooper always stood apart. He made it clear he wasn't to report to a hired detective, even one who's connected to the president."

"But how does that connect him to the bomb?"

"It doesn't, of course. But what does is that one of my best men, Chambers, found a half-burned telegram in Cooper's fireplace. I'd asked Chambers to keep an eye on him. Luckily, part of the message was still legible. It said, 'Proceed as planned. Kiel. No one left. Deal with Pettit separately.' It was unsigned."

"I can see that might be suspicious, but it's not definitive."

"Oh, don't be so stupidly naive, Jason!" Ellis was surprised at the ferocity in Andy's voice. "Don't you see? They can't send a telegram that says, 'Kill Senator Ellis and King Wilhelm in Kiel, leaving no one alive. Kill Pettit later if he survives.'"

"But . . ." Ellis stopped. He didn't want to be stupid or naive, but if Andy had just killed a man on the basis of this telegram . . .

"What else did you know about Cooper?" Patricia asked.

The expression on his face made it obvious Pettit hated being the one interrogated, since it was usually the other way around. "I know because I did my own investigation. He'd only worked at State for a month and was selected because he speaks German fluently. The notation on his hiring record says simply 'highly recommended,' which is always code for some political appointment."

"So he has a sponsor somewhere?" Ellis knew he had to be careful now, or Andy would clam up.

"He was planted there specifically for this mission." Before

Ellis could question him about that, he added, "He's out of New York, Jason. He was connected with some very shadowy figures there. He should have never been appointed to State, but they're casual about such things when a person comes recommended the way he was."

Jason nodded his head. "Meaning someone paid a great deal of money into someone else's campaign fund."

"But why would he want to kill Jason?" Patricia's voice was tinged with desperation.

"That's why I needed to talk to him. After the telegram, we increased our watch, but it was State that was coordinating security at the yacht club, so we couldn't get close to the planners. After the attack we were able to talk to them, and I found two witnesses who saw Cooper talking with the fellow with the bomb. When I confronted him just now, he pulled a knife on me, which is why I bumped him at just the right moment."

Patricia tried to suppress a gasp but was unsuccessful.

"I know," Pettit said. "I didn't come here to kill anyone. But I also didn't come here to be killed."

"Of course not," Jason said. He stared directly at Andy for a few moments, his mind recalling the years they'd known each other. The only conclusion he could come to was that Andy was telling the truth. His loyalty had been proved far too many times to question it now. "What do we do now?"

"I assume the German authorities will figure out what happened, so I'm sure I'll be interrogated."

"Maybe not. After all, you've been credited with helping save their king's life. Somehow I think that'll go a long way in a country like this."

Andy shook his head. "I doubt it. The Germans are nothing if not efficient. Sentimentality is not likely to enter into their interrogation techniques." He took a deep breath. "The main thing is I have to send that telegram before I turn myself in."

"What's in the telegram?" Patricia asked, clearly trying to keep her emotions under control.

"He's going to get his own people looking into who Cooper's sponsor was," Ellis said quietly. "We've got to find out who is behind all of this, and this is the first solid clue we have." He turned to Andy. "Am I right?"

"Exactly right. Awful as this is, we finally have a lead we can follow. Somewhere along the line someone made a mistake. Someone will have left another clue, and we'll find it."

Jason stood, which gave permission for Andy to stand. "Well, then. You go send your telegram. I'll contact the Kaiser's people and let them know what happened. I think it will be better coming from me. It was self-defense, after all. Still, it will complicate things back home."

"We could just say he was with us the whole time."

Jason and Andy turned toward Patricia, both astonished. "What do you mean?" Jason asked.

"All you need to do is get rid of that hat you like so much, and you'll look like anyone else in the crowd down there." When Pettit glanced down at the hat he'd been wearing on the street, Patricia stood up, picked it off the coffee table, and walked over to the fireplace. "Knowing how effectively you can move through a crowd, I sincerely doubt there's anyone who will connect you to the accident. And if there are, let them come to *us*, not the other way around." With that she tossed the hat into the fire.

"But they'll know he's in our delegation. That would raise questions," Jason said.

"And we'll say that we know little about this Mr. Cooper from the State Department, but that we feel terrible about the accident. He must have been distracted and stepped off the curb at the wrong time." She walked closer to Jason. "Listen, my dear, we couldn't tell from here what happened for sure, and we were looking directly at Andy and Cooper when it *did* happen. People passing by wouldn't have paid any attention to Cooper until after he fell."

Ellis looked at Patricia and smiled. "You continue to amaze me, dear." Turning to Andy he said, "It would simplify things a lot if it was just an accident. And if the Kaiser's people suspect anything, they're likely to keep it to themselves to avoid any scandal connected to the throne."

Andy nodded. "I'm lucky to have you two."

"It was our lives you were saving, so go send that telegram." Andy walked over to the coatrack by the door and chose one of his jackets. "Wear this just in case someone happened to notice you before. This will change your appearance."

Pettit nodded and then departed through the door, leaving the Ellises to sort out their thoughts about what had just happened.

New York City
April 7, 1908

"Your man failed, and now you must tell us why."

Kozlov looked at the European with dispassionate eyes.

"And just what does *his* failure have to do with me? I was not there."

"You were given the assignment, and it failed. We must determine if it was because of incompetence or disloyalty." With that, the fellow raised the gun he had presented immediately after entering Kozlov's office. "You are to return with me to Europe, where you will explain yourself."

"Ah. The attempt on the Kaiser's life was a failure, and so I'm to be killed. Even though I'm the one who told you it was a stupid thing to do in Germany. 'The fuse is ready to be struck in Russia,' I said the last time you saw me. 'The German workers love their king,' I said, but you didn't believe me. And now I'm proved right, and you come here and threaten me. Why is that the case?"

"Because reports from the scene suggest your man was going for Senator Ellis first, and that is the reason he failed. It was this Mr. Pettit who thwarted the attempt. Now word is out in Germany we have bungled yet another assassination attempt, and the Kaiser is extracting a heavy price for it. We left it in your hands, and you chose your own personal vendetta over the plan. The mission was bungled. And now we have reached the . . . what do the Americans say?"

Kozlov grimaced. "They say 'the end of your rope'—you have reached the end of your rope."

"Yes! That is it. We have reached the end of our rope. So my dear Kozlov, you must come with me right now."

Kozlov very carefully raised the glass of sherry he'd been nursing and drew a tasteful sip. He was fully aware he wouldn't be making a trip to Europe. Once outside his office, he'd be killed and his body disposed of. That was simply the price of failure. *But I am* not *a failure, you ignorant maggot!* Setting the glass of sherry down on his desk, he looked directly at his handler from the chair behind his massive desk. "Have you ever heard of a silencer? A very innovative American invention."

"What are you talking about, Kozlov?"

Kozlov put his elbows on the desk, templed his fingers, smiled wanly, and lightly tapped his foot on a lever along the inside of the bottom of his desk. There was a muffled whuffing sound accompanied by a small puff of smoke that drifted up from the front of the desk, and the man who'd been threatening him suddenly had the most startled look on his face Kozlov had ever seen. A dark stain grew on the fellow's chest, and he slumped backward into the chair directly behind him.

The man's eyes bulged, and his hands trembled as they tried to find the spot where the stain was spreading through his dark wool vest.

"Ah, but you're not dead yet, I see. You have time to appreciate that *I* killed *you*, and not the other way around." He walked around the desk, reached down, and took the handgun from the man's now limp hand. "There will be even more questions for me to answer to Europe, but now they'll know better than to trifle with me." Kozlov walked back to his desk and slipped the man's revolver into a side drawer. "It would have been better all along if I'd organized this whole operation myself. Bolsheviks may be smart when it comes to politics, but they're still ignorant in the affairs of the daily world—the world in which I operate." He walked back to the chair and reached down to push the man's eyelids closed. Nothing was quite so disconcerting as being stared at by a dead man's vacant eyes.

He walked to his liquor cabinet and poured himself a shot of whiskey, which he downed in a single gulp. Then, going to the door, he stepped out and said to his secretary, "Please summon Tom Scanlon."

"Yes, sir. Right away."

He walked back over to the chair, where he rested his hand on the dark oxblood leather above the corpse. "Another job for Tom. This time he may not be so willing—this will challenge his loyalty. It will be sad when he knows so much I can no longer trust him."

Tom Scanlon knocked a moment later. "Come in, Tom," Kozlov said casually. "I need your help in a small matter."

CHAPTER *21*

ALL THIS WAY FOR NOTHING

St. Petersburg
April 13, 1908

"The joy's gone out of it," Jason Ellis said to Andy Pettit. "Patricia would have loved touring the Peterhof, the tsar's summer palace, and yet you sent her home from Germany."

"It was the only prudent thing to do. Now we know you're a target, you really couldn't risk the children losing both of you."

"And you're sure she'll be safe when she gets home?"

"As safe as human beings can make her." Andy turned to Jason, wishing he could take away his uncertainty. "I've put my very best people on it. I know each of them, and they're trustworthy. I promise you that."

Ellis nodded as they walked down the sculptured steps between two of the terraced waterfalls of Peter's House—a modest name for a pretentious palace. The water cascading directly from under the great summer palace was the perfect way to frame the great structure built by Peter the Great to show the world how modern and European Russia had become.

Many assumed that St. Petersburg had been named for Tsar Peter, the most powerful of all the Russian tsars, but Peter insisted it was in honor of St. Peter the Apostle, the first bishop of the Christian Church in Rome and the impetuous apostle of Jesus who cut off a soldier's ear, exactly the kind of man Tsar Peter would choose as his patron saint. That they shared the same name was a bonus. That way, everything that bore the name of St. Peter indirectly bore the name of the tsar who honored him.

This grand palace was built to challenge the grandeur and glory of the splendid palace of Versailles in France, emblazoned as it was with the words *Á Toutes les Gloires de la France*—"To All the Glories of France." From what Ellis could tell, the Peterhof was every bit as grand, particularly with its ocean access that allowed Peter to come and go easily into the Baltic. Now it was the summer residence of the current tsar and tsarina, Nicholas II and Alexandra.

Like his cousin Wilhelm II, Nicholas II was also Queen Victoria's grandson and the current English king's nephew. Letters between Nicholas and Wilhelm were always signed 'Nicki' and 'Willy.' Yet somehow Jason Ellis doubted their family ties would mean much if their countries ever found themselves at odds with one another.

Jason sighed. "Ah, well. We carry out the charade. We pretend the incident in Germany was nothing more than an inconsequential disturbance at our luncheon, and the international community has treated it as such since the actual deaths were suppressed by the German crown. 'A suspicious object was found on the grounds but was quickly neutralized before anything could happen.'" He shook his head. "The official explanation is always a dumbed-down version of events, but this one takes the cake. To have lived through it and yet to have no acknowledgment of it, makes me think I imagined the whole thing. I'm not sure Roosevelt will believe it when I tell him."

"Well, it's true. And while I doubt we're out of danger yet, with Cooper out of the picture, I'm now settled about the men who continue to travel with us." Andy Pettit looked around at the immaculately groomed gardens. Few would guess he had a weak spot for gardens, and there was much to appreciate here. "I think you're safe. The tsar rules with a tight coterie around him. There are still many in Russia who hate him, so security's unlike anything I've ever seen. Still, an American in St. Petersburg presents a tempting target, even for those who have no connection to the incidents that've already happened in your vicinity."

Ellis laughed. "Incidents in my vicinity." He and Pettit wandered into one of the hedgerow mazes that so delighted the children of kings and queens. "And here I thought I was a popular fellow—but someone wants to kill me."

"You still don't get it, do you?"

"Get what?" Ellis showed a hint of irritation, as he always did when Andy lectured him.

"They always go for popular leaders. It seldom has anything to do with whether they *like* you or not. It has everything to do with who'll get the most newsprint. That's why anarchists kill presidents and princes. Haven't you noticed that sometimes the assassin is one of the victim's closest friends or servants? They murder because they want maximum public exposure."

Jason nodded thoughtfully as he pondered this new insight. "And just how did you learn all this? I'm not aware of any textbook on the subject."

"There isn't—and that's a problem. At this point there's no formal science behind what we do. The Pinkertons have great methods, but how does that help anyone but the Pinkertons?"

He stopped walking and turned directly to Ellis. "That's why I think you should create this new Federal Agency of Investigation. If those of us who work in this field are to ever have a chance of holding our own against the anarchists, bank robbers, and murderers, we must have a way to share information and advance our methods. Who cares if people lose some privacy—losing their lives is a lot worse."

Jason bit his lip. Making those kinds of concessions was a sign of maximum stress. And then he sighed, his way of releasing stress. "I suppose you're right. But once we give a freedom away, it's gone for good. When Pandora opened the box, there was never a chance of getting all those troubles back inside. Even as threatened as I am right now—and it would be almost impossible for anyone to feel more threatened than I do—I'll miss what we give up when it's gone."

"Not to show a lack of sympathy, Jason, but it seems to me that you *chose* to give up a lot of privacy the moment you went into public service. If you'd stayed in the private sector, there's a good chance none of this would be happening to you. In the end, aren't investigative agencies about bad people and public people?"

Jason laughed. "A self-inflicted wound, is it?" Then he grew serious. "I'll support the legislation. If this trip has done nothing more than to convince me of that, it's been worth the effort. We must make an increased effort to fight the enemies of civilization. This is a place where America can provide leadership. Just consider: The English were afraid to let us meet with Scotland Yard for fear it would attract the zealots, and then we very nearly got a king and a senator murdered in Germany for the same reason. And now we've spent a week in Russia touring palaces and gardens, with virtually no interaction with the tsar. I seriously doubt we'll get to meet Nicholas."

"That's about where I am. Fortunately, the security people here really know their business. These people are ruthless in their methods, but they know what's going on," Pettit said.

"So, from your point of view, this leg of the trip is worthwhile?"

"Absolutely—I've learned more here in a week about how to deal with terrorism than in all my previous experience put together."

"Well, then, I'm glad we came."

"One thing that's curious is how often they ask about your friend Maxim Kozlov," Pettit said.

"Kozlov? I wonder why. I haven't thought about him the entire trip."

"He's apparently well-known by at least some of the people in the ministries."

"Are they raising any alarms about him?" Ellis asked.

"No, no alarms. They're confused about him, wondering how he became such a successful capitalist. They mostly ask if he's really as fabulously wealthy as they hear he is. I think they must be jealous."

"He *is* extremely wealthy. From everything I know, he does exceptionally well. My investments with him have done fine, although I've kept him on a tight leash."

"In what way?"

Ellis shrugged. "Short selling is sort of the antithesis of the American attitude. Most of us make our money when businesses succeed. People like Kozlov make money when they fail. It's the rich taking from the poor."

Andy Pettit shook his head as they emerged successfully from the maze. "It seems to me that characterizes everything I've experienced here in Russia. People seem to boast of their failure." He looked up at the exquisitely finished powder-yellow walls of the Peterhof, trimmed in elegant white facades and trims designed to draw attention to the most spectacular showpiece of the palace, the dazzling gold-leaf-covered dome of the palace chapel. It was breathtakingly beautiful. As Andy looked up at the dome, he added, "They take pride in their palaces, but their people live in squalor. And when they talk about the lack of respect the Russians get on the international stage, they simply shrug their shoulders as if to say it's always been that way."

"Which probably explains their curiosity about Kozlov. There are always a handful of resourceful people in the world—even in Russia—and someone like Maxim must stir a little pride."

"I suppose." Pettit was thoughtful.

"Well, let's go find out if we get to meet His Majesty or not. I, for one, have seen all the palaces I need to see. I'm more than ready to head home. My time here has not been as useful as yours."

"My bet is we won't get to meet him. Maybe tonight at the ballet, but not a private visit. The Russians prefer to keep their foreign affairs centered on Europe, not America. And they're well aware of the attack in Kiel. So aside from tonight's performance, I think an audience with Nicholas is off the table."

Jason nodded his head. "That's right—we get to go to the ballet tonight." They walked in silence for a time, and then his sullen mood returned. "Patricia would have loved it."

"You should enjoy it for her."

Jason paused. "You're right. I should enjoy it. We're here now and not likely to ever return, so I need to savor the experience. I'm glad you're here to keep me thinking straight."

CHAPTER *22*

DRAWING CLOSER TO THE END

Chicago
April 13, 1908

"You idiot! That parcel's marked 'Fragile,' and you throw it around like it's a piece of garbage! I don't know how they do things in New York, but here in Chicago we take pride in our work, or we leave. Are you too stupid to understand something that simple?"

Angel Casimer's cheeks blazed at the rebuke, and he wanted to hurl the infernal little package straight into his fat supervisor's face. *Baubles for a millionaire's mistress—while workers are paid one pathetic dollar per day! Why should I not go shove this down her lipstick-daubed mouth!* Casimer desperately yearned for the time when he could say such things in public.

Since arriving in Chicago, he'd been thinking furiously about how to communicate his legacy. If he was shot to death after the assassination, how would the world ever know why he did it? Big Jim had assured him that he would speak on his behalf, but Casimer had come to doubt his master's sincerity. *You are becoming just another politician who will use the uproar of the assassination to further your own personal ambitions!* He could see quite clearly Fitzsimmons would use the turmoil to move up in the union, and then out into politics as a senator or mayor or another position where graft would make him wealthy. *Which means that you are just like all the others. There are so few of us who act out of pure motive, only a handful are willing to lose their life for the greater good!* Without fully realizing it, Casimer was already thinking of himself as a martyr. Which is why he had to figure out how to communicate his outrage directly to the world. Otherwise, his sacrifice would be meaningless.

"I ASKED YOU A QUESTION! ARE YOU BOTH STUPID *AND* DEAF?"

Casimer jumped and then turned to his supervisor, imagining as he did how it would feel to put a bullet right between his two fat eyes. "I am careless, Mr. Smith. And that is very foolish. My sincere apologies. I assure you that I will exercise greater care."

Smith shook his head. "If I could fire you on the spot, I would. But apparently I can't because of your connections. But if you keep bungling important deliveries like this, I assure you that I will at least get you transferred—hopefully to the district of Alaska, the farthest point away from me, you stupid Cossack. Now get on with your work!"

Casimer turned away, his heart pumping. His hand twitched as he fantasized about killing the man. *It is worth it. I have made a dozen deliveries to the arena, and I am making friends with the guards.* It was likely Casimer's definition of a friend was different than the guards'. *They know me and will not think twice when I make an approach during the convention.* In that regard he was correct, and it showed that he still had at least some hold on reality, even if it was tenuous.

St. Petersburg
April 13, 1908

"My deepest regrets, Senator Ellis, but His Majesty will not be able to attend tonight's performance after all, and tomorrow he leaves for Moscow. Affairs of state are pressing, you see."

Jason Ellis bowed slightly to the tsar's minister, who'd been dispatched to deliver the news to him and Andy in the opera box where they were sitting. At least the aide was high ranking, which turned the message into a gracious snub.

"I am sorry to hear that. It would be a signal honor to meet such an eminence as the tsar. But I understand. The affairs of the Russian people come first in His Majesty's thoughts. Please convey our deep appreciation for the courtesies extended to us during our brief visit to your magnificent city."

"Most certainly. And there will be more. Tsar Nicholas asked that we prepare a grand banquet in your honor, to be attended by those of the highest rank." The fellow smiled an insincere smile, which really aggravated Ellis.

"That is a wonderful gesture. But I'm afraid we must decline. I've received news from America that requires my prompt attention, so we will be departing soon. I'm afraid that we must content ourselves with the contacts we've already made." Even Jason was surprised at how cold he'd managed to make his voice sound. Judging it a bit much, he smiled and said, "But our visit to this great land will be a highlight in our memories. Thank you for your hospitality. I trust that you'll deliver our regrets?"

Now it was the minister's turn to bow. "Of course. We regret that you must leave so quickly, but such seems to be the fate of those who govern." He looked up and smiled a now cynical smile, indicating that he understood precisely what had happened. The Americans had been rebuffed by the Russians, and Ellis had returned the insult. "I will make sure that every effort is extended to help you prepare for your departure, including some special gifts the tsar has requested for you."

"Thank you. Perhaps now is the appropriate time to deliver a gift from President Roosevelt and the people of the United States to the tsar." Moving slowly to not startle any of the guards, he reached down cautiously to a small bag and opened it. Pulling out two small packages, he said, "This is from our Tiffany's in New York City, where I'm from. They are matching diamond pendants created exclusively for the tsar and tsarina. I hope their majesties find them fit for a king and queen."

"They will wear them with pride, of that I am sure." The minister took the gifts, bowed, and departed.

And just like that it was over. Andy's time had been well spent, and Jason was lonesome. Left alone, the two friends sat down in the elegantly upholstered chairs at the front of the opera box. Ellis was irritated to find himself peevish. He considered the possibility of leaving.

"You don't really think they'd take the chance of putting you in the same room as the tsar after what happened with the Kaiser, do you?"

Jason turned at the sound of Andy's voice. "What?"

"The chance of an attack in Germany was rated very low. The chance of something here in Russia is very high. The fact that the anarchists tried in Germany and failed puts the risk of someone going after you or the tsar right off the scale. Don't take it personally."

Andy was whispering now because the house lights had dimmed.

"But it was a rebuff," Ellis replied.

"It was what it was," Andy said coolly. "And frankly, it's a relief to me since I'm responsible for your safety. Sit back and enjoy the ballet. Don't you think it's rather remarkable that two kids from upstate New York are sitting here at all?"

Jason checked himself and then settled back against the plush seat. "You're right again. It *is* remarkable to be here." Cheered, he soon allowed himself to become lost in the rich musical tapestry of a ballet set to the music of Frederic Chopin.

"Angel, my friend. Did you have anything to do with this?"

"Do with what?"

Fitzsimmons laid a two-day-old copy of the *Chicago Morning News* on the table in front of Casimer. Pointing to a small article, he asked again, "Does this have anything to do with you?"

Angel Casimer cast a quick glance at the paper. "A man was killed by thieves. It happens all the time in Chicago. Why would you think of me?"

"Because, Angel, the man was your supervisor. And it's well-known that you didn't get along. His throat was slashed in a most brutal manner, which would not be expected in a simple robbery. The people in New York who got you this job are alarmed. That's why I am here."

Casimer slammed his fists on the table and looked at Fitzsimmons furiously. "I am glad the man is dead! He was a pig who deserved to die. But *I* did not do it."

Fitzsimmons thought seriously about reaching across the table and choking the life out of Casimer. It was probably the safest thing to do. But then everything up to this point would be wasted.

"The thing is, Angel, we have less than a month to go. If the police discover that you're involved in a crime, you could find yourself in jail while the Republicans have their great party. And then our opportunity would be lost." He frowned. "And that would be a great tragedy, wouldn't it?"

"I told you—I didn't do it."

Fitzsimmons stood and moved to Casimer's side of the table. "I hope not, Angel." He paused for effect. "Because if I find out that you did, or if you do anything else to draw attention to yourself in these next four weeks, I will put my hands around your bony little neck and squeeze until your eyes bulge out of their sockets, and then I will keep squeezing until the bones in your neck crack under the pressure. And even then I will keep squeezing until you have no air in your lungs, and there's no more life in your body!" He rested his enormous hands heavily on Casimer's shoulders. "Do you understand, Angel?"

He felt Casimer's slender shoulders tremble under his hands. *He's probably thinking how to kill me for talking to him like this!* It troubled Fitzsimmons that a man could transform himself as completely as Casimer had. He knew from his conversations with Angel that he'd almost failed to activate the detonator at Union Station out of moral revulsion at killing. Now he was willing to kill anyone who crossed him. *I've created a monster.* He reconsidered as he thought about the invisible man who paid for all this. We've *created a monster.* "Do you understand me, Angel?" he said softly, almost kindly.

The small man turned and looked up into Fitzsimmons's eyes. While Big Jim had no idea what he expected to see, he was unnerved to find the light in Casimer's eyes had faded completely. There was nothing there but hate. Fitzsimmons felt the skin on his neck crawl and wondered if he'd have to dispose of Casimer after all.

CHAPTER 23

COUNTDOWN TO TERROR

New York City
June 5, 1908

Having returned from Europe, Senator Ellis scheduled several weeks in his home district office for meetings with constituents while staying with his family on Long Island, where they attended church together for the first time in several months. It bothered him that his schedule had kept him from family and his friends for so long, and visiting after church had almost made the world feel normal again, though it was not.

Staying in New York also gave him a chance to follow up on some suspicions he had about the terrorist attacks. He asked his secretary to clear his calendar before placing a phone call.

"Andy, it's Jason Ellis. I've found something interesting that you should see. Yes, I think it has bearing on the attacks, and suggests something bad's about to happen. No, I know you love Katz's Deli, but it's in the Russian district, and that's not a good place to meet. How about Delmonico's? I'll arrange a private dining room. 12:30? I can make that. See you soon."

Ellis replaced the earpiece of the wall-mounted telephone on its hook and leaned against the wall on the opposite side of the hallway. He used the fingers of his hands to massage his temples, though it did little to relieve his headache.

Chicago
June 5, 1908

"Thirteen days, my friend. You have just thirteen days to wait, and then your moment will come." Big Jim smiled broadly at Angel Casimer. He worried for a moment that Casimer looked out of place in this upscale steak house, but realized Chicago was not nearly as formal as an East Coast city. No one would take notice.

"I will enter from the service entrance on Sixteenth Street. You will have the package ready for delivery?" Angel responded.

"It will be labeled as coming from a Mr. John Schumster in New York City for Congressman James S. Sherman. Most observers think Sherman will be the vice-presidential nominee, so it's certain he'll be invited to the dais when Senator Taft arrives at the Coliseum. And since Sherman is from New York's 27th District, no one will question a package arriving from one of his prominent supporters—they'll assume it's a gift."

"And you will send it from New York so it has all the appropriate seals? They search for such things, you know. If it is not authentic they will turn me away."

Fitzsimmons raised his hands and smiled even more broadly. "Naturally it will have all the right seals, Angel. I have a man who will see to it personally."

"But how can you make certain it will arrive at the right time? What if it arrives early? What if it is late?"

The smile faded on Big Jim's face. "It *will* arrive at the correct time. That's not your concern. You just need to be ready when it does arrive."

Casimer clenched and unclenched his hands nervously. "It is just that I like to prepare the weapon myself. How will I know it is loaded properly? What if it misfires because the charge is improper? These are things I should control."

Casimer's eyes darted furtively side-to-side, the wild look Fitzsimmons had come to distrust now very evident. To calm him, Fitzsimmons rested his enormous hands on top of Casimer's petite ones. "Angel, the gun will be fully ready to use. I have taken care of that personally. You know that they'd find a gun if it were concealed on your person, and then you'd never get inside the Coliseum. You'd be arrested quietly, and you would die in a lonely cell. The authorities would make certain that no one ever knew your name. But by using this package as our delivery device, you can get the weapon to the place you've selected, and then you'll quietly wait for the big man to arrive. Then you'll change history itself!" he said with a flourish. When Casimer failed to respond to his enthusiasm, he shoved a photograph of the intended victim across the table.

"I know this is the person I am supposed to kill. Why do you give it to me again?"

"Because there will be many people in the crowd, and it will be confusing." He showed him a second photo, this time of Jason Ellis. "It is important that you shoot the right men. If you make a mistake, you may end up harming the movement rather than helping it. I'll be there to help you find the right men."

"I know who I want to shoot—Theodore Roosevelt. You

called him King Roosevelt. Why do you not let me do as I please?"

"We've been through this, Angel. Remember that it is not my decision to make. There is science in determining who should live and who should die. You are to strike the fuse, but we must make sure that there is an explosion at the other end. We have determined killing Roosevelt would hurt our cause. But these targets will help because they are on the side of the capitalists." He paused. "So do you agree that the package is the right way to get you where you need to be, and that you'll do this exactly as we have rehearsed?"

Casimer nodded. "Yes. It is a good plan." He tried to smile but was unable to fully control his facial movements.

"You haven't been sleeping well, have you, Angel?"

"I sleep all right." His jittery eye movements betrayed this as a lie.

Fitzsimmons reached into one of the pockets on his jacket and pulled out a small package. "Take this with you, Angel, and place a few drops on your tongue tonight so you'll sleep well. You need to be rested."

"What is it?" There was alarm in Casimer's voice.

"Nothing harmful—just a small amount of laudanum. It's safe and recommended for anxiety and sleeplessness."

"It is opium! I can't be drugged when the time comes. I must be fully alert."

"Which is why you need to take this for the next seven days, and then taper off." Fitzsimmons tightened his grip on Casimer's hands. "Angel, you must ask yourself if I've done everything I promised I would do. Have I done that for you?"

"Yes," Casimer said sullenly.

"Then trust me on this. You need to remain calm for just

thirteen more days, and then you can unleash your anger. But until then I must know you're sleeping. A man is far less able to perform without sleep than under the influence of something as harmless as opium." *And under its influence you will not be so moody and nervous.* Still holding Casimer's hands under his own, he bounced their interlocked hands lightly on the table. "Will you do what I ask of you, Angel?"

"Yes. I will do what you ask."

Fitzsimmons withdrew his hands. "That's good, Angel. That's good." He reached into his pocket and pulled out a second package, an overstuffed envelope. "Now, my dear friend, this is for you."

"What is it?"

"Cash. I want you to have fun this coming weekend. You've played a serious role in all this, and I want you to enjoy this final week before the great event. Go for a ride in that new invention, the roller-coaster, at Riverview Amusement Park. I hear it's great fun."

"But I can't do that. I am about to do something momentous."

"No one will fault you for enjoying a weekend." Fitzsimmons shoved the envelope to the center of the table where Casimer couldn't help but take it. "Do with it what you like, Angel, but for heaven's sake do have some fun." He paused. "Then go home and get some sleep. You'll do both those things, Angel?"

Casimer nodded. Then he smiled. "I will. I will go to this Riverview Park. I have always wanted to see this new roller thing."

"And now you will ride it!" Fitzsimmons's smile was warm and sincere. *After all, a condemned man deserves at least one last weekend of joy.* Fitzsimmons reflected that just that morning he'd made the penultimate payment to the Chicago City police officer who would shoot and kill Angel Casimer just moments after everyone would be able to identify him as the man who shot and killed Senator Ellis and the Republican vice-presidential candidate, James Sherman. He'd made the payoff in a dark barroom. Fitzsimmons was confident the policeman couldn't identify him if for some reason it ever came to that. But it wouldn't, since the policeman would be hailed as a hero for striking down an assassin before he could harm someone else. Then the policeman would get his ultimate payment, the country would be in an uproar, and no one would suspect Fitzsimmons's role. The world could erupt in flames.

Fitzsimmons smiled, and Casimer smiled in return.

New York City
June 5, 1908

"Yes, Mr. Kozlov?"

"Who were you talking with, Tom?"

"What?" Tom Scanlon turned toward the empty spot where Maxim Kozlov was pointing.

"Who were you talking with?" Kozlov smiled, but it was a cold smile.

"Senator Ellis," Scanlon replied, perhaps more nervously than he would have wished.

"That's what I thought. And what did the good senator want?" Kozlov watched Scanlon carefully.

"He wanted to know about some of the transactions in his account. Nothing detailed. Quite routine, in fact." If Scanlon was trying to hide something, Kozlov couldn't detect it. The man was nervous—anyone observing their conversation would have seen that—but then, Scanlon was always nervous, particularly after he'd had to dispose of the dead Russian in Koslov's office. He now lived in fear of other such incidents.

"Ah. That's fine then. I wish you'd told me he was here. I would have liked to say hello."

"Oh, I'm sorry, I didn't know. I would have—"

"It's all right, Tom, it's all right. I just like to greet our best customers. There will be another time."

"Yes, sir. Of course. I'll make certain of it." Scanlon shifted uneasily.

"That's all. You can return to work."

Tom Scanlon scurried away, much like a mouse that managed to escape the paws of a cat.

As he watched him leave, Kozlov spoke quietly to himself. "I'm sorry I didn't get to say goodbye to you, Senator Ellis. I should have liked that." Kozlov smiled. It was turning out to be a very good day. The Europeans hadn't pressed him on the disappearance of their man, and he imagined they respected him for taking action on his own. Now he'd been asked to travel to Europe in August to report on his activities. "And that's good, because by then my plan will have succeeded, and I will have a seat at the master table." Of that he was sure.

Washington, DC
June 5, 1908

"Well, my dear, we're off to Chicago." Theodore Roosevelt gave his wife a one-armed hug.

"Rather exciting for me. After this, I get my husband back."

"Not until next March. I still have nine months."

"Yes, and unlike most presidents who lose influence at the end of their term, you still have a great many things to do."

He smiled at her. "Well, I shall miss all this, but there's no sense brooding about it. I made my decision to not run, and now I shall make the best of it."

"Bully," she said.

"Yes, bully." Theodore Roosevelt straightened his tie. There would be stops all along the route to Chicago for his presidential train, which is why they were leaving so early. He wanted plenty of time to meet people, to encourage local politicians, and to get his own sense of how the country was feeling. "At the very least, we shall have a great time in Chicago."

"You shall have a great time. You'll be in meetings from early in the morning to late at night, making deals and brokering alliances. And in the end they'll choose the candidate you want them to choose."

Roosevelt went over to help Edith with her dress. "I shall do my best. If I'm to have a legacy, it will start in Chicago. My own ambitions will now succeed or fail in the hands of my successor. So you're right. I must be optimistic and positive, and then things will turn out right."

New York City
June 8, 1908

Jason Ellis took a long sip on the six-ounce bottle of Pepsi-Cola served with his plate of haddock. He'd grown very fond of this quirky-tasting drink in the ten years it had been available for sale in bottles. Most restaurants mixed either Pepsi-Cola or Coca-Cola syrup with soda water, but that always led to uneven sweetness. Ellis's precise nature preferred the predictability of the bottles. Setting the small bottle on the table, he looked up at Andy Pettit. "I've thought about it a lot, and something just doesn't feel right about these latest moves by Koslov."

"He's short sold multiple stocks in multiple sectors? You're sure of that?"

Ellis nodded. "Normally I wouldn't even be notified if he borrowed and sold my stock, since trust companies don't have to square up their books with clients until well after a transaction has taken place. But I think his man Scanlon was worried about him doing it with me again after I raised such a stink about the Union Life short sale. Scanlon sent me a note on company letterhead as a courtesy."

Pettit pursed his lips. "I think I'm fairly smart, but not smart enough to tell what's going on in your head. Tell me why you think this new round of short selling is significant now."

"I have certain friends on Wall Street." He dropped his voice. "Actually, J. P. Morgan helped me. Kozlov has been doing some kind of work for Morgan, but Morgan turned the tables on him when I asked him to make some discreet inquiries about Kozlov. Whenever an order goes down to the Exchange, it is recorded in a journal, and Morgan's man alerted him to this activity." He looked into Andy's eyes. "It was actually you who started my train of thought on this."

"How'd I do that?"

"When you told me about the inquiries about Kozlov in St. Petersburg. Do you remember us having a discussion about short selling then?"

Pettit nodded. "One of several."

"Well, I had trouble falling asleep that night—probably because I'd enjoyed the ballet so much. At any rate, I thought about our conversation, and then my brain somehow connected to the thought that Kozlov had short sold some of my holdings just before the bombing at Union Station and again before the fire at the restaurant. The biggest sale of all was in Union Life stock just before the assassination."

"Were those the only times he did that, or was it a coincidence?"

"No, those were the only times. And he made a great deal of money on the first two. He would have really cleaned up on Union Life if I hadn't intervened in the market."

"And now he's borrowing all kinds of stock?"

Ellis nodded. Andy was one of the smartest men he knew, but he was still learning about finance. "He must be betting on a general market decline, which means he has a reason to believe the whole market is going to tumble. If it does, he'll make a profit regardless of what stocks he buys. It's one thing to short a company you think is having trouble, but quite another to bet against the whole market—particularly when the fundamentals are indicating a good year ahead."

"Let me tell you what I think you've told me. You're saying that if Kozlov has actual foreknowledge of an event, he has no risk in short selling because he *knows* a stock's going to drop."

"That's right."

"And the only way he could have had foreknowledge of either the Union Station bombing or the restaurant fire is if he had something to do with it."

"What else could account for the timing? Pure luck seems a weak explanation."

"And if he's now selling short across the board, then he thinks something will rattle the entire stock market—something he may have a hand in?"

"My man on Wall Street confirms he's borrowed stock from nearly every major brokerage house. He must be putting *all* his assets at risk."

"And you've formed this opinion based on a tip from one man."

Ellis shook his head. "First of all, the tip's from Morgan's man, so it's reliable. But I also spoke with Kozlov's man, Tom Scanlon. He's a good fellow. Perhaps a bit too loyal. He confirmed his note indicating that Kozlov had borrowed and sold my stock. And then he added an odd twist I wouldn't have expected from him."

"Which was?"

"He said, 'Rather remarkable how fortunate Mr. Kozlov is in timing the market, isn't it?'"

Ellis was offended when Pettit replied in an annoyingly sarcastic voice, "Why, yes, I see—heaven forbid anyone ever says anything like that about me: 'He's good at his job.'"

"Knock it off, Andy. It was the way he said it. There was an element of disgust in his voice I can't describe but I know was there. It was as if he was trying to get me to understand something."

"And you believe what he's suggesting is that Kozlov's connected somehow to the terror attacks—and he knows something new is coming."

"I know it sounds crazy. Kozlov could even be the mastermind, I don't know. If it were that simple, I think Tom Scanlon would have told me outright. But I'm sure Maxim's manipulating the stock market based on inside information. I have no question of that."

"What's coming up that could rock the whole stock market?"

Ellis bit his lip. "A lot of things. There are sporting events all around the country. The prizefighter Tommy Burns is going up against Bill Squires on June 13th, which will attract a huge crowd. And that John Krohn fellow is starting his walk around the perimeter of the entire United States, which means public celebrations in any city through which he passes. And virtually any day is a good day for an attack on Wall Street. It's puzzling to me that New York's been spared any major anarchist threat recently. And the Republican party convention is in Chicago on the 16th through the 19th of this month. There are plenty of possibilities."

Andy drew his breath, then laid his head back against the red velvet upholstery of the booth in which they were seated. "I'd put my money on Chicago. They're going after Roosevelt again. I've always thought the Union Station thing was aimed at the president."

"I'm not sure it's Chicago. New York seems more likely to me. But even if it is the Republican convention, they could aim their attack at Senator Lodge, the chair of the convention, or against any of the eight leading candidates for president. And anarchists love launching attacks randomly against innocent citizens. That's the problem—how can we know if my theory's true, and if it is—how do we know how to stop it? If Kozlov's involved, he already hates me for what I did in the Union Life rescue, and he'd be perfectly happy to have me killed if he even suspects I'll get in his way again."

Pettit sat up quickly. "Kiel! Do you see a connection?"

Jason nodded his head slowly. "That makes sense. Which means I may still be a target."

Pettit gave Jason a grim half-smile. "The only way to react is to narrow the field. We must eliminate the least likely places and concentrate on the points of greatest risk. So, here's what needs to happen next . . ."

CHAPTER 24

UNFORTUNATE EMPLOYMENT

New York City
June 10, 1908

"Wha—!" Tom Scanlon's voice was silenced before he could develop any volume, and the small man's frame jerked from the force of being ripped from the street he was walking down into a side alley. "Be quiet, Mr. Scanlon, or bad things will happen to you!" The whispered voice in his ear was fierce and frightening.

Scanlon couldn't have said anything anyway with a hand gripped firmly over his mouth and his right arm pulled up hard behind him. "Will you be quiet if I uncover your mouth?" Scanlon nodded and felt great relief as the pressure was reduced on both his mouth and his tortured arm. "There—now come with me."

"But who are—" Scanlon winced and cried out in pain as his arm was twisted even harder than before.

"No questions!" said the man savagely. "Just come this way."

Scanlon was embarrassed to feel hot tears rolling down his cheeks, but he knew better than to say anything more. In a matter of moments, he felt himself being pulled through a door that opened very briefly and then shut decisively behind him. Before he could figure out what was happening, he was thrust down into a plush, overstuffed chair very close to the ground, his long legs bending up at an awkward angle, making it impossible for him to get up quickly on his own. Looking frantically around the room, he saw a shabby little table and curtains drawn shut to keep the light out.

"Hello, Tom." Scanlon whipped his head around at the sound of Jason Ellis's voice behind him.

"Senator Ellis?" There was an odd mixture of indignation and relief in his voice as he said this.

"And this is a friend of mine, Andy Pettit. Sorry to be so rough with you, but we didn't want to attract any attention."

"Pleased to meet you, Mr. Scanlon," Andy Pettit said easily, stepping out in front of Scanlon.

Scanlon's eyes darted back and forth between the two men who had now come into view. "What do you want? Why have you done this to me?" His eyes moved even more quickly when Ellis sat down on a kitchen chair directly in front of him. The single light bulb hanging from a long cord directly behind Ellis hurt his eyes. "Well?" he said, trying to choke the emotion out of his voice.

"Tom," Ellis said, "we have reason to believe you've been a bad person, and we need to talk to you about it. Right now."

"Bad person? I'm not a bad person!"

Ellis noted a twinge of panic had replaced the indignation that was there a moment earlier.

"Ah, but you have been," Pettit said, his voice much harder. Pettit moved to a spot directly to Jason's left, but not enough to block the light from striking Tom's eyes. "It seems a trunk was dumped into the East River a few weeks back."

"A trunk? I don't know anything about a trunk!"

"But you *do* know about the trunk, because we have two eye-witnesses who identified you as the man who shoved it into the river."

"How can anyone make such a claim? No one can make a positive identification."

"They can when they see this." Pettit handed Scanlon a black-and-white photo showing him directly in front of the First Commerce Trust Company building.

"How did you get this? I never allowed anyone to take my photograph."

Pettit nodded. "It was hard, I admit that. A person must stand still for a long time to get a good photo that isn't blurred, which is why that attractive young woman who accosted you on the street the other day spent so much time talking with you. While she asked for directions, my photographer took your photo from behind her back. It took a great deal of care to set it up exactly as we needed it, but fortunately you're very punctual. Your movements are easily predicted from day to day." Pettit stepped aside and placed another chair directly next to Ellis's.

"In fact, that's how we knew you'd be on this street tonight at exactly this moment. And so now you're here with us."

"But, but—"

"But Tom, there was a dead body in the trunk, and *you're* the one who put it in the river. If you don't cooperate with us, you'll be arrested and tried for murder."

"Murder? But I didn't kill the man! Mr. . . ." His voice trailed off, and he slumped back in the chair. His knees hurt from being so much higher than his hips, but it was no use trying to get comfortable.

"It was . . . Mr. Kozlov?"

Tom Scanlon scowled at Pettit but said nothing.

"Tom, you'll face the electric chair for sure unless you cooperate with us," Jason said.

"I'll face a worse fate if I cooperate."

"Only if you're the one who killed that Russian," Jason said, "and I can't imagine why you would have. It's not in your nature. That is, unless Maxim Kozlov *ordered* you to kill him, and you're a very different kind of man than I imagine you to be."

"I told you I didn't kill anyone."

Pettit leaned forward. "And yet there's a very soggy corpse down at the coroner's office."

Scanlon's eyes darted wildly, and for a moment his knees twitched as if he were going to try to get up and run. But then his shoulders slumped. "I'm a dead man, no matter what I do. Either you'll convict me of murder, or Mr. Kozlov will have me killed."

"Like he had this man killed? The Russian was a Bolshevik, you know. We know where he came from, and since this discovery, we've learned that Kozlov has been sending money to a Russian dissident named Vladimir Lenin in Austria. It seems Kozlov's business operations have been directed at raising money for stirring up trouble in Russia and continental Europe."

"He didn't have the man killed," Scanlon said sullenly.

"What do you mean?" Pettit asked, curious.

Scanlon looked up, his eyes red. "He didn't have him killed because *he* killed him. Mr. Kozlov killed the man himself."

Jason's response was soft, but also tinged with an edge of fear. "That's good, Tom. Tell us what happened, and maybe we can help you."

Scanlon shook his head. "He'll kill me for sure."

"We can protect you."

"No, you can't. But at least I'll die with a clean conscience." With that, Tom Scanlon, Maxim Koslov's loyal lieutenant, broke his reserve as words started to tumble out of his mouth.

The Drake Hotel, Chicago
June 14, 1908

"You look handsome, Senator Ellis. Did you acquire a new addition to your wardrobe on your trip to Europe?"

Ellis smiled at Edith Roosevelt. "I have a weakness for London tailors. Thank you for noticing."

The president's wife turned to Patricia. "He really is too handsome for his own good, isn't he?"

Patricia smiled cheerfully. "Which is why I had him purchase a stylish but very short leather leash to go with his new tails. That way I can hold onto him."

"Really," Theodore Roosevelt said to his wife. "Is this necessary?"

Jason laughed. "Please, Mr. President, it's so seldom I have attractive women talking about me, I'm rather enjoying it."

Roosevelt harrumphed, and the conversation quickly turned to the dinner at Marlborough House and Patricia's impression of the new British royalty now that Queen Victoria was gone. After listening to the women for a few moments, Roosevelt motioned for Ellis to follow him.

"You'll forgive us, my dear," Roosevelt said, "but I do have a slight matter of business to discuss with Jason."

"Of course. We'll be fine." Roosevelt knew that Edith

preferred being in the company of close friends, which is why he was comfortable leaving her with Patricia.

As Ellis and Roosevelt made their way through the crowd, the president was obliged to shake many hands along the way and engage in idle chitchat with party luminaries from around the country. But eventually they made their way into a small vestibule reserved exclusively for Roosevelt just so he could have this kind of private talk. "Are you quite sure of all this, Jason?"

"We can't be absolutely sure about all of it. But we do know some things for certain. First, once Andy knew to focus his investigation on Kozlov, we were able to use some of the contacts we developed in Europe and Russia to identify a connection between Kozlov and the Bolsheviks in exile in Germany and Austria. Many telegrams have gone back and forth—as well as the help we received from J. P. Morgan when one of his men at Kozlov's clearinghouse confirmed large sums of money have been wired to Europe over the course of the past three or four years. Chances are very high that Kozlov's activities here were originally funded by Russian dissident money, and he's been using our markets to improve their fortunes."

"That's just what I need to hear—our stock market is being used to finance Bolshevism. This Mr. Kozlov is a very clever man."

"Clever, lucky, or blessed with uncanny foreknowledge of certain events."

Roosevelt nodded with a scowl. He had dealt with moneymen often enough to know exactly what Ellis was suggesting.

"Third, we know that Kozlov murdered one of the Bolshevik intermediaries right in his own office. His man Tom Scanlon broke down and confessed everything when Andy Pettit confronted him."

"And how could Pettit have known about that?"

"How does Andy know anything? From what I gather, he un-leashed a small army of detectives to ask about any peculiar go-ings on around the First Commerce Trust building, and it wasn't long before some street vendor told him he saw both Kozlov and Scanlon lug a large trunk out of the building late one night, and then Scanlon departed with it in a small wagon—"

"And knowing the date and time that it took place, Andy was able to find informants up and down the length of Manhattan to figure out where the wagon ended up," Roosevelt said.

"I see you remember how detective work gets done from your days as police commissioner, Mr. President."

"The East River?"

"What?"

"The East River—I assume that's where the wagon ended up?"

"Ah. Yes. I thought I'd said that. Once Andy found a vagrant who saw Tom Scanlon push the trunk into the river in an obscure spot, it was easy enough to have divers go down and retrieve the trunk. The fellow inside had been shot through the chest."

"So Mr. Scanlon is guilty as an accomplice."

"A very disturbed and unwilling accomplice. As I said, he broke down when confronted. We're sure he had nothing to do with the murder, but he did assist in disposing of the body."

"And what else did you learn from this Scanlon person?"

Jason sighed, the memory of his interrogation of Scanlon stir-ring up feelings of guilt. "We learned that Kozlov had sent him to an obscure saloon in Baltimore on a number of occasions to deliver envelopes stuffed with cash to an unnamed person."

"Come on! Scanlon must know whom he was meeting with."

Ellis shook his head. "I don't think so. I honestly think he convinced himself that it was a business deal."

"If he's a man of integrity, he'd have to make up a story like that to justify what he was doing." Roosevelt was silent for a time. "Baltimore was close to the Union Station and restaurant fire but far enough out no one could easily connect them."

"That's our thinking."

"Where is this Scanlon fellow right now? Has he given you any sense of where the next attack is going to take place?"

Ellis shook his head, then took a deep breath and exhaled slowly. "Tom Scanlon turned up in a local morgue the day after we met with him. His throat had been slit. We promised him that he would be safe, but now he's gone—"

Roosevelt frowned. "A very ugly business."

"I feel responsible for putting Scanlon in that position. Andy says his murder was expertly done. But Tom Scanlon made it easier. He insisted he had to go back to Kozlov and act as if nothing had happened to keep him from becoming suspicious. Whoever murdered Scanlon did it not far from where we met him. Unfortunately, we may have tipped our hand in the process of interviewing him. Kozlov may be aware of what we're up to."

"I doubt it," Roosevelt said. "My guess is Tom Scanlon was as good as dead the night he helped Kozlov with the body. A man like Kozlov leaves nothing to chance. Assuming you and Andy were discreet in where you met him—and I can't imagine that Andy would be anything but—then Kozlov was likely unaware he talked to you. That means Scanlon was killed as part of a pre-arranged plan."

"I hope you're right, because right now there's nothing we can do to accuse Kozlov. All he'd have to do if arrested is say Scanlon was the murderer, and he was simply trying to conceal a scandal.

Without Scanlon to testify otherwise, Kozlov's lawyers could easily create reasonable doubt."

"What are you going to do next?"

"A couple of things. Andy's doing his best to figure out who Scanlon was seeing in Baltimore. We hope to have a break on that very soon. If that works out, we can begin to figure out what role he's been playing and how far the conspiracy goes."

Roosevelt nodded. "That's good. But what about Kozlov? Are you going to confront him?"

Ellis shook his head. "It would do no good. He can rationalize everything that's been going on."

"But he might call off the attack."

"We don't think so—chances are high that the die's already cast and the assassin's acting on his own. Andy assures me it's the only way an operation like this can happen without implicating people up the line." Ellis smiled. "But there may be a positive turn of events in this."

Roosevelt raised an eyebrow.

"If Kozlov were to suspect his operation is compromised, he'd close out all his short positions to limit his risk. But my contacts down at the Exchange are watching very closely, and so far he hasn't pulled back."

"Ah," Roosevelt said. "So if you can thwart the attack, Kozlov will suffer financially. No assassination, no drop in the stock market, and no chance to profit."

"I think it's even worse than that for Kozlov. Since it's likely that the markets will go up when Taft is nominated, which I'm sure you'll see to, Kozlov will have to close out his positions at a loss. Even a modest increase in price will bankrupt him when he has to buy that much replacement stock at higher prices."

"Play with fire, and eventually you'll get burned."

Ellis nodded. "But only if we thwart the attack."

Roosevelt stood up. "You've created quite an operation, Jason. I should name you the director of our new federal investigative agency when it gets through Congress."

"And give me a heart attack? No thanks—this isn't the kind of stress I'm cut out for."

"So where's it going to be, Jason? I know you don't have all the facts yet, but what does your intuition tell you?"

"I'd like to say we don't know enough, and that's true. But we're sure it's going to be here in Chicago. Two or three days from now when the convention's going full steam."

"Am I the target?"

"We don't think so."

"But why? They tried once before at Union Station. What could send a more powerful message than to murder two presidents in a row?"

"I'm not sure you were the target in Washington. And if you were, your popularity will protect you now. When McKinley was shot, it ended up hurting the anarchists and all the others calling for civil destruction. You're perceived as a friend of the workers, so killing you would be just as pointless. It would trigger a sympathetic response, exactly the opposite of what they want." He took a quick sip on his drink. "They need someone prominent but not as well-known. Someone seen to represent business interests oppressive to the workingman."

"Ah." At this news Roosevelt sat down next to Jason. "So is it you or Howard Taft?"

"Wish I knew. Either of us would be a good target. But so would James Sherman. I hear he's on track to be nominated as vice president. If so, he has a high enough profile to be a target. Since we're both from New York, we don't get a lot of sympathy from the average worker." He inhaled deeply and let the air out quickly. "All I know is that if we don't figure it out tonight or to-morrow morning, someone could very well be dead by tomorrow night, and Kozlov will make a fortune. That someone could be me."

"Then go home, Jason. Go back to New York or to Washington. Go right now and we'll take care of the convention."

Ellis's eyes narrowed. "Sorry, Mr. President, but I can't do that."

"And why not? It's the only prudent thing *to* do."

Ellis looked down and into his drink. "Two reasons—if I leave it could tip them off. But more than that, it's become personal. Very personal." He looked up, a cold, determined look in his eyes.

"Ah. I see." In Roosevelt's world of honor and chivalry, Ellis's decision made complete sense. "Better to die a brave man with honor than to live a coward."

Ellis nodded.

CHAPTER 25

FIREWORKS AND MUZZLE BLASTS!

Chicago
June 15, 1908

Andy Pettit read the telegram carefully and passed it to Jason Ellis. "I think we have it. I think this is the man who arranged all of this."

Ellis studied the telegram and then nodded. "Makes sense, doesn't it? If so, what's next?"

"We can do this one of two ways. We can do our best to find this fellow and waylay him, or we can prepare to act when he emerges."

"What do you think is best?"

"I don't want to divert manpower trying to find him when the attack could take place at any time in any number of locations. It could be right now at the Coliseum, or later this afternoon at a hotel, or it could be tonight at any of the dozen or so formal dinners scheduled to take place outside the convention hall. I think we need to have our men at the most likely locations and be ready to react when we discover him. It's much easier to let someone come out of the darkness than to try to search through all the shadows." Andy paused. "Besides, we don't know if he's acting alone or in partnership. The few descriptions we have of the Hartford assassin suggest he was a small, almost petite, man, which is different than the fellow I have in mind. My guess is there are at least two involved. If that's right, it does us no good to capture one but not the other."

Ellis walked over to the window of his apartment at the Drake Hotel and looked out on Lake Michigan, a magnificent sight that would have inspired him on any other day. Turning to face Andy directly, he said, "You know as well as I do you can narrow your list to where I'm scheduled to be. The only way to make this work is for me to take the risk."

"That would make it easier to catch them. But it would be smarter to get the hell out of town."

Ellis shook his head. "And all that would accomplish is I'd have to wait for the next time they try something." His face hardened. "We *must* do this now. I won't live like this any longer. This is our country, and I will not live in fear."

"So you've made your decision?"

Jason Ellis nodded.

"All right, then. I'll distribute this photo to all our men. And you and I will rehearse our parts for something I hope doesn't happen."

In his apartment, Angel Casimer straightened his tie and smoothed his jacket. As an accredited courier, he had to look the part perfectly. Plus, these clothes would show up in all the photographs when the newspapers chased him down after it was over, and he had enough pride that he wanted to look good. He then reached down to the table and carefully folded the sheaf of papers that contained his handwritten "Manifesto to the World." It documented all that he'd done in the cause: the bombing in Washington, DC; the assassination in Hartford; the Army lieutenant he'd shot in the back in Cuba because of his incompetent leadership; and his plea to workers everywhere to rise up and throw off their taskmasters. He expressed his admiration for Lenin and Trotsky and all the courageous Bolsheviks in Europe. And lastly he named Big Jim Fitzsimmons as his contact and confidant. "I know you do not want to be known for this, my large friend, but you must be made to stand up for what you say you believe, just as I am willing to do." Carefully placing the folded papers into his inside vest pocket, he adjusted his hat. Then, preparing to leave the apartment for the last time, he looked down at the ticket stub from the wonderful new roller-coaster. "Soon all people will have such days as I had, whether they have money or not. All things will be owned in common, and the world will be at peace!" He wanted peace—few would understand that because he and others like him would be the cause of untold blood, flames, and death before it happened, but that was the price that was required for something as wonderful as world peace. A new world could rise only from the ashes of the old. First, the old world must be consumed in flames. *And now it is up to me, Angel Wilhelm Casimer, to start the fire.* He pinched his lips to confirm his determination. *And today is finally the day!*

Chicago Coliseum
June 18, 1908

Jason Ellis's heart was pounding so hard under his shirt he was quite certain people could see his necktie pulsing against his jacket. He was all alone now at the base of the stairs that led to the dais. In just a matter of moments Senator Howard W. Taft and Congressman James S. Sherman would be walking through the tunnel to these stairs so they could emerge triumphant to the roar of an excited crowd. He looked out and saw the firemen carefully priming the charges for the fireworks that would be ignited the moment Taft burst into view.

"Perhaps it will happen in the tunnel . . ." If this was the time and place for an attack, as Andy suspected, it would be better in the tunnel. Andy Pettit had many good men stationed there. He and they had occupied the same spot the day before, but nothing had happened. Which is why Andy told Ellis earlier that morning that he was convinced it would happen today or not at all. "It's most likely to happen up on the stand in view of all the assembled delegates, where it would have maximum effect." That's why Andy was stationed across the roped-off aisle watching as people came and went into the tunnel. Ellis felt better knowing that Andy was there. Looking around, he took note of the Chicago policeman standing directly next to him and felt a bit comforted. More than anything in the world he wanted to cast a sideways glance at the man Andy Pettit was watching so carefully, but he knew it might draw the fellow's attention. He forced himself to keep his eyes focused down the tunnel, even as his brain registered the increasing crescendo of the speaker's voice bellowing out from the platform, warming up the crowd prior to bringing out the men almost certain to be the next president and vice president of the United States. *I wish whatever's going to happen would happen soon. The suspense is killing me!*

Casting a glance at Andy, he was startled as he heard motion coming from the end of the tunnel. He turned to see what was happening. "Oh, my! And there he is—our good Senator Taft."

The sunlight coming from behind Taft through the open door at the end of the tunnel made it difficult to see anything but shadows, but Taft was a large man, and his silhouette was unmistakable. That must be Sherman next to him. *Dear Lord, please help us now.*

He was surprised that amidst this much tension, his mind brought up an image of Patricia and the children on their sailboat off Long Island. It was a strange thought for a moment like this. *I hope I get to go there again.*

"What do you want?"

"I have a parcel for a Mr. James Sherman from New York City." Angel Casimer struggled to keep his voice steady. "It says it is to be presented to him from the dais!" Casimer showed the man the properly stamped address and instructions.

"I'll take it to the podium."

"No!" Casimer said. Then, forcing himself to sound calm, "This is registered. I must present it to Mr. Sherman personally." He looked up and smiled. "It's all part of the show, you see. The man who sent it is a backer of Congressman Sherman, and he owns the company I work for. It is essential that everyone in the crowd sees my uniform so they know who sends the gift. I'm sure Mr. Sherman is expecting it."

The security guard grunted. "That's not going to happen. If you want to present it to him at the base of the stairs, that is fine. But I can't allow anyone without credentials up on to the dais."

Angel Casimer shrugged and bit his lip. *Less glory, but people will still find out when they hear the gun go off.* "All right. I will meet him by the stairs."

"Fine, but just don't get in anyone's way. If he doesn't want it now, get off the stand immediately."

Casimer took a deep breath while convincing himself not to shoot this imbecile on the spot. "Of course," he said to the guard, "we *are* taught to be discreet!"

He moved quickly into the tunnel while unobtrusively reaching his right hand into the package from the underside through the slit he had put there earlier. In a moment his hand closed around the weapon, and he quickly had his finger on the trigger. "Now, I just point through the box and fire. No one will see the gun or know what's happening until it is too late." Casimer walked quickly until he was at the front of the tunnel, near the base of the stairs that led up to the dais and paused. He could hear the commotion of the famous men coming closely behind him. He cast a glance at a prearranged spot and was relieved to see Fitzsimmons standing there. He turned slightly when Fitzsimmons moved his eyes in the direction of Senator Ellis, and then Casimer nodded slightly in return. Finally, as the moment drew near, Casimer looked down to see if his necktie was straight. He'd never been so exhilarated in all his life!

"And now, my fellow Americans—my fellow patriots—it is my honor to present the next president of the United States, the inimitable Senator William Howard Taft!"

Ellis glanced over at Andy Pettit, whose face looked as if he were in a trance, so much so it almost seemed he wasn't paying attention. Then, like a lightning bolt, Andy pointed and shouted, "It's Sherman! Save him!" Andy lunged in front of Jason toward the other side of the tunnel. Blood pounding in his ears, Ellis forced himself between the gunman and the vice-presidential candidate, shouting, "Get down, James! Get down!" He really didn't need to say it, since his forward momentum sent both he and Sherman sprawling. Taft had already mounted the steps to go up on the stage, and the noise was so loud in the auditorium he was unaware anything was happening behind him.

But happening it was. As Ellis spun around, he saw Andy Pettit pin a small man against the tunnel wall, and then he thought he heard the retort of a weapon—a retort that just barely preceded the sharp crack of fireworks going off in the auditorium as a shower of dazzling sparks went up to the sky, sending the crowd into a fury of jubilation.

"What's going on?" Sherman shouted in his ear.

"An assassination attempt, James! Stay down!" Pulling himself up, Ellis forced himself to go over to Andy, who lay crumpled in the hallway. It was then that he saw the half-crazed eyes of a man wearing a delivery uniform. "Death to the capitalists!" the man shouted. "Death to Jason Ellis!" At that point the man's right arm came up, his hand oddly concealed inside a small box.

"No!" Ellis heard himself shouting as he tried to get out of the way, but he knew it would be too late. A bullet travels much faster than a man can fall. "No!" Suddenly he realized how badly he wanted to live. He thought he felt a sharp pain in his side as he crashed into the wall of the tunnel, but as he hit the wall, it also registered that the Chicago policeman who'd been standing next to him had fired at the delivery man at point-blank range. He felt the flash on his face as the officer's gun went off a second time. And then he felt the delivery man falling against him. As the small man's body collapsed next to him, he felt the man's life drain away. "I am Casimer. I did this!"

CHAPTER 26

A TERRIBLE PRICE

Chicago Coliseum
June 18, 1908

Jason Ellis shuddered at the realization that a dead man now rested on him, and he struggled to scoot out from under the body.

"Senator Ellis, are you all right?"

"I'm all right." Glancing down, he saw a sheaf of papers in his hands, papers passed to him by the shooter. Skimming the first page, his eyes widened as he recognized a name. He quickly slipped the papers into his vest pocket. Once the body was lifted away, he was pleased to see James Sherman standing in front of him. "James? You're alive! It failed!"

"Yes, thanks to you. Are you okay?"

Ellis felt up and down his side, fully expecting to find blood. To his surprise there was none. "I guess I am. I thought I'd been shot."

"I did too." By now a small crowd of Andy's detectives had gathered around. "James," Ellis said, "you've got to get up on stage. I don't think anyone in the crowd heard it. You're safe now. Go up there!"

"What? Are you sure?"

Ellis nodded. "I'm sure. We don't want anyone to know about this if we can help it. It'll ruin everything if it gets out. Go, James! And don't say a word about it. Not to anyone!"

Pettit's men confirmed that it was all right, so Sherman made his way to the stairs and onto the stage, which naturally caused a new explosion of cheers. Jason wondered what sort of expression the next vice president could muster in view of what just happened.

To the detective standing next to him he said, "It's insane to try to hide it, but it would be so much better if we could!" Then he quickly surveyed the area and decided that if anyone in the crowd was aware of what had happened, they didn't show it. "Too much noise!" said the detective. "That and the fact that everyone in the immediate area was working for Mr. Pettit."

Ellis became aware of something warm against his leg and looked down to see the motionless body of the assassin. "Is he dead?" The detective kneeled down, put his hand on the man's carotid artery, and nodded. "He's dead."

Ellis leaned back against the wall. "I'm glad. I shouldn't be, because now we can't question him, but I'm still glad. Maybe all of this is finally over."

"Senator—" One of Pettit's men pointed to Ellis's right.

"Andy!" Ellis moved quickly to kneel at the side of Andy Pettit, who was slumped against the tunnel wall. "Andy! What—?"

"It looks like I got myself shot trying to wrestle the gun away from our young assassin. Who'd have known it hurts so much to get shot in the stomach." Andy struggled for breath. "He got the best of me, but at least I kept him from getting you or James Sherman."

"We need an ambulance!"

"We've got one just outside." The detective raised Ellis to his feet. "We're going to take him out right now. You should walk with us, Senator."

"I'll go to the hospital with him."

The detective, John Penrod, nodded. "I'd appreciate that, Senator. We'll take care of everything here."

Ellis's legs were wobbly enough he didn't mind that one of the detectives stabilized him as they walked down the tunnel. After a few steps, he hesitated. "Big Jim Fitzsimmons—the union leader. He's in on this. The assassin confirmed it. You've got to find him, or there may be another attack!" Ellis heard the renewed sound of panic in his voice.

"We've already taken care of that," John Penrod said.

"You have?"

"Sure; it was Fitzsimmons's eyes that told Andy where the assassin was. He was watching him the whole time."

"He was?" Ellis shook his head. "I mean, yes, I guess I knew he was watching someone." Ellis wasn't sure he could even re-member his own name, let alone recall what he was supposed to know. His best friend was shot, he'd been the intended victim of an assassination, and a dying man had fallen on him. How could he remember anything when all he wanted to do was get out of here and go back to the hotel to be with Patricia? By this point they were near the exterior door to Sixteenth Street, and Andy's men were loading him into the ambulance.

"But how did you get Fitzsimmons?" Ellis asked, mounting the steps to the horse-drawn ambulance.

"We had three men in the vicinity. In the ruckus, they whacked him a good one with a billy club. He went down with-out a sound, and we dragged him out before anyone in the crowd could react. He'll be taken into hiding for the time being. It all went according to Mr. Pettit's plan."

Ellis reached down and took Andy's hand in his. "Your plan. You were three steps ahead of us all along." He felt a lump come up in his throat as he held his unconscious friend's hand. "You better live, Andy. Please live."

CHAPTER 27

MORGUES AND HOSPITALS

Chicago
Late evening, June 18, 1908

"Are you Senator Ellis?"

Jason looked up from the chair he was sitting on in the hospital waiting room. He'd been rehearsing the events of the past six months in his mind, trying to figure out how to connect all the pieces of what had happened to him. "Yes, I am."

"There's a phone call for you. I was told it's quite important."

"Where can I take it?"

"In our administrator's office. I will take you there." He followed the young man who had been sent to find him, and in a few moments he found himself talking to Theodore Roosevelt's secretary, who quickly handed the phone to the president. Ellis realized that he would have to be very guarded in what he said, since phone lines were open to anyone who happened to share the line, including the hospital operator and anyone else on that circuit.

"Jason, is that you?"

"Yes, sir. Thank you for calling."

"I just heard about the . . . disturbance. Is everything all right?"

Ellis stammered for a moment as he tried to form his thoughts and say them in a way that would keep the conversation controlled. "I think everything is better than it was. We found the men we were looking for, and they have been, uh, taken care of. They won't cause any more problems. I can tell you about it later tonight if you like."

"That's good. And our friend?"

Ellis felt his throat tighten. "Not doing so well. That's why I'm here. He's in surgery. I've been waiting." Jason couldn't figure out what else to say. The doctor had looked serious when Andy disappeared into the operating room. "Will you tell Patricia I'm fine? I look forward to joining her later tonight." He paused. "Unless our friend still needs me."

"Patricia's with us. We already had a report that you were all right, but I'll reassure her." Roosevelt was distracted. "She'd like to join you."

"I'd like that. Andy would too."

"I'll see to it. I don't think I should come—"

"No, that wouldn't be good."

"All right, then. Well, keep me informed. I'll see you at the hotel?"

"Yes, sir." He replaced the earpiece on the cradle at the side of the wall phone. As he left the room, he thanked the young man and made his way back to the surgical wing of the hospital. As he arrived, he saw the surgeon walking in his direction. "Dr. Stoddard—may I ask how things went?'

The doctor looked up, startled. "And tell me who you are again?"

"I'm Jason Ellis, senator from New York. Your patient, Andy Pettit, is my best friend. I came here with him."

The doctor eyed him narrowly. "Tell me how this happened?"

Ellis swallowed hard. Just as he'd entered the ambulance, Andy's man John Penrod had crawled in and whispered in his ear, "We're going to say that this was a robbery attempt gone bad; nothing more than that." So, doing his best to lie, Ellis repeated that line to the doctor.

"Well, I'm afraid that it didn't go well for your friend."

Ellis's pulse quickened. "You mean . . . he died?" The words seemed quite surreal, even as he said them.

"No, no—I didn't mean that. I'm sorry." The doctor arched his shoulders, which had to be exhausted from spending more than three hours in surgery. "I mean fragments of the bullet lodged in his spine." He hesitated. "I'm afraid it's very likely your friend is going to be paralyzed from his lower waist down."

"Paralyzed?"

The doctor nodded. "We couldn't remove all the fragments— the bullet shattered inside his body. Some of the pieces were simply too close to important nerve bundles, so they'll have to stay there. He will have the use of his arms and hands, but there's not much hope for his legs . . ." The doctor's voice trailed off.

Jason Ellis was too dazed to even reply. This was something that he'd never considered.

"We did the best we could. And it's possible that I'm wrong . . ." The doctor sounded miserable.

Ellis took a deep breath. "I'm sure you did everything right. This was a very bad thing, and I'm grateful that you saved his life. That's what's important."

"We did do that. He would have died without surgical intervention; we were at least able to suture up all the internal wounds and stop the bleeding."

"Of course." Ellis squeezed his hands together behind his back to calm himself. "Can I see him? How long before he wakes up?"

"I honestly don't know. It will be at least an hour or two before the ether wears off. But he won't be in any condition to visit until tomorrow at the earliest. You should go home. If you were a witness to all this, you'll need some rest yourself."

Ellis steadied himself. "Can I ask one thing of you, doctor? Can I be there when you talk to him about . . ." For the first time since everything had happened, his voice cracked, " . . . about his legs? My wife and I are very close to him."

"It would be better if you're there." The doctor hesitated. "Does he not have any family?"

Jason shook his head. "He's not married, and his mother lives in upstate New York. My wife and I are the closest thing he has to family here, so we should be with you."

"How can we reach you?"

"That's easy. I'll be here." That, at least, was one thing Jason Ellis could control in the insanity that had become his life.

"John, I didn't want anyone else to see this, but I need you to keep this safe for me."

"What is it, Senator?"

"The shooter forced it into my hands when he fell against me. It says his name was . . . something . . . Casimer, I think . . . and that he and Jim Fitzsimmons were responsible."

"Casimer." Penrod accepted the papers.

"It's the assassin's 'manifesto,'" Ellis said, "and it makes for some very disturbing reading."

Penrod glanced through it quickly.

"This will be helpful. With it we can backtrack through everything that's happened."

"You told me you had picked up Jim Fitzsimmons, the union organizer?" Ellis asked.

"We have him on ice not far from here. Care to come with us to interrogate him? For the moment I'm leaving him all to himself to break down his reserve."

"I'd like to be there, but I don't dare leave Andy."

"I should stay here too, then."

"No," Ellis said, shaking his head, "you should leave me here and go talk to Fitzsimmons. Try to make some kind of sense out of all this. If Andy's never going to walk again, then the least we can do is find out why all this happened." He closed his mouth tight for a moment to steady his voice. "It needs to have some meaning—some purpose. Otherwise, the price is simply too high."

John Penrod nodded. "All right. I'll get on it." He looked down the hall to Pettit's room. "He's the very best you know—absolutely the best. There isn't a man on the squad who wouldn't have taken that bullet for him."

Jason nodded in rhythm to John's words. "I know. Instead, he took a bullet for me. Now I must help him figure out how to keep his spirits up and adjust to this new reality." He accepted Penrod's extended hand. "I'll let you know if we need anything."

New York City
June 19, 1908

"Mr. Kozlov, there are some men here to see you. They say they are from the Exchange."

Maxim Kozlov looked up and scowled. He'd just been looking

at the stock ticker and noted that prices had gone up—not down, as he had expected. He'd even called one of his contacts at the *New York Times* to check into the news out of Chicago, only to be told that Taft had been nominated, and the Republicans were in their usual orgy of delight.

"It's failed. Against all odds, the attempt has failed." Kozlov said this to no one in particular.

"Pardon me, sir?"

"Nothing." He shook his head, and then stood up. Kozlov was not a man to feel fear, and yet, perhaps for the first time in his life, he experienced a deep sense of dread, mixed with indignation, as a wave of anxiety washed over him. "Show the men in. I'm sure they have important business to discuss with me."

Chicago
June 19, 1908

"So you're alive?"

Jason Ellis jerked awake at the sound of Andy's voice. Despite his best efforts, Jason had drifted off to sleep for a few moments. As he shook his head to clear it, he looked at the clock on the wall and realized that he'd been asleep closer to half an hour. "Yes, I'm alive. And so is James Sherman. The only person who died was the man who shot you."

"Any idea who he was?" Andy's voice was groggy, and when Ellis looked down into his eyes he saw that they had a faraway look in them.

"Casimer, a man named Angel Casimer. He left a manifesto that explained it all."

"I wondered about him."

"You knew about Casimer?"

Pettit nodded, and then shifted uncomfortably. "He was one of the guys we had on our list of suspects. He was sometimes seen with Fitzsimmons. Little guy, a war veteran."

"That's right."

Andy shifted yet again. Then he turned and fixed his gaze directly on Ellis. "I can't feel my legs, Jason. What do you know about that?"

Ellis felt his lip quiver. As drugged as Andy was, he could easily postpone telling him anything. He probably wouldn't remember this conversation anyway once the anesthesia wore off. But Andy wasn't that kind of man. "The doctor says that the bullet fragmented inside your body and damaged your spinal column. His opinion is you'll be paralyzed from the waist down, but that you should have full function in your arms and torso." He was shocked at how clinical he sounded but reassured he'd managed to get it out without breaking down.

Andy nodded his head slowly. "I kind of wondered if that's what happened. Even at the Coliseum I couldn't make my legs move."

Ellis reached over and took his hand. "I'm so sorry, Andy. You did it to protect me and James."

Andy shook his head. "I did my job, Jason. No need to be sorry." His eyes fluttered closed, and then opened, and then closed again. "I did my job."

Jason Ellis watched as Andy drifted back to sleep. As he sat back down in the chair, fully aware that he'd have to have this same conversation with Andy again, he was struck by the absolute integrity of what Andy had said. And then a wave of despair rushed over him unlike any that he had ever known.

CHAPTER 28

THE PERILS OF A NAKED SHORT SALE

New York City
June 23, 1908

"But you can't go in! I don't care who you are!"

The young secretary's voice was shrill as he tried to bar Ellis and two members of the Secret Service from entering Maxim Kozlov's stately office.

Once inside, the man stammered to Kozlov that he'd tried to stop them, but Kozlov raised a hand to quiet him. "Why, Senator Ellis," Kozlov said, rising behind his desk. "Come to gloat?" He paused long enough to dismiss the young male secretary. "Do come in. I'd offer you a drink, but I'm sure these gentlemen aren't supposed to drink on the job."

"No, they're not. And as for gloating, I'm afraid that far too much has happened for me to take any pleasure in seeing you."

"I'm the one who lost everything to the officers of the stock exchange, and yet you pity yourself."

Ellis shook his head. "Maxim, there's no need to play coy. My best friend is in a hospital, paralyzed, and I was very nearly murdered. Let's not compare our misery." He cast a glance around. "Your office is in disarray; is it possible you were leaving?"

"I'm sure that's none of your business. My creditors will all be dealt with in time, including you. Surely my financial ruin is satisfaction enough."

"I would feel sympathy for you, Maxim, if I didn't know that your losses are the result of murder and your attempt at market subterfuge. We're here to talk about your options."

"My *options?*" Kozlov raised an eyebrow. "And what does a United States senator have to do with my *options?*" His voice was calculated and cold.

"I'm here because the Treasury Department wants me here. My experience on Wall Street has helped them unravel the awful game you've been playing. Now we're here to take you into custody for market manipulation and the murder of Tom Scanlon. And indirectly for the assault on Andy Pettit by your hired man."

"Murder?" There was no emotion in Kozlov's voice. "I'm not guilty of murder. Tom Scanlon was guilty of murder. He killed one of my Russian associates, and then, to keep scandal away from our doors, I helped him."

Ellis nodded. "I expected you to say that, Maxim. You realize we have witnesses of you carrying the trunk out at night, so you admit to being part of it, yet blame a dead man who cannot testify of the truth."

"I'm the one telling the truth, Senator. Whatever else you think is a lie."

Ellis held his ground. "Witnesses saw you and Scanlon with the trunk, we discovered the body, and we have connected you to Jim Fitzsimmons of the Baltimore dockworkers union. He's been connected to Angel Casimer, who was killed at the Chicago

Coliseum while acting under your direct orders to assassinate James Sherman and me. These things are known!"

"Direct orders? Really? I do not remember issuing any direct orders to anyone, let alone some person in Baltimore. I've never been to Baltimore, so how could I have done that?"

"We can connect the cash to you, and the orders of whom to kill and when. The thing is, Mr. Fitzsimmons is something of a meticulous person, contrary to his appearance. He saved all the notes that accompanied the cash payments, and our handwriting experts have confirmed that you wrote the notes. Your handwriting is very distinctive."

"Which is why it's so easy to forge." Kozlov shifted his weight behind his desk. "At least that's what my attorneys will say to create 'reasonable doubt.' Isn't that a wonderful phrase—reasonable doubt—your American justice system is so helpful to people who are falsely accused. And besides, it'll be such an embarrassment to you to take me to trial. I notice that the only mention of the events in Chicago in the New York newspapers is that a common thief was killed by a Chicago policeman. So where is this conspiracy that you speak of? The fact is that there was no conspiracy, and yet this fellow from Baltimore has chosen, for whatever reason, to try to implicate me. But he cannot."

"Why don't you come with us, Maxim? Let's talk and explore your alternatives."

"I prefer to stay where I am." Kozlov's face hardened as he said this.

"Well, we believe the Justice Department can make a case against you. And even if they fail, you've still lost all your money, including the money from the Bolsheviks who bankrolled you in the first place. I'm sure they're on their way here to find out what happened to the substantial sums of money you promised to deliver to them after the Chicago convention."

Kozlov's face flushed. "Whatever I do with my money is *my* concern, Jason Ellis, not yours!"

"Not when it promotes international anarchy. Then it becomes our concern. It becomes *my* concern when you try to have me assassinated—not once, but at least three times. So, you *will* talk to me about your alternatives!"

Kozlov sighed. "You have no good cards to play, Senator. I will not submit to you, and if arrested I will demand a public trial where you will have to admit to all that happened in Chicago. It will stir up panic and lead to the very kind of laws that you seem to despise."

Ellis took a breath. "Perhaps you're right, Maxim. Perhaps we should not involve American courts. In which case we will simply turn you over to the tsar's attaché for expatriation back to Russia. I'm sure you'll find the tsar's justice less friendly than ours, particularly when we turn over all the files we have on you and your failed financial transactions to our counterparts in Russia. That was one of the positive developments of my overseas trip earlier this year—meeting people who know you and who are interested in you." He should have stopped, but couldn't stop himself from adding, "And I think it will be viewed very badly by the regime in St. Petersburg that you have given so much money to this fellow Vladimir Lenin and the Bolsheviks who seek to overthrow them, don't you?"

Kozlov growled, his anger boiling over. "You're such a fool, Ellis! A prudish fool. You have no idea what kind of game you're playing."

"Either submit to our system or to theirs. You have ten seconds to make your decision!"

Kozlov's naturally dark countenance grew even darker. "I've failed in many ways, but I shall succeed in righting one wrong! I shall make up for all the incompetents who were supposed to deal with you but who failed!"

With that, he stomped his right foot on the lever under his desk. The noise it caused was so sharp that Ellis winced. But nothing more happened.

"What?" Kozlov looked down at the floor. He stomped on the lever a second time, cursing as he did so.

"So you were going to kill me right here, right now?" Ellis smiled. "And in doing so, you've given us just what we need to arrest you on an easy-to-prove charge of attempted murder!"

Kozlov stomped on the lever a third time, looking up at Ellis with pure hatred in his eyes. "What do you know about this?"

"The gun you have mounted under your desk was disabled last night."

Kozlov's face changed color yet again. "What? But how?"

"My friend Andy Pettit placed one of his detectives on your cleaning crew. He took care of it after you left for the evening."

"But how could Pettit know—"

"From the angle of the bullet that struck the Russian we pulled from the East River. It was a fair certainty he wasn't expecting to be shot in your office, so there had to be an element of surprise. And the upward angle of the bullet suggested it wasn't you who pulled the trigger directly, since you are too tall for that when standing, and the angle would have been much shallower if you'd been sitting. Pettit surmised you must have had something like this weapon mounted near or in your desk. Our man confirmed it last night and made certain it was disabled. He replaced the bullet with a blank cartridge."

"You came in here to entrap me. To get me to take this action so you could accuse me."

Ellis smiled a humorless smile. "All's fair in love and war."

"And what if I had repaired this today? Were you so stupid as to trust your life to this man's work last evening?"

Ellis's countenance darkened. "It would have been worth getting shot to have you executed. After what you did to Andy Pettit—and to so many other innocent people—it would be an honor to die if it sent you to the gallows."

Kozlov stepped back. "So your hatred of me has come to equal mine of you. Perhaps that's some small consolation for the trouble you have caused me."

Jason Ellis wanted to step forward and beat Kozlov senseless, but he controlled himself. He could not imagine how he'd become the focus of Kozlov's rage, but clearly he had.

"Well, you've done what was needed." Ellis motioned to the Secret Service to place Kozlov in handcuffs.

"Do I still have the option of going to Russia?"

"I'm afraid not, Maxim. Attempted murder, as well as everything else we can attach to you for these attacks, means you'll be sent to a prison here and tried for your crimes. If justice is served, you'll have a date with an executioner."

"I see. Are you a betting man, Senator?"

"Occasionally. But unlike you, I even bet when I *don't* know the outcome in advance."

"Well," Kozlov said, nodding his head slightly, "let me give you a tip on an absolutely certain bet. Wherever you take me in this savage country of yours, it will not be sufficient to keep me from being murdered by my Russian friends. They'll have their revenge before you get your chance. I nearly lost my life when you thwarted me in the Union Life episode. And now that I've lost everything, they will not allow you Americans to have the pleasure of being my executioner."

Ellis nodded slowly. "I can't imagine how, but you come from a resourceful people. We will see." With that he motioned for the Secret Service agents to take Kozlov away.

When the others were gone, he allowed himself to sit down. His legs were trembling, and he didn't care to admit how frightening it had been when Kozlov tried to shoot him. "*Nicely played, Jason,*" he heard Andy Pettit's voice in his mind.

"*But too late, my friend. Too late for you.*"

"*Take what satisfaction you can. He tried to destroy you, and in the end you engineered his destruction. It was the right thing to do.*"

"*Ah, Andy. Kozlov was right—I came to hate him, and I have never felt that way about a man before. I feel as if I've lost myself in all this. And you've lost your legs. What, old friend, shall become of us?*" There seemed to be no answer.

"Well, enough of this," Ellis said to the air. "You should go downstairs and swear out the complaint against Kozlov." With that, Jason Ellis exited the elegant office of the once mighty Maxim Kozlov.

Chicago
June 23, 1908

"Mr. Fitzsimmons. Do come in and sit down." John Penrod, Andy Pettit's right-hand man, motioned to a scrawny chair in the center of the room that likely groaned at the thought of Fitzsimmons sitting on it.

"I want to see a lawyer."

"And just what makes you think you're entitled to a lawyer?

We're here to find the truth. If, after that, you go to trial, you can have a lawyer."

"There's nothing to learn. I'm a union organizer from Baltimore, here to observe and perhaps arrange pickets for the convention. Your men waylaid me, and you'll have to answer for it. There is nothing more to it than that."

"Yes, we know who you are. But thank you for giving us your version of events."

Fitzsimmons scowled but said nothing.

"Now let me give you our version. It's simple. Things weren't moving fast enough for you, so you decided to go into the terror business. You found a young protégé, Angel Casimer, who was willing to do your bidding. You ordered a bomb to be placed under the tracks at Union Station. Then you arranged for a restaurant fire in downtown Washington. Your little pal murdered a businessman in Connecticut. And finally, you got your man appointed as a courier here in Chicago so he could murder James Sherman at the Republican Convention. All of which would stir up a great deal of animosity between the mostly Republican owners of industry and the working men that you hope to lead. In the end, you'd move to the front of the pack, so to speak, and up whatever ladder it is you hope to climb." Penrod pursed his lips. "How'd I do?"

"You have a great imagination, that's for sure. You talk about a man I don't even know."

"Casimer? How is it, then, that we have eyewitnesses who place you at his dinner table on at least three occasions here in Chicago, and that the courier company's representatives in New York say you made the call to get him appointed?"

Fitzsimmons's face darkened. "How could you know such things when they're not true? Besides, even if I did know the

231

man, which I'm not saying I do, I certainly didn't know that he was a murderer. And now that he's dead, it would be impossible for him to say otherwise."

"You'd think so, wouldn't you?"

"Think so? What kind of an idiot are you? He's dead; he can't say anything."

"Well, as it turns out, even dead men can speak." Penrod reached into his pocket and pulled out a stained sheaf of papers. "Sorry for the condition of this. That's Casimer's blood on it. He gave this up just as he was dying. Of course, you saw all that since you were there."

Now the color drained from Fitzsimmons's face. "I have no idea what you're talking about. I just happened to be standing there when that incident took place."

"It was your eyes that told us who the intended target was. You motioned to Casimer and then looked at Congressman Sherman just before Casimer raised his arm to shoot the congressman."

Fitzsimmons stood up. "I said I want a lawyer. I'm sure I'm entitled to a lawyer!"

Penrod remained sitting, and quite impassive. "It's like this, Fitzsimmons. Just before he died, Casimer handed over these papers to Senator Ellis. And this little 'Manifesto to the World' of his makes it certain you were involved. He names you in every event I cited."

"But he's dead—he must have done that just in case he got caught. It's the oldest trick in the book—blame someone else so you don't get the death penalty."

"Well, in this case, I think it's going to work. From what our troubled Mr. Casimer had to say, he claimed full responsibility for all the murders, but he also implicated you. He apparently suspected that you would disavow him when it was all over, which is why he went to such great lengths to make sure that the world knows of the important role you played in all this. You're likely to face a hangman's noose. Or the electric chair. I'm not sure what they use here in Illinois. Personally, if I were in your shoes, I'd hope it was the noose. Being fried alive is an awful way to die. They say your skin turns black, and smoke rises up from your fingers and toes while the electricity squeezes the air out of your lungs." Penrod shook his head. "Just plain awful."

Now Fitzsimmons was sweating. "Can I have a drink?"

"Of water? Sure." Penrod stood up and moved to a table on the opposite side of the room.

"I was hoping for something a little stronger," Fitzsimmons said under his breath.

Penrod came back and handed Fitzsimmons some water. He awkwardly drank it, hampered by the handcuffs he wore. Besides the handcuffs, there were two armed guards standing at each side of him, so there was no risk of Fitzsimmons hurting anyone.

"What are you going to do with me?"

Penrod nodded his head slowly. "That's the big question, isn't it? The easiest would be to turn you over to the district attorney. Chicago takes care of things like this very quickly. You'd likely be pushing up daisies inside a couple of months."

"But?" By now it had dawned on Fitzsimmons that Penrod wasn't acting on behalf of the police. Or even in a federal capacity. "Who are you, anyway? And what right do you have to be questioning me?"

"Right? I have no right. I just happen to have *possession* of you." Then Penrod leaned forward, and his face and voice went very, very cold. "I'm also a guy who works for Andy Pettit, who's now paralyzed from the waist down because of your stupid schemes. And if I wasn't under direct orders from him, I'd do the same thing to you, and then leave you begging for pennies on the street in the middle of Chicago!"

"You're not even the cops?" Fitzsimmons was indignant. "You've got to let me go. You can't hold me."

It would have been better if he hadn't said that, because two seconds later he found himself in a very uncomfortable position on the ground. Penrod had kicked the legs of the chair out from under him, and then proceeded to kick him in the ribs on his left side while the other two detectives pummeled him from above.

"All right, all right—I've had enough!" Fitzsimmons wiped the blood that dripped from his mouth.

Even at that, one of the detectives had to pull Penrod back from launching another kick. "Listen," Penrod hissed, kneeling down so his face was even with Fitzsimmons's on the floor. "What we *should* do is just take you out and let you sink to the bottom of the lake out there just to see how long you can hold your breath."

"But?" Fitzsimmons wanted to seem tough, but he was scared to death. He was especially horrified at the thought of the electric chair. He'd touched a live electric wire once, and the jolt had almost broken his shoulder, the muscles contracted so tightly. The thought of being killed that way was terrifying, particularly since the electric chair sometimes had trouble killing large men.

Penrod stood up and motioned for the other two to help Fitzsimmons up. He found a new chair for him. Then, pulling his own chair forward so their knees almost touched, he said quietly, "But Andy has other ideas for you."

"What kind of ideas?"

"He has the idea—which I think is crazy—you could go to work for us."

"Go to work for you?"

"Yeah—he wants a despicable guy like you. I hope you say no, because you don't deserve anything but the electric chair."

"I can't go to work for you. Why would I?"

"The way Andy explained it is that it would be inconvenient for all this mischief about Casimer and Congressman Sherman to come to light. Somehow, whenever one of these crazies does something in public, it brings out all sorts of other idiots who want to get famous. So, we want this thing to just go away."

"And if you were to put me on trial, it would be in all the newspapers."

"Something like that."

"What sort of work would I do?"

Penrod raised an eyebrow. "What would you do? You'd do exactly what you already do. You'd be a union organizer who gets up and gives stupid speeches to get people all worked up. You'd organize strikes and work slowdowns. You'd continue to be the pain in the neck you're so perfectly suited to be."

Fitzsimmons's eyes widened. "But how does that help you?"

"Well, you'd also inform against any anarchists in the union. You'd let us know when someone was planning to do something beyond the legal activities of your union. And you'd help us run a sting operation every once in a while on guys as bad as you."

"You want me to be a snitch?"

"We want a lot more than that, Mr. Fitzsimmons. We want to own your very soul. Think of it this way: if you agree to our terms, you'll spend the rest of your life in constant fear the people you rat on are going to find out or we're going to change our mind and bring this little manifesto out into the open." He leaned very close to Fitzsimmons. "You've got to remember there's no statute of limitations on murder. If you ever double-cross us, or get arrogant in any way, then this little arrangement we're proposing will go away."

"And if I don't go along?"

"Then you may find yourself with a bullet in the back of your head for trying to escape while we're taking you in. Like I say, we don't want this to get out. So, either you work for us, or you join your sleazy little friend Casimer in the hell where murderers end up."

Fitzsimmons looked as if he was going to throw up. "But if the people I rat on ever figure out it's me, they'll . . ." his voice trailed off.

"Which is why you have to get very good at playing a double game." Penrod stood up. "But then, you've been doing that for a long time already, haven't you?" He extended a hand to help Fitzsimmons stand up. "Now's the time to decide. Either you work for us on the terms I've described, or your next stop is the Chicago police precinct down the block. The only problem is that we're clumsy, and if you were to try to escape we'd have to, you know . . ."

"Speaking of the police, what happened to the policeman who shot Casimer?"

"The hero who saved the day?"

Fitzsimmons snorted. "Some hero."

Penrod smiled. "If you're saying his motives may not be entirely pure, then I advise you to keep it to yourself. He did what any police officer should have done. We've made sure he'll get a commendation."

Fitzsimmons shook his head. "The only thing that will ever mess up your boss's plan is if I up and shoot myself." He shook his head even harder. "And if I had even a shred of integrity, that's just what I'd do."

"Fortunately for us, you don't." Penrod walked over to the second table and motioned for Fitzsimmons to follow. As he got there, Penrod took the handcuffs off him and gave him a pen. "Now, sit down, Mr. Fitzsimmons, and write down everything you know about Angel Casimer and about your part in the murders in Washington and Hartford and what happened here in Chicago."

"But why? You told me I was going to work for you."

"And you are. But you will be a better employee if we have your statement in a safe, won't you?"

"That little idiot—I knew I should have killed him after Hartford. I knew he was coming unglued. But I didn't, and now he's left his little manifesto."

"Yes, and if it had stopped there, you might have got away with all this, but your ego wouldn't allow it." Penrod shoved Fitzsimmons down into the chair. "Now write!"

New York City
June 23, 1908

"May I ask what's happening, Senator Ellis?"

Ellis looked at the young man who'd replaced Tom Scanlon. "I can't really say, Dick. But you're smart enough to know your boss played some short sales very badly, and the Exchange is closing out all his positions. I've been in talks with Pierpont Morgan, and I'm pretty sure that he's going to take over First Commerce. If it works out as I hope, you and your fellow employees will still have jobs."

"Thank you. But what about Mr. Kozlov?"

"Mr. Kozlov has some difficult things to answer for. In fact, I need to be going right now to be with him. But I promise we'll be back with answers. Try to keep everyone calm, and we'll see what works out."

The fellow nodded and then held the heavy brass door open so Jason Ellis could exit to the street. As he did so, he saw the unmarked police wagon they'd ordered had pulled up. Jason walked over to the curb to stand next to Kozlov, debating whether he should ask him why he did what he had done.

"All right, Mr. Kozlov, it would be better if you got in with little fuss." This, from one of Andy's detectives.

"Well, Senator Jason, it looks like you've won this round. But the game isn't over. You know it isn't over."

Ellis considered this was the first time that Kozlov had ever called him by his first name.

"I never had any ill will for you, Maxim. I don't know why—"

Whatever Ellis was going to say was quickly drowned out by the sound of a motorcar careening around the corner, tires screeching on the cobblestones as it did. Having had more than his fair share of unexpected experiences lately, Jason wheeled in time to see the muzzle of an automatic pistol extend from the automobile and heard himself shouting at people to duck. Of course, there really wasn't time to duck since the person with the gun had the advantage. Before his mind could fully register it, Ellis saw the blast of the muzzle and heard the quick succession of retorts from the gun. And then he heard Maxim Kozlov cry out as multiple bullets smashed into his chest. Ducking behind the police wagon for safety, Jason somehow noted that one of the guards had been hit as well. His heart pounding, he still heard the sound of the motorcar speeding away down the street.

When it was gone he quickly moved back to where Kozlov

had fallen and knelt down beside him. Kozlov's eyes were clouding over. "I told you they'd get me."

"Be quiet, Maxim. We'll get you help."

"Do you want to know why I hate you?" It was difficult for Jason to understand Kozlov, as he was now choking on his own blood. Ellis leaned closer, and Kozlov tried to say something, but all Ellis heard was a gurgling sound, and then he felt Kozlov go limp.

Ellis slumped onto the street. His mind was numb. At what point does the cumulative weight of tragedy and terror finally overwhelm?

"Are you all right, Senator?"

He looked up at the Pettit detective and extended his hand. The fellow reached down and helped him to his feet. "We'll get you out of here, Senator. Perhaps you should get into the wagon so people don't see you."

Ellis nodded and quickly climbed into the privacy of the police wagon. As he sat on a bench along the side, he rubbed his temples. Thinking of Kozlov, he said to himself, "I guess it really doesn't matter why you wanted to destroy me, does it?" But it did matter, and looking at the dead body of Maxim Kozlov being loaded into the wagon with him, Ellis sighed, understanding that he would never know.

CHAPTER 29

AN UNOFFICIAL PRESIDENTIAL CITATION

The White House
December 27, 1908

"Happy birthday, Andy," President Theodore Roosevelt said. Andy Pettit looked up from his wheelchair.

"Thank you, Mr. President."

"Three months and you can call me . . . 'ex-President Roosevelt' or 'former President Roosevelt.'" He turned to Jason Ellis and asked, "What do you think? Which should I go by?"

"You should go by 'Mr. President,'" Ellis said. "It's a lifetime title, even though the office passes into other hands."

"Not to friends. You shall all call me Theodore, my preferred name." Turning back to Pettit, he continued, "At any rate, happy birthday, Andy. Remind me how old you are."

"He's forty-eight years old, just like me," Patricia Ellis said. "We were both born in 1860. That's why Jason has always treated us with such scant respect; he's older by a year and a half, you know."

Jason shook his head but said nothing.

"Which makes Jason the same age as I am," Roosevelt said

cheerfully. "And look where we've all arrived in our lives. Not too bad for a few ordinary kids from New York state."

It was at this moment that Jason Ellis finally understood why he had such great respect for Theodore Roosevelt. As a man, he was full of contradictions, bluster, and bravado. But in this moment he was completely unaware of how his remarks about where they had arrived in their lives might strike someone like Andy, who was now destined to spend the rest of his life in a wheelchair. Because of that innocence, Andy had to know that Roosevelt still considered him perfectly fit and able. And that attitude was Roosevelt's greatest strength.

"We haven't done too badly, have we?" Andy said. "I can imagine worse places to spend one's birthday than in this house on this street in this city."

"The home of the greatest country on earth," Roosevelt said enthusiastically. "We may have our problems, but no one is our equal. And if anyone can solve the problems that face the world, it is we Americans as we play a leading role with our allies."

"Here, here," Jason Ellis said, raising a glass. Everyone joined him in a toast.

"How is your recovery coming, Mr. Pettit?" the president's wife asked quietly. Perhaps she was concerned about how Andy might interpret all of this.

"It's harder than I would have thought," Andy said. "But because of all the exercise they put me through to strengthen my arms and chest, I think I'm in the best physical shape I've been in for years. And I'm getting used to the wheelchair. I think I'll be all right."

"That's the spirit," Roosevelt said. "And what about your business? Are you going to be all right on that account?"

Andy nodded thoughtfully. "It's interesting. We've taken on

new cases, and I find myself in an interesting new role." He closed his eyes for a moment as a wave of pain coursed through the nerves in his lower back that no longer connected to anything. Everyone in the room could see what was happening but were kind enough not to say anything. When the pain subsided, he opened his eyes and said, "What's interesting about it is that I find myself in a consulting role now. Since I can't get out and do the work myself, my detectives must bring all the information to me, and then I sort through it. It's amazing how much you can discern when you're detached from the investigation. In some ways, I think I'm sharper than I've ever been."

"And he also lacks a little patience when his men bring him an incomplete set of facts," Jason said.

Andy looked up. "Is it my fault some of them are incompetent? They have a perfectly obvious trail of facts emerging before them, and they fail to grasp where it's taking them. I'm forced to prompt them with the next questions to ask and what details still need to be investigated." Andy said this with no trace of humor, which made it funnier.

"Andy's never been one to suffer fools easily," Jason said.

"Well, I think it's heroic of you to have such a fine attitude," Patricia said. "While others would have complained and withdrawn from the world, you've simply forged ahead."

"They call that resilience," the president said, "and it's the mark of a true man and a true woman. I hope I have it."

"I'm not sure it's all *that* noteworthy," Andy said. "The simple fact is that I can do nothing else. I saw the man raise his weapon, I reacted, and I was shot. When I found Jason sitting by my hospital bed the next day, he told me I'd never walk again. What good is it to fret about something that's beyond your control?"

The others nodded; their admiration increased by his modesty.

"Well, I for one am glad you solved the Casimer case," Jason said. "One or two more murder attempts on my life and I'd have lost it—of that I'm sure." He said this good-naturedly, but the truth it portrayed was reality. Even these many months later he frequently tossed and turned from nightmares of men being killed and blood splashing on him. Fortunately, Patricia was patient and would wake him to help him calm down.

"Well, I'm hungry," Jason said, and he moved behind Andy's chair to push him to the table where a beautifully decorated birthday cake had been set out. The others crowded around as they prepared to sing a birthday song and cut the cake.

"If I could," the president said, "have just a moment of your time before we proceed." Naturally the room quieted down. "Everyone in this room is among the select few who know how close we came to a horrific event in Chicago. But because of our good friend Andy Pettit, aided by our rightfully paranoid Jason Ellis, disaster was averted." Everyone clapped in appreciation. "But," Roosevelt said, "not without a price. And that is why I invited you here tonight." He motioned to a steward, who brought two small boxes to him. "Because it makes sense to keep these events out of the public eye, I can't do anything in an official capacity to recognize your heroism or your sacrifice. If I could, I'd have a commemorative gold coin struck by the Treasury in honor of you both. But then we'd have to explain ourselves."

Ellis nodded to show his agreement.

"But that doesn't stop me from expressing my personal appreciation and my admiration." The president walked first to Jason, handing him one of the boxes, but with an admonition to wait just a moment before opening it. Then he bent down and handed the second box to Andy Pettit. "All right, gentlemen, please open your box and see what we"—he gestured to all around the table—"see what we feel about you and what you've done for our country."

Each of the men fumbled with their small wooden box, finally opening the small clasp that opened to reveal a brilliant medallion.

"I had this medallion cast in your honor. They are the first and only Theodore Roosevelt Medals of Appreciation. Each is cast in solid gold."

Ellis lifted his medallion, which had a likeness of a bald eagle on the Great Seal of the United States and the words of the citation written in the outside ring of the medallion. Just under the eagle was the name "Jason Ellis," followed by "1908."

"Mr. President," Ellis said, "this is magnificent. Thank you." He'd learned long ago that at a time like this, false modesty only detracted from a gift. To accept it with appreciation was the best way to show respect for the one who gave it.

Andy Pettit took longer to form his words as he gazed intently at his medallion. Not an emotional man in ordinary circumstances, he struggled to compose himself. Finally, looking up, he managed to say quietly, "This means everything to me, Mr. President. Everything."

The women in the room had to bring out their handkerchiefs, and even the president had to brush his cheek. "Yes, well, words will never describe the appreciation I have for you both."

This was one of those moments you want to last forever, but everyone knows it can't, yet no one knows for sure how to end it. Fortunately, the quick-witted Patricia Ellis knew what to say. "The best thing about these medals is that no one will ever know what you did to earn them. A hundred years from now when someone finds them in a drawer, or perhaps in the Smithsonian, they will be shrouded in great mystery. And that will add immeasurably to their value."

"Here, here," Roosevelt said. "To mystery, and to Jason Ellis and Andy Pettit!" With that, everyone gave them three hurrahs, and then they sang "Happy Birthday to You," a recently written song by Mildred Hill that was increasingly becoming the way to recognize someone's birthday. Andy Pettit leaned forward to blow out the single candle on the cake, and the celebration moved forward.

It was perhaps an hour later as they were preparing to leave that Roosevelt motioned to Jason and Andy to come over to him privately. Kneeling at Andy's side, the president spoke in a quiet voice. "Gentlemen, I'm afraid there's been another threat—this time on the life of the president-elect. Some socialist fellow making bold statements. I hate to impose, but perhaps you could look into it?"

"I'm a US senator," Jason said defensively, "not a private investigator."

"Yes, the US senator who chairs the new oversight committee of our new Bureau of Investigation under the redoubtable Charles Bonaparte. So, I'm afraid this *is* your concern, Jason."

Ellis shook his head, but then changed it to a nod.

"And you, Mr. Pettit, are to look into it as an interested citizen. Something tells me you have special insight into these sorts of people."

Andy smiled. "We do have some resources at our disposal. One of our best informants is just a few miles away in Baltimore."

"That's what I thought." Roosevelt grew serious. "You'll have something to me about all this in a week or two?"

They nodded in the affirmative.

ACKNOWLEDGMENTS

I'd like to especially thank Derk Koldewyn, my Shadow Mountain editor, for his edit of the manuscript, and for the masterfully written chapter notes that he created to support the narrative.

My thanks to Chris Schoebinger, Shadow Mountain publisher, who reviewed and accepted the book, offering encouragement as he did so, and for Chris's own initial edit.

Thanks to Shadow Mountain's art director Garth Bruner for his masterful execution of the cover, along with all the other employees at Shadow Mountain. They work to make my writing the best it can be and to bring the book to you. Thank you!

CHAPTER NOTES

Chapter 1

Union Station in Washington, DC, was designed by the famous architect Daniel Burnham (noted for being the Director of Works of the "White City" of the 1892–93 Chicago Exposition as well as the architect of New York's Flatiron Building and San Francisco's Merchants Exchange). The station was announced in 1901, and was to unite the Pennsylvania Railroad and the Baltimore and Ohio Railroad in one station, less than a mile from the Capitol Building; its creation allowed the railroads to remove their lines from what is now the National Mall. It opened on October 27, 1907.

One feature of the station was a separate entrance and terminal, the "Presidential Suite," for foreign leaders and other distinguished guests to be greeted by government officials as they arrived in Washington.

Union Station, Washington, DC, circa 1910.

Chapter 2

The now-famous New Year's Eve ball drop made its first appearance on New Year's Eve, 1907, a change from the usual fireworks show sponsored by the *New York Times*, to commemorate the opening of the *Times'* new building on Times Square in New York City. The ball has been redesigned only six times in its now-118-year history, mainly to update the technology available. In 1907, it was illuminated with incandescent light bulbs. Now, it's illuminated with LED lamps and the outer surface is changed yearly to reflect a specific theme.

Quotes from Senator Ellis and President Roosevelt were adapted from Jim Rasenberger, *America, 1908: The Dawn of Flight, the Race to the Pole, the Invention of the Model T, and the Making of a Modern Nation* (Scribner, 2011), Kindle edition, pages 12–15.

Chapter 3

While the machine politics of Manhattan's Tammany Hall had waned somewhat from its zenith during the "Boss Tweed" days of the mid- to late-1800s, it was still a formidable force in New York politics in 1908. It wasn't until the mid-1920s that machine politics in New York began to wane under the reformist administration of Franklin Delano Roosevelt.

Chapter 4

John Pierpont Morgan was one of the Gilded Age's most famous financiers; at his death, his estate at his death was $68.3 million (adjusted for inflation, about $2.2 billion in 2024 dollars). He and Theodore Roosevelt had a rocky relationship, since Roosevelt was seen as a trustbuster, trying to break up the monopolies that barons like Morgan, Rockefeller, Gould, Vanderbilt, and Carnegie were busy creating.

Chapter 5

What we now know as the FBI, the Federal Bureau of Investigation, began just previous to the events in this book as a small federal agency named the National Bureau of Criminal Identification. While its task was mainly to identify criminals in order to pursue crime across state lines, Theodore Roosevelt wanted to make it more robust to track down the anarchists that were threatening both national and world peace during his administration. It went through several iterations—the Bureau of Investigation (BOI), founded in 1908, initially employed just thirty-four people, including agents hired away from the Secret Service. Then, in

1932, it was renamed the US Bureau of Investigation, and then again in 1933, changed its name to the Division of Investigation (DOI). Not long after, in 1935, if finally landed on "Federal Bureau of Investigation," its name today.

Chapter 6

The Westcott Motor Car Company, incorporated in Richmond, Indiana, in 1907, produced automobiles in the early twentieth century. One early model was the 1908 Westcott Runabout, a compact, two-seat vehicle made for personal transportation. It featured a simple, open-body design typical of other runabouts in that era.

Auto production moved to Springfield, Ohio, in 1916, and the company made vehicles until 1925. The Westcott Runabout was a notable example of early American automotive design, bridging the gap from horse-drawn carriages to motorized vehicles.

Chapter 7

The Pinkertons first attracted notice when Allan Pinkerton foiled the "Baltimore Plot" to assassinate President Abraham Lincoln in 1861. Lincoln hired him and his associates as his personal security and as spies against the Confederacy, leading eventually to the formation of the Secret Service.

Chapter 8

One of the more publicized assassinations in this era was the bombing of former Idaho governor Frank Steunenberg in front of his house in Caldwell, Idaho. A miner associated with the Western Federation of Miners eventually confessed (under interrogation from a Pinkerton detective), and implicated several leaders in the WFM organization. The trial for those three men ("Big Bill" Haywood, Charles Moyer, and George Pettibone) was publicized nationally and featured attorneys William Borah, the newly elected senator from Idaho, for the prosecution and Clarence Darrow for the defense.

Chapter 9

With only 8,000 automobiles in the whole of the United States, if there were any motorcars in Hartford, they were not available to the Pinkertons or Angel Casimer at this time.

Chapter 10

Angel Casimer fantasizes about there being a "Ballad of Angel Casimer" sung after his death. Protest songs have been a feature of American history since "Yankee Doodle" was first sung by British troops and then subverted by American forces in the Revolutionary War. The union movement and its association with the anarchist movement in the early 1900s also spawned protest songs, most notably by the IWW ("Wobbly") union organizer Joe Hill, who was active during this era.

Chapter 11

In earlier drafts of this chapter, I mentioned that Jason Ellis also had an apartment in lower Manhattan for the many times he worked in the city. As a senator, he set up his primary field office near Trinity Church to be close to Wall Street. Historically, senators first held meetings at their desks in the Senate, and as that became unworkable, some rented offices in boarding houses or hotel lobbies. From 1891 to 1905, senators were given renovated space in the former Maltby apartment building, but it was condemned in 1904 and senators had to revert to their old system until 1908, when the Senate Office Building (now the Russell Senate Building) was completed. (See https://www.senate.gov/about/historic-buildings-spaces/office-buildings/maltby-building.htm for more information.)

Chapter 12

The Library of Congress was first authorized in 1800 when the US national capitol was moved from Philadelphia, Pennsylvania, to Washington, DC. Two years later, President Thomas Jefferson created the position of Librarian of Congress, and it is still a president-appointed position. President Jefferson also saved the library during the War of 1812, when the small collection housed in the Capitol was burned by the British in 1814. Congress bought Jefferson's substantial personal library (of nearly 6,500 volumes) to replace the burned books.

Today, the Library of Congress collects every book published by American publishers. In 2016, "the Library's collection of more than 162 million items [included] more than 38 million cataloged books and other print materials in more than 470 languages; more than 70 million manuscripts; the largest rare book collection in North America; and the world's largest collections of legal materials, films, maps, sheet music, and sound recordings" (https://www.loc.gov/about/history-of-the-library/time line/; see also https://www.loc.gov/about/history-of-the-library/).

Chapter 13

"Big Jim" Fitzsimmons carries a Colt revolver. The ultimate "cowboy gun," the Colt Peacemaker (or Single Action Army) was produced for more than 100 years, and carried by US Army cavalry officers in the late 1880s, including General George Armstrong Custer. In later US military history, General George Patton, who began his career in the cavalry, was famous for carrying a custom Colt Peacemaker with ivory grips, acquired during the "Pancho Villa Expedition" in 1918 (during which his opponent, Pancho Villa, carried a Colt Bisley—a Peacemaker variant—with mother-of-pearl grips).

Chapter 14

The history of the Communist Party in Russia is convoluted and full of intrigue, but one of the first and largest factions was the Russian Social-Democratic Workers' Party (also known as the Russian Social Democratic Labour Party). It eventually split into two parties, the Bolsheviks and the Mensheviks (which mean, respectively, "majority" and "minority," though the Bolsheviks were a smaller group than the Mensheviks until the Russian Revolution in 1917). The leader of the Bolsheviks was a young academic named Vladimir Ilyich Ulyanov who went by the pseudonym Vladimir Lenin.

Chapter 15

Senator Ellis mentions some of President Theodore Roosevelt's many accomplishments. An engaging resource for more information is the three-volume biography of Roosevelt by Edmund Morris: *The Rise of Theodore Roosevelt* (Modern Library, 2001); *Theodore Rex* (Random House, 2001); and *Colonel Roosevelt* (Random House, 2010).

Chapter 16

Much of "Big Jim" Fitzsimmons thoughts are typical of union organizers from the time. One such (mentioned above in the note to chapter 8), was "Big Bill" Haywood, a miner, union organizer, and a founder of the International Workers of the World (the "Wobblies"). His autobiography, *Big Bill Haywood's Book*, is an interesting look into the labor movement and its origins in America.

Chapter 17

Sir Winston Churchill is best known for his service as Prime Minister of Britain during World War II, but his biography rivals that of Theodore Roosevelt, including similar service as First Lord of the Admiralty—Roosevelt was Secretary of the Navy—including promoting innovation in combining British naval and air power. A good resource is the one-volume biography *Churchill: Walking with Destiny* by Andrew Roberts (Viking, 2018).

Chapter 18

Maxim Kozlov talks about an attack by Jean-Baptiste Sipido on King Edward in Belgium in 1900. For more information on this attack, see Christopher Hibbert, *Edward VII: The Last Victorian King* (St. Martins-Griffin, 2007).

Chapter 19

There were actually several racing yachts owned by Kaiser Wilhelm II named *Meteor*; this one would have been *Meteor III*, which was replaced the next year by *Meteor IV*. The Kaiser had a love of sailing and a keen sense of competition with his cousin, King Edward, but never managed to beat him in a race. A good biography of "Kaiser Bill" is *Kaiser Wilhelm II: A Life in Power* (Penguin UK, 2009).

Chapter 20

"Using an improved version and without her husband's knowledge, [Karl] Benz's wife Bertha and their two sons Eugen (15) and Richard (14) embarked on the first long-distance journey in automotive history on an August day in 1888. The route included a few detours and took them from Mannheim to Pforzheim, her place of birth. With this journey of 180 kilometers [about 112 miles] including the return trip Bertha Benz demonstrated the practicality of the motor vehicle to the entire world. Without her daring—and that of her sons—and the decisive stimuli that resulted from it, the subsequent growth of Benz & Cie. in Mannheim to become the world's largest automobile plant of its day would have been unthinkable" ("The first automobile," *Mercedes-Benz.com* [website]; available at https://group.mercedes-benz.com/company/tradition/company-history/1885-1886.html).

Chapter 21

While the dates aren't exact, there's a very good chance that Andy and Jason could have attended a ballet titled *Chopiniana* at the Mariinsky Theatre in St. Petersburg on April 13, 1908—it was premiered there on March 8 of that year. (See https://www.mariinsky-theatre.com/performance /Chopiniana__Le_Carnaval__Schhrazade/.)

Chapter 22

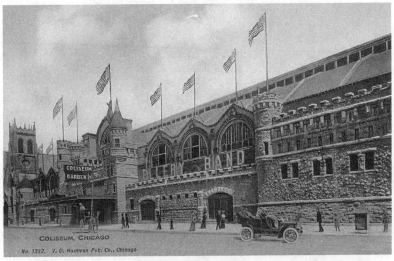

Chicago Coliseum, site of the 1908 Republican National Convention.

Chapter 23

Pepsi-Cola was first called "Brad's Drink," named after its inventor, Caleb Bradham, a pharmacist in New Bern, NC. Because of its alleged digestive qualities, it was renamed "Pepsi-Cola" in 1898. (See https://pepsi store.com/history/.)

Chapter 24

Theodore Roosevelt as New York City police commissioner.

Chapter 25

Interior of the Chicago Coliseum, Republican National Convention, 1908.

Chapter 26

The first ambulance service in Chicago was organized through the police department in 1890 "with a donation from Mrs. Ada Sweet," who "provided funds for an ambulance that . . . was simply a [horse-drawn] patrol wagon equipped with a stretcher and bandages. The [officers] assigned were trained by a [doctor] in basic medical techniques" ("History," *ChicagoPolice.org* [website]; available at https://www.chicagopolice.org /about/history/).

Chapter 27

Andy Pettit would probably have been rushed to St. Luke's Hospital at 1435 S Michigan Avenue, just around the block from the Chicago Coliseum. It was founded in 1865 and moved to that location a little while later, eventually "merging in 1956 with Presbyterian Hospital and Rush Medical College" (see "Hospitals," *Encyclopedia of Chicago* [website]; available at http://www.encyclopedia.chicagohistory.org/pages/602.html).

Chapter 28

Big Jim Fitzsimmons is threatened with death by hanging or the electric chair. "Illinois used death by hanging as a form of execution until 1928" (see "Capital punishment in Illinois," *Wikipedia.org* [website]; available at https://en.wikipedia.org/wiki/Capital_punishment_in_Illinois), but the electric chair became New York State's method of execution in 1889, with the first prisoner executed in 1890.

Chapter 29

While military honors were sparse in early American history, the Medal of Honor was created in 1861 by Abraham Lincoln (see "Medal of Honor history," *VA.gov* [website]; available at https://www.cem.va.gov /history/Medal-of-Honor-history.asp). Civilian honors usually took the form of commemorative coins struck in the civilians' or a special occasions' honor (see, for example, "Commemorative Coins from 1892–1954," *USMint.gov* [website]; available at https://www.usmint.gov/learn/coins-and -medals/commemorative-coins/commemorative-coins-1892-1954). The civilian Presidential Medal of Freedom is relatively new, having been authorized by President John F. Kennedy in 1963.

IMAGE CREDITS

Page 249: "Union Station,[Washington, D.C.]." Photograph. Between 1909 and 1932. From Library of Congress: National Photo Company Collection. https://lccn.loc.gov/96511846 (accessed November 21, 2024).

Page 255: "Coliseum." Photograph. From Wikimedia Commons: V. O. Hammon Collection. https://commons.wikimedia.org/wiki /File:Coliseum_(NBY_416192).jpg (accessed November 21, 2024).

Page 256: "Theodore Roosevelt when he was a New York police commissioner." Photograph. Between 1890 and1900. From Library of Congress: New York World-Telegram and the Sun Newspaper Photograph Collection. https://lccn.loc.gov/2013650911 (accessed November 21, 2024).

Page 256: "Republican National Convention, Coliseum, Chicago, June 16, 1908." Photograph. Chicago, Illinois. 1908. From Library of Congress: Geo. R. Lawrence Co.; June 17, 1908. https://lccn.loc.gov/2007663938 (accessed November 21, 2024).